MASHAKA

MASHAKA

And the Journey to the Land of the Rainmakers

A Novel

Ben S. Wasike

iUniverse, Inc.
New York Lincoln Shanghai

MASHAKA
And the Journey to the Land of the Rainmakers

iUniverse books may be ordered through booksellers or by contacting:

iUniverse
2021 Pine Lake Road, Suite 100
Lincoln, NE 68512
www.iuniverse.com
1-800-Authors (1-800-288-4677)

Because of the dynamic nature of the Internet, any Web addresses or links contained in this book may have changed since publication and may no longer be valid.

This is a work of fiction. All of the characters, names, incidents, organizations, and dialogue in this novel are either the products of the author's imagination or are used fictitiously.

ISBN: 978-0-595-47208-6 (pbk)
ISBN: 978-0-595-91487-6 (ebk)

Printed in the United States of America

Contents

PART I

THE JOURNEY BEGINS

Prologue

The silence was shattered by the sudden outburst of barking coming from the neighbor's compound.

The children froze.

Someone was approaching their house. *Is it mother?* But their mother always called out whenever she got home. So who could that be?

Then they heard the footsteps.

At first is sounded like the soft rustling of dry leaves outside. But the more keenly the mortified children listened, the clearer it became that indeed, someone was approaching their house. And for sure it was not their mother. Furthermore, the person was walking very slowly, very purposefully, and, very stealthily. The children stared at each other in horrified silence, none of them brave enough to utter a word.

Up to that moment, the four children were sitting alone in the semi-darkness of the room waiting for their mother, who left for a far off village late that evening. Usually she would not leave them by themselves this late but a pressing emergency forced her to make the impromptu journey. It was a long walk to the village and it was well over three hours since she left.

The flickering light from the oil lamp reflected softly on their solemn faces as it cast long shadows that danced like ghosts on the dark walls. The sound of distant thunder only added to the eerie atmosphere in the room. Occasionally, an accompanying lightning bolt would flash through the cracks on the old wooden windows, momentarily lighting up the room in a ghostly fluorescence.

"Do you think something happened to her?" one of the children, a young boy, asked.

"Shh, don't talk like that. You will bring bad luck to mother," his older sister admonished him.

"But I am scared."

The sister tried to comfort him. "She will be back soon. She probably got caught up in bad weather."

"I am hungry."

As if to confirm the statement, the boy's stomach grumbled slightly.

"You know it is dangerous for us to cook without an adult present," the sister warned.

The children fell silent, just staring at the flickering lamp.

"I wish father was alive," the boy broke the silence again.

"Will you stop it!" his older snapped at him

"Don't shout at me."

The two other children just watched their arguing siblings in silence as the distant thunder rumbled on. It probably came from a storm coming down on a far off village. The children kept staring at the lamp's flame in silence, lost in their thoughts and worries. No one could have known what they were thinking about, but one could have wondered though.

That was about the moment they heard the footsteps approaching their house.

Then came the knock.

It was so soft it was hardly audible even in the ominous silence.

"Open the door, it could be mother," whispered the boy.

"How do you know it is her?" the sister replied.

"Then how will you know it's not her if you don't open the door?"

"You think you are so smart," she sneered at him.

The girl tiptoed to the door and peeped through the rusty keyhole. There was nobody outside. But then the soft knock came again. One more time, the girl peeped through the keyhole and jumped back in surprise. She saw something this time. But she could not recognize what it was because it flashed across the keyhole in a blur. She hesitated, looking back at her frightened siblings.

"Just open the door," the boy mouthed.

Shaking visibly, the girl opened the door slightly. The rusty hinges squeaked noisily as the worn door slid open. She froze in her step, staring at the strange man standing at their doorstep. He was dressed in a tattered old robe and his gray beard hung so low it almost reached down to his chest. His gaunt face was lined with numerous wrinkles and his large piercing eyes stared right at her. The lighting flashed once more, illuminating his bony face in a very chilling manner. The girl froze in her step. She was too shocked by the sight of the man she could not muster the will to slam the door on his frightening presence. The man also carried a strange walking stick on which he leaned his old emaciated body as though his life depended on it. On his right hand was a shiny silver bracelet glinting in an eerie contrast to his wasted varicose wrist.

In a raspy and tired voice, he begged the girl to let him in.

"But mother told us not to let any strangers in," the girl declined the request, holding fast to the door handle.

But the man sounded desperate. "Have pity on this old man. Would you let your dear grandfather stay out in the cold of the night if he was in my place?"

"No ... no ... I would not," the girl stammered in a scared but guilty whisper. She opened the door some more.

Without further hesitation, the man stumbled into the room and made straight for the three children cowering by the small lamp. They scuttled back, huddling together in a small mass of horrified innocence. The girl made as if to grab the man but stopped short. He was just rushing in to grab a stool for himself. The man then sat down and stretched his wizened old hands towards the lamp's small flame.

"Thank you for letting me in children. It's so nice and warm in here," he rasped.

"Who are you?" the girl asked, huddling by her siblings and trying to put as much distance between them and the strange man.

"I am a traveler from a far off land. You are the first people who let me inside their warm house. Thanks for letting me in. I mean no harm to you."

The children just stared at him. They were shaking visibly in his presence.

"Don't be afraid of me little ones. I am just a harmless old man. Look, can I tell you children a story?"

The offer took them by surprise. The children looked at each other in confusion until finally, the boy blurted out.

"Yes, I would like a story."

The girl quickly elbowed him lightly, sending him a warning look.

"What?" he whispered at her. "It is just a story."

"It is okay children, no need to fight over a story. I have plenty of them."

"Then go ahead and tell us one," the boy insisted.

"All right then. Now get ready for a story you have never heard before."

The children stared at him in silence as he continued.

"Children, get ready because I am about to transport you to a far off land. I will take you to a world full of fantasy. It is a world so unlike anything you have ever imagined. This is a story even the oldest person in your village is yet to hear. In fact, you will be the very first people to hear my story."

The children looked eagerly at the old man. *Probably he is not that strange after all.*

"But you have to promise me one thing children," he whispered sharply and raised a long bony finger towards them. Again, they scuttled back in renewed fright.

"You have to promise me you will not tell a soul about my story. This will be our little secret. You see if you tell others, they might try to go into the fantasy world and destroy it forever. Would you want that to happen?"

The children shook their heads vigorously.

"Well then children, have you ever heard of a place called Amani?"

They looked at each other and shook their heads again.

"Okay. Now, are you all ready to go with me to Amani?"

The children nodded their heads anxiously as their faces lit with anticipation.

"Amani is a place that existed a very long time ago," the man explained. "It existed in a time period simply known as the near ancient. You see the world was divided into three time periods back in the day. There was the era of the old ancient, which was followed by the era of the near ancient. Soon after that came the era of the new ancient. But that is a very, very, long time ago children."

The old man paused to adjust his old robe.

"My story begins one morning in Amani ..."

CHAPTER 1

The Attack

It was a new day in Amani.

Amani was one of the small scattered villages lying in the sparsely populated area off the slopes of Mount Elgon. The villages stood on top of the rolling ridges formed millions of years ago when hot molten lava flowed freely from the then newly formed mountain.

But that is a very long time ago.

Now, these ridges rolled on and on, corrugating the landscape into endless furrows. They were covered by a lush carpet of green grass sprouting from the fertile volcanic soils beneath. Being a tropical world also meant there was a steady supply of rain. These conditions provided the perfect environment for agriculture and that is what the villagers did.

Life was peaceful and over the years the village prospered in this tropical heaven. One or two unsettling incidents occurred in the past but the industrious villagers soon put these away and moved on—except for one incident.

This was an incident the villagers would have preferred not to stick at the back of their minds. But it did; sticking fast to their memories the way pollen sticks to a bee's legs, the way soot sticks fast to an old chimney, or the way grass sticks its roots deep into the soil. These dark memories hung at the back of every villager's mind. Since the day the incident occurred, life in the village was never the same again. It was as if an evil rapist snatched the chastity right out of the innocent villagers. People did not talk the same again, children did not play as freely as they did before, and people no longer trusted their neighbors.

But time is probably the best panacea the world has ever seen. As the years rolled by, the effect of this incident healed and the people almost forgot all about it. But the incident had the most significance to one village resident. Although it changed the life of every villager, it defined the life of one young village resident. Now it was about to change his life forever.

But this was a new day in Amani and the villagers did what they did best. They went about their daily chores; farming, cleaning, hewing wood, and so on.

It was about mid morning as three young boys went about their business. Their task today was to take the cattle out to graze in the lush pastures just outside the village outskirts. This was a day long task since cattle can graze for hours on end. The early morning sun shined bright but not too hot. The boys' chatter mingled with the occasional moo of a cow and the chirping of the active birds in the trees. It all seemed very ordinary. It all seemed very peaceful.

"What do you mean your sling is steadier than mine? My sling is so good I can hit two birds with a single stone," proclaimed the first boy.

"In your dreams," laughed the second boy. "Last time you used your sling you missed a bird so bad your own sling hit you in the face."

"Not as bad as I punched you in the face the last time you tried talking to me like that. Show me some respect."

"Respect? What do you mean respect? You are not an elder, and furthermore, you did not hit me in the face. That was a coward's blow you threw me. How about we do it face to face like real men right now?"

"I am ready for you anytime ..." He lunged at the boy mid sentence.

"Stop it you two!" interjected the third boy. "Remember what my father said about fighting when we are out in the pastures? That was the last warning he gave us. I don't want to be a human scarecrow chasing birds from the crops all day."

"Yeah, that sounds like a childish chore," the second boy concurred.

The first boy nodded in agreement then inquired. "When are we having lunch?"

"We just took breakfast. You have the appetite of a man-eating ogre," the second boy mocked, mimicking the gluttonous eating manner of an ogre.

But the first boy was defensive. "My mother says if I eat a lot of food I will grow to be as big and strong just like my uncle."

"Your uncle was born big. You were born short."

"Well, forget you. You are not too much taller than me anyway," the first boy replied lamely, giving up the argument.

The two boys chattered back and forth as they lead the cattle through a small thicket in a single file. Occasionally, a clever cow would leave the herd and try to make its way from the rest. The boys would round the stray animal and bring it back in line with the others. They carried thin poles that had long leather whips attached to one end. They swung these whips in the air to produce sharp clapping sounds to discourage the cattle from the leaving the herd.

Just when they reached midway through the dense woods, the cattle at the head of the line stopped cold in their tracks. With ears pointing in the air, heads held high in anticipation, the cattle refused to proceed any farther. Cattle only do that when they see danger or when they are about to engage in a fight. But then the chirping birds took off shrieking. The thicket went cold and silent as man and animal froze, not knowing what lay behind the bushes.

"What's wrong?" whispered the first boy.

"I don't know," replied the second.

"Shh. Keep it down," warned the third boy.

The boys scanned the bushes around them but saw nothing.

"It's probably hyenas trying to attack the cows," the second boy suggested.

"Hyenas don't attack in broad daylight!" corrected the first boy.

"Then what is it?" agonized the third boy.

They could hear rustling sounds coming from the left. They turned to look but saw nothing. The rustling sounds then emerged from their right but they saw nothing on that side either. Then a low menacing growl sent the cattle jostling against each other.

"What was that noise?" the third boy asked.

"I think it sounded like a lion," the first boy replied.

The second boy looked at him askance. "And what was the last time you saw a lion in this area?"

"Oh no, do you think it could be the …" The third boy did not finish the sentence. An eerie bloodcurdling howl cut rudely through the silence as if to confirm his unfinished sentence.

The cattle start backing up, tripping over each other as the boys desperately tried to hold them back. It was a futile effort. The sheer size and force of the animals were too much for the young boys. The animals took off in a mad stampede, knocking the boys down and almost trampling them beneath their thick hooves.

The boys took off after the cattle. As they ran, they kept screaming out one word.

"*Damu!*"

Hot at their feet were the dreaded *Damus*. The creatures quickly caught up with the boys and surrounded them. The trapped youngsters remained in one spot, huddling together, hands joined in fear and despair. An iridescent light shot from the *Damus'* eyes, sending powerful beams of light at the boys. The local people claimed this light had the capacity to hypnotize whoever looked the creatures in the eye.

"Whatever you do, do not look into their eyes," the third boy pleaded to his friends.

The boys shuddered as the menacing creatures encircled them. The *Damus* seemed to take their sweet time with the boys. Occasionally they would taunt them with menacing growls so guttural they could churn a grown man's innards. Other times the creatures would snarl their snort-like mouths and display sharp sets of fangs that seemed to run forever inside their long mouths.

It is hard to describe these creatures since they took on the characteristics of different animals. Whereas they were lithe and feline, they were covered by a thick coat of long dirty fur similar to that of a hyena. In fact, their bodies were dotted with spots just like those of a hyena. But they were much larger in size and structurally they looked exactly like very large wolves. But their mouths were different. These were long and thick like a pig's and ended in a sharp snort and inside the mouths were sharp and irregular teeth. Hanging from the tip of their mouths were two long thick saber-like fangs under which darted several long and forked tongues like those of a snake.

While their front legs were pawed, their hind legs were hoofed. This means that while they circled the boys, they scratched the ground and at the same time stamped their hooves. All the while the huge thick porcupine spikes on their backs kept rising and falling every time they growled. Occasionally they would also lunge at the boys and bark just like dogs.

Legend had it that the *Damus* were known to stun and hypnotize their victims with the powerful glare from their eyes. With the victim stunned in temporary paralysis, they would then lunge at his throat and suck all his blood and eventually snatch his soul. No one had ever survived a *Damu* attack.

No one could argue against the grotesque evidence these creatures left behind—mummified human carcasses devoid of blood. The remains would lay there, eyes still open in a hypnotized gaze, teeth grinning in a ghostly manner, and the dry ashen skin clinging fast to the lifeless bones.

Ghastly images of the victims ran through the boys' minds as they stood trapped by the *Damus*. As they stood shaking in fear, the boys knew very well the fate that was about to befall them. Well, at least two of them. The third boy reacted differently. His body went rigid and his eyes glazed over then brightened up in a strange and powerful glow.

The *Damus* stopped circling the boys and froze in place, looking straight at the one boy. With their bushy tails tucked between their legs, the creatures started backing up while making squealing noises. The glare from the boy's eyes grew even more powerful, sending the creatures scampering away into the thicket.

The boys remained huddled together, too shocked to move and too paralyzed to speak. Just as quickly as the glare in the third boy's eyes appeared, so did it disappear. He fell to the ground in a heap, dazed and spent.

"Mashaka, Mashaka!" the two boys called out to him as they tried to pick him up.

They had to shake him several times before he finally came to. Wobbly, dazed, and confused, he struggled to his feet.

"What just happened … where are the *Damus*?"

"They are gone," replied the first boy. "We have to run back home."

The boys took off as fast as their young feet could carry them.

"Children," said the old man, "this is a story about a boy named Mashaka. This is a boy whose destiny was determined long before he was born. He was about to set off on a journey that would take him to the very end of the world. This is a journey that would take him to places so fantastic they defy human imagination. But you have to promise me one more time children. This will remain our little secret. No one else hears my story, right?"

Impatiently, the children nodded in agreement. They were completely absorbed in the old man's story and they could not wait to hear the rest of it.

"Now, I want each of you touch my bracelet and swear you'll never, ever, tell my story to anyone."

The children took turns touching the man's bracelet and promising him their secrecy.

"Good. Now that I have your word, let me tell you what happened next."

CHAPTER 2

The Rain

It was a few days since the *Damus* attacked the boys and the village was still in shock. Fear of a new attack made everyone including adults to shudder at the mere sound of a breaking twig. The villagers walked in a tense and subdued manner. An aura of helplessness hung over Amani just as the shroud of darkness covers the earth on a stormy night. Although no one wanted to admit it, most people knew exactly what was likely to happen next.

The village elders forbade anyone to go past the village limits lest another resident fell victim to whatever monsters lay out there. No one would deny that the *Damu* attack was an omen of more evil to come. The memories that had been hanging at the back of the villagers' minds for so long now unfurled to fill their brains and their whole beings. What they had tried so hard to forget and bury in their past re-awakened. Now they would have to live through the terror one more time. It was a prospect no one in the village wanted to entertain in their mind. It was a calamity no one in the village would wish on his or her worst enemy.

But the damage was already done. The wheels of evil were already in motion. No human, not even the mightiest, could now stop these powerful cogs of evil as they ground against each other. The ocean of doom was already boiling in anger and it was about to unleash its fury. The wrath of the one who no one dared mention his name was about to release upon the poor villagers. But even among the most forgetful, the villagers had ironically waited for this moment—a moment that had been in the making for fifteen years.

That was when the incident occurred.

It was a day to remember; it was a day to forget.

The incident was a culmination of events that tore the village apart and created rifts between the residents. People argued until civil debates turned into full-fledged fist fights. Residents threatened to abandon the village and relocate elsewhere. Mothers begged their husbands to take their children to safer environs, and for once, even the elders almost lost control of the village. Amani would never be the same again.

It all started with Malaika, a young girl from a far off village. Chastity was a virtue all girls were required to carry to their matrimonial bed. Those who broke this tradition faced a lifetime of rejection, shame, humiliation, and even ostracism.

Being the daughter of a village elder, Malaika was held to an even higher standard. However, she did not live up to this expectation. At least not in a rational way, for she mysteriously conceived a child. The fact that no one knew the father aggravated the situation even further. The shame was too much for her father to take and hence he threw her out of his house and eventually out of the village.

For days on end she wondered in the wilderness, surviving on a diet of wild berries and spring water. Her emotional despair only compared to her physical deterioration. She had almost succumbed to the elements when some hunters from Amani found her lying half dead on the outskirts of their village.

Not knowing who she was, the villagers took her in and nursed her back to health. When she finally broke her story some of the village residents wanted her kicked out immediately. They believed she was the person the Seer prophesied about. The prophesy was that one day a girl from far off would show up in the village bearing a child of mysterious conception. The Seer went on to prophesy that this would not be an ordinary child. He would be a child born free of corruptible human spirit with powers no other human possessed. The child would be the only person with the capability to bring the evil Lord Kifo down and restore peace to the whole world.

But the lord of death would not rest until he had vanquished the soul of this innocent child. For everyday that the child lived, then his mysterious powers would grow. In return, the evil lord's powers would be spent. The evil one would spare no resources in trying to destroy this child. Those who came between him and his target would face the full force of his wrath too.

The village residents feared that if they allowed Malaika to stay, they would face the wrath of the evil lord.

And that is exactly what happened that day, fifteen years ago.

The day started out much like any other and the village residents went about their routine business. The young boys took the cattle out to pasture; the young girls went out to fetch firewood; mothers, with their babies strapped to their backs, went out to the springs to fetch water, while the men worked the fields.

It was the screams from the young girls out to fetch firewood that heralded a new era of terror for the people of Amani. The men dropped their digging tools and rushed to the girls' aid. But it was too late. The *Damus* had already claimed their first victims from Amani.

The two girls lay there, eyes open in deathly amazement, dry skin tightly hugging their skulls and bones. Their teeth were exposed through their wafer thin lips in a ghostly grin. Their mummified bodies looked ages old, yet they had been attacked just a few minutes earlier.

Instinctively all eyes turned towards Mount Elgon, home of the evil lord. The mountain lay north of Amani and that day it looked different. Ominous black clouds had gathered over the mountain and as they boiled angrily, the villagers could hear distant thunder coming from that direction. It never rained this early in the year. Furthermore, rain always approached from the east and not from the north.

The villagers scurried back into the confines of their village and hastily buried the two victims. By tradition, funerals were elaborate ceremonies that took days of rituals to complete. These rituals were done to ensure the deceased had a peaceful passage to the otherworld. But fear that evil might have lingered inside the two young victims' remains meant they had to be buried as quickly as possible.

The women threw their hands in the air and wailed. The men beat their chests and mourned bitterly. The mothers of the two victims were inconsolable and repeatedly tried to jump into their daughters' graves as if to make a last minute attempt to redeem their young lives. As the last handfuls of fresh soil filled the graves up, the wind picked up, signaling that rain was approaching.

If the villagers had looked to the north, they would have noticed that the amount and intensity of the clouds over Mount Elgon had increased. The dark clouds churned and boiled in a sinister brew all day. Towards evening, they would slowly float towards the village.

Late that afternoon Malaika went into labor. What no one noticed however was every time she had a contraction, the dark clouds over the mountain would spew bolts of lightning. As the first few drops of rain fell, the villagers ran inside for shelter.

Then it happened.

Thick sheets of rain relentlessly pounded the roofs of the simple village houses. Golf ball sized hailstones fell through the trees, shredding the leaves into thin strands. Huge bolts of lightning descended, striking and splitting whole trees in two. The din from the rain and the hail drowned out any sound including Malaika's screams as she continued in labor.

But this was no ordinary rain. No, this was perhaps the evil lord's most dreadful manifestation—the rain that comes to life. This was the rain through which he begot his vicious minions, the *Vuas*.

The *Vuas* were a demonic force that manifested though this type of rain. They started out as misty figures in the rain but they quickly absorbed the water to form gigantic ogre-like rain monsters that stood well over ten feet in height. They would then take on human characteristics. This means that they could walk and talk, but whenever they opened their horse-like jagged watery mouths, they would spit out lightning bolts that torched houses, humans, and livestock alike.

The monsters pounded on the simple roofs which caved in easily, sending the poor villagers cowering in corners under the leaking roofs. The *Vuas* pounded on the simple wooden windows, shooting lightning bolts through them. They would then break through the charred windows, insert their frightful heads inside and spray the frightened habitants with powerful jets of water and high voltage lightning bolts.

Some villagers thought it wise to run outside for safety. That was a big mistake. The *Vuas* would simply shoot them with their lightning bolts, instantaneously burning them to a crisp. Their remains would fall to the ground and break into several brittle pieces of human charcoal. Others faced the wrath of the huge hailstones. The *Vuas* used their evil powers to redirect the stones into deadly trajectories that went straight for the victims' heads. The victims would be dead long before they hit the ground, the hailstones still lodged deep inside their bleeding skulls.

The onslaught intensified as Malaika's labor pangs grew. The *Vuas* were out to destroy her and her baby. But they had to do it with the child still inside its mother's womb. For once he was born, he would sap their powers instantaneously. They had to find the baby and they had to do find it quickly.

"Push!" screamed the midwife.

"I can't," pleaded Malaika.

But the midwife was in no mood for her pleas. "You have to!"

"I can't do this, I can't do this."

"You can do it!" the midwife shouted as she raised her hand, feigning to give Malaika a slap across the face. "Do you know how important it is for you to bring this child into this world?"

"Now you want to hit me?" Malaika screamed at the midwife. "It is my child and I can do whatever I want!"

"It is not your child," the midwife snarled back. "This child belongs to all of us. This child is our only hope. Now I don't care what you say or think, but I will be long dead before I allow the evil lord to destroy this child. Now you must push!"

Too weak to argue against the animated midwife, Malaika just whispered. "But I am too weak to push anymore. Just let me die with the child inside me."

"Don't you see that what is happening to the ..." The midwife was cut mid sentence as a lightning bolt ripped through the window. A powerful stream of water burst into the room, pushing both her and Malaika into a corner.

"Haaaaaaah, I have found you at last!" roared one *Vua* as it peeped through the smoking opening.

It then proceeded to enter the room in the most bizarre manner. It seeped into the house though the hole in the burnt out window, practically pouring in through the hole as if it was a huge tap of water. After it all poured in, the *Vua* then quickly reconstituted itself and slowly and menacingly approached the two women.

They stared back at the watery monster in disbelief. They knew the end was near.

"Haaaaaaaah!" the monster roared again, opening its jagged horse mouth and spraying them with more water.

The two women crouched in the corner in fear, shaking and soaking wet.

"I will not let you do this!" shouted the midwife as she lunged at the monster. She sailed right though it's watery insides.

"Haaaaaaah! And what do you think that will do?" mocked the *Vua*.

"I will be dead long before you touch that baby!" the midwife shouted in defiance. Once again she lunged at the monster but sailed right through it.

"Then I shall grant you your wish. Woman, you are as good as dead. Have it your own way!" the monster shouted back and opened its mouth, hitting the poor midwife with a series of lightning bolts.

Still on her feet, she convulsed in a violent death dance as the high voltages roasted her from inside out. All that time her mouth remained open in a silent scream. Soon the charred pieces of her remains fell and scattered on the floor, smoldering and steaming under the leaking roof.

It was too much for Malaika to take. She braced herself on the wall, took a deep breath and pushed with all her might.

The cries of the newborn baby mingled with the pounding rain and the screams of the hapless victims outside.

"Noooo!" screamed the *Vua* as it laid its eyes on the newborn. "It cannot be, it cannot be."

With that scream, it contorted painfully, twisted into a liquid spiral, whirled through the burnt out window and exploded into tiny drops of water outside. It expired not too far from the spot where another *Vua* had a young boy trapped against a tree. The monster had its mouth open ready to roast the poor boy. Knowing his last moment on this good earth was upon him, the kneeling boy just covered his eyes with both hands and waited for the worst. But then a powerful shower of water hit him, sending him sprawling to the ground. Still lying flat on the ground, the boy opened his eyes slowly and peered around. *I'm I dead?* All around him the *Vuas* were dissipating one by one.

The dark clouds melted into the sky and the evening sun broke through, shining on the carnage below.

Malaika held her son close, tears dripping from her eyes.

She whispered softly, "Mashaka."

CHAPTER 3

The Send Off

"Order, order!" shouted the elder.

Everyone fell silent.

This was an emergency village assembly. The mood was somber as the villagers sat facing the council of elders. The council members sat on their ceremonial stools, draped in their ceremonial robes and headgear. The rare crimson robes the council members wore were special only to important council meetings. Otherwise, the elders wore simple white robes whenever they attended to their daily duties. These elaborate ceremonial robes were hand stitched strictly by mature women who had to have had grandchildren born to them. Their headgear was made up of matching turbans with rare cowry shells sewn in all around. Their long beards only added to the aura of seniority. On their feet, the elders wore leather sandals that had colorful beads sewn in into intricate patterns.

In each elder's hand was the official ceremonial stave. No one but the elder ever touched the stave. That was taboo. It was said that if a young boy touched the stave, he would suffer stunted growth for the rest of his life. A young woman who touched the stave would be rendered barren for all her life. A pregnant woman who touched the stave doomed her unborn baby into a stillbirth, and if a man touched the stave he would instantly turn blind. Nobody had ever broken these rules since no one wanted to suffer the severe consequences. Each stave held its own supernatural powers and only its bearer knew what these powers were.

The council of elders called the meeting to discuss the village's fate after the *Damu* attack a few days earlier. The council was made up of five elders who made all the decisions in the village. Their functions varied from conducting marriage ceremonies to deciding when the village would go to war. In between, they settled land disputes, conducted funeral ceremonies, and took care of other traditional rituals.

To sit on the council, one had to have demonstrated extraordinary capabilities. Two elders had successfully led Amani to war several times and their battle wounds were testimony to this. Their dexterity and battle savvy leadership techniques were legendary. Their fame did not end within the village's boundaries. Mention of their names sent cold chills down peoples' spines even in far off villages. Many a song was composed about their bravery. Children were regaled with sumptuous servings of mind-boggling tales about the men and their war exploits.

The third elder had wisdom unparalleled by anyone. He was responsible for creating proverbs and maxims that were now core to the culture of Amani. His wisdom had seen numerous disputes settled in an amicable and agreeable manner. Not once had a quarreling party come to him and left in conflict. He possessed the unusual power of seeing intricate patterns in human relationships and without him many residents of Amani would be at constant loggerheads. He was also a renowned orator and whenever he spoke his words were like magnet to the ear. For these reasons, he was the council's spokesman.

The fourth elder was a renowned medicine man. His knowledge of herbs, illnesses, and natural remedies made him vital to the health and well-being of the whole village. Many people, both children and adults, owed their lives to his forte. They say as a child, he spent hours in the forest honing this skill. People came from far and wide to tap off his knowledge of herbs and remedies. Once, a mysterious pandemic almost wiped out the livestock of a warring village. The elders from that village came begging for his help. Practically on their knees, they promised to cease all hostilities towards Amani. Within weeks their livestock were restored to bountiful health.

The fifth elder was perhaps the most intriguing. For one, no one really knew how old he was. He might as well have been as old as the village itself. He was known as a great traveler whose journeys took him to far off lands. But his fame lay, not in his odysseys, but in the mysterious powers people said he possessed. They said he could foretell events in the deep future. People also rumored that among all the staves the elders carried his was the most powerful. No one even knew what type of material the stave was carved from. Rumor had it that his stave was so sturdy no man-made weapon could put a scratch on it. But nobody knew much about him for sure, not even his name. That is how long he had been around. That was how mysterious he was to the villagers. Everybody simply knew him as the Seer.

The crowd murmured quietly, occasionally glancing at Mashaka who now sat in isolation between the villagers and the elders.

"People of Amani, we gather here in deep fear and trepidation. We all know we have angered the evil lord," the council spokesman said, his voice reverberating with authority.

The villagers broke into a murmur.

"Silence!" the spokesman shouted.

The villagers quieted down respectfully.

"We all know the reason we face the wrath of the evil one. We also know that we do not stand a chance against his power. Our kindness is bound to be our downfall."

The villagers wearily nodded their heads in agreement.

"The council of elders has gathered here today to decide what we shall do with the evil lord's target!" he continued, his voice resounding with more authority.

All eyed turned towards Mashaka.

"We took the boy's mother into our village in good faith. Our fathers and their fathers had a custom. Do not reject the helpless when need still abounds in this world. For no one, and I mean no one, knows when the tables will turn and you will be the one in need."

He paused for dramatic effect and it worked perfectly. The crowd was hanging on to his every word.

"But it comes a time when a man has to face the reality staring him in the face. It comes a time when a man has to make tough choices. When a fly harasses your nose, don't you raise your hand to swat away at the nuisance? Don't you?"

The villagers chorused their agreement.

"That time has come for us, people of Amani. It tears my heart in two just thinking about it but we have to do what we have to do."

He paused and started pacing up and down. His eyes studied the villagers who by now were totally transfixed by his words. Like reflex action, their eyes followed his every footstep.

"This boy," he said softly, turning to Mashaka, "has lived among us as one of our own. But we have paid a great price for his presence. No man or woman in his or her right state of mind will claim to have forgotten what happened here fifteen years ago. Yes, that day when the evil lord paid his first visit to our humble village."

The villagers stirred uneasily as the horrific images from fifteen years ago flashed through their minds.

"Yes! I see fear, I smell fear. I know most of you can taste fear in your tongues," the elder said, pointing his stave at the villagers.

Each time he swung his stave their way the villagers would scuttle back en masse, hands held up defensively. Who knew what powers that stave held.

"But that day that died so long ago is back to haunt us. The terror is now reborn, people of Amani. The evil one has reawakened and now he comes to finish off his nemesis. He has come back to settle a score he failed a long time ago. He has come back, he has come back, and he has come back for you Mashaka!" he screamed as he ran, leapt high into the air, landed right in front of the boy and pointed his stave directly in his face.

The trembling boy scrambled back, his mouth gaping in amazement, his eyes wide open in fear.

"No, don't kill my son!" Malaika jumped from the crowd and ran towards her son. But the villagers quickly subdued her and held her down.

The elder then turned to the villagers, looking at those in the front row straight in the eye. One by one he whispered out to them sharply.

"But we shall pay the price no more!" He repeated that statement at least five times, each time whispering in a harsher tone.

Malaika sat huddled in the middle of the crowd, whimpering helplessly as her son's fate was debated.

"Like we all do with all council matters, we are going to vote. We are going to vote on whether to keep the boy here and face the extermination of our village, or send him off and avoid the wrath of the evil lord."

"Please don't send my son away," begged the mother. "Please, I beg of you."

"Hush your voice woman!" shouted the elder. "The council members will vote and the council's decision is final!"

He turned to face the council members.

"May all of you in favor of saving our village raise your staves," he called out, raising his ceremonial stave.

Three staves went up.

"Seer, do you wish doom upon our village?" another elder inquired of the Seer, who had declined to raise his stave.

"I do not wish harm upon the village," the Seer answered softly. "But tell me councilman, of what good is it, sending this poor innocent child off into the wilderness?"

"Because we have to save our village, that's why," the medicine man whispered sharply to the Seer. "Now raise your stave!"

"I shall not be party to the destruction of an innocent life," the Seer declared firmly.

He took a long look at Mashaka, then at Malaika, and then hung his head, his gaze fixed to the ground. He knew there was nothing he could do to change the council's mind.

"Well, so be it. It is one against four. The council commands that the boy leaves the village!" the spokesman announced.

The crowd gave a collective gasp as the spokesman announced the decision.

Meanwhile, Malaika, overcome with grief and shock, simply passed out. The spokesman walked over to Mashaka, leaned over and raised the boy's chin with his stave. He proceeded to give him his marching orders

"You will leave the village first thing in the morning."

※   ※   ※

It was predawn when Mashaka finally left the village. His departure was marked with no fanfare. Only a handful of well wishers came to bid him goodbye and wish him luck on his journey into the unknown. He carried a few supplies his mother packed for him. It was mostly dried food to last him a few days. He carried that in a worn leather sack that he slung over his shoulder. To protect him from the cold, he draped a heavy cloak woven from rough sisal threads over his back and a similar hood over his head. Additionally, he carried his machete and sling in case he had to hunt for more food, or probably if he had to defend himself.

Malaika put up a vicious struggle trying to hold her son back but again she was quickly subdued. She scratched and clawed against the women holding her. All the while she screamed at the top of her voice begging the elders to let him stay. Even as the village women held her back firmly, she flayed out her arms desperately as if to pull her son back using invisible ropes. Exhausted with her futile efforts, she just went limp and stared at her departing son as the women held her up.

As he walked away, Mashaka could not tear his eyes from his mother's sad stare as she feebly waved at him. He waved back, tying to feign a brave and composed demeanor. But deep inside, his spirit was torn to shreds. He had never been away from home, not to mention away from his loving and caring mother. His younger siblings hung on their mother's side, crying their little hearts out.

Earlier on he promised his mother he would return one day. His mother just looked at him solemnly and all the words she could muster were:

"May the spirits of your ancestors travel with you my son."

He set off in a random direction not knowing exactly where to head. Tears welled in his eyes but he held them back bravely. He promised his mother he would come back to see her one day. He knew however that as long as the evil lord existed the village would never let him return. At the back of his mind he knew he would have to face his nemesis eventually. How? He did not know.

He trudged past the pastures he led his adopted father's cattle everyday. He went past the clear springs from which the village people fetched their drinking water. Farther on he crossed the shallow stream in which he and his friends swum to beat the heat from the punishing midday sun. It had all seemed so perfect. But now it was all gone. Gone the way the morning dew evaporates in the blazing morning sun. He would never see his friends again. He would never see his mother again. He would never see his little brothers and sisters again. More tears welled in his eyes again.

He trudged on.

The early morning birds were already chirping in the trees. From a distance he could hear the early rooster crowing to announce a new day. Meanwhile, the dew stuck to his feet as if to give him a reluctant goodbye hug. The cold early morning breeze blew through the trees as he walked farther and farther away from the village. He was now well past the village outskirts and was so deep in thought and sadness he did not notice the shadowy figure trailing him. It was the sound of a breaking twig that alerted him that he was not alone. He quickly reached for his machete, ready to defend himself against any assailants.

"Massshakaaa!" Like a sharp knife, the whisper cut through the predawn semi darkness.

Mashaka scanned the woods around him but he did not see anything.

"Shh it's me, now turn around," the whisper came again.

He did, but there was nobody. He almost jumped out of his skin when someone tapped him on the shoulder. He jumped around and blurted out.

"Seer, you scared me!"

"It's okay my son. I came to wish you farewell. You have a hard and treacherous journey ahead of you. But you know that your troubles have just begun. The evil lord has regained most of the powers he lost when you were born and now he wants to avenge you. If he kills you, he is bound to defeat all mankind and rule the whole world. But as long as there is a whiff of life inside you, he dares not advance from his evil home."

The Seer paused, looked deeply into Mashaka's face and continued.

"Mashaka, you know you were born for a special purpose. You were born with an enormous gift no other human being has ever possessed. You were born to destroy the evil lord and restore peace to the whole world. My son, everyone depends on you."

"I was not born for a purpose!" Mashaka interjected rudely as the emotions that had been building up inside him let out. "I am destitute! I have been cast out of the only place I called home. I will never see my mother again. I will never see my friends again. You call that a purpose?"

"Listen Mashaka …"

"No I won't listen! I do not even know who my real father is. I do not know where I am going. I might as well be dead. The evil lord is out for my life and I am out here alone!"

"You are not alone. You will never be alone."

"I wish I knew my father. I wish I knew where to go. I wish I knew why you keep saying I was born for a special purpose." The tears he'd been holding back all this time now came streaming down his cheeks.

The Seer took a deep breath and replied. "The answers will come to you with time my son. I promise. It's just that you are not ready for them yet."

"And when will I be ready? Will I be ready when I finally get buried into the ground? Will I be ready when I have been consumed by wild animals in the wilderness?"

"When the answers come to you my son, you will understand. Now here, take this," the Seer said, handing Mashaka his ceremonial stave.

"But I can't. This is your ceremonial stave."

"This will protect you from the evil you will face in your journey. Remember, the stave is very powerful, but it only obeys the one it is handed to. Now Mashaka, I hand it to you. Go ahead and hold it."

Visibly shaking, Mashaka extended his trembling hand towards the stave. No sooner did his fingertips touch the stave than it gave an ear piercing shriek. He dropped it and jumped away.

"What is that?" he asked, moving farther away from the stave.

"Ha-ha-ha," laughed the Seer. "See, I told you it is a very powerful stave. It even talks. Now go ahead and pick it up."

Mashaka took a few hesitant steps towards the stave. He picked it up and caressed it slowly. It lit up with a bright golden glow and purred like a sated cat.

"It likes that!"

"Yes it does. And it also does a lot of other things too. Now listen very carefully my son. You will head east to the land of the Rainmakers. It is they who hold the answers that you seek. It is they who hold the key to destroying the evil lord. But even with that, they still lack the power to confront and defeat him. Only you have the power to destroy the evil lord."

Mashaka listened intently but doubtfully. "But I am just a young boy. How can I destroy the evil lord?"

"Mashaka, when you get to the land of the Rainmakers ..." The Seer's words trailed off as he chocked with emotion. "Mashaka, it is true! Only you can save this world. The evil lord has come back with a vengeance. He is about to destroy the whole world. Mashaka, he will destroy every human being including your family. We don't have too much time."

"But how do I reach the land of the Rainmakers?"

"Just head east and your instincts will guide you."

"Then why don't you travel with me to the land of the Rainmakers? You are a great traveler. You know the way and we will reach there much faster."

"Mashaka, I am an old man. The journey will be too hard on my old bones. In fact, I would slow you down if I accompanied you. But you see if I stay behind, I can keep an eye on your mother while you are gone. How does that sound?"

"Well, at least I have your stave. Furthermore, what do I have to lose? I have been banished from the village."

"My son, do not talk like that. Their eyes will open soon enough and when they get to see the reality of who you are, they will be very eager to have you back among them."

Mashaka nodded his head slightly.

"Oh, before I forget, here take this." The Seer handed him a silver bracelet.

"What is this that you … a bracelet? Of what use is that, Seer?"

"It is a very powerful bracelet. If you concentrate very hard that bracelet will let you communicate with me anywhere."

"Oh really?"

Mashaka put the bracelet on his wrist and instantly felt a tingling sensation run through his arm.

"I can feel it Seer, I can feel it!" he whispered in childlike amazement.

"Now you have to be on your way. You don't have too much time to reach the land of the Rainmakers. I wish you the very best my son."

Mashaka looked down at the stave and then at the bracelet.

"Thanks so much … Seer, where did you go?"

But the Seer was nowhere to be seen

"Thanks Seer," Mashaka murmured.

He turned around and headed east.

CHAPTER 4

The Chase

Mashaka held firmly to the stave. It didn't feel like a piece of wood. It felt warm and alive. It reminded him of when, as a small boy, he used to hold to his mother's hand. He wondered what would happen to his mother now that he was gone.

After the council meeting, his mother did not say a word. She did not even break into tears while she quietly packed his meager travel bag. He looked into her eyes and saw the sadness in them. But he also saw something else. It was a glint of hope. It was very faint but it had been there. Somewhere deep inside he knew he would see his mother again.

The morning sun stood bright in the cloudless blue sky. Mashaka knew he needed to hurry before the midday sun moved in with its punishing heat. Although he had not looked back towards the village since his departure, he was sure it would be a good distance away by now. He did not wish to look back but his urges got the better of him. He climbed a tree and gazed back towards the place he once called home. He could see the village at a distance and sharp pangs of nostalgia set in. Once again, tears welled in his eyes.

From where he was, he could not make out any distinct features in the village but he noticed something different that morning. It was a huge plume of smoke rising from one end of the village. Although almost inaudible, he could also hear distant wails wafting through the morning air from the direction of the village.

What could that be? There were no ceremonies taking place at this time of the year. Furthermore, no one lit a huge fire unless …

His heart fell into despair as he contemplated the possibilities. A fire that big was lit only on two occasions; during the initiation ceremonies of young boys and when an adult died.

"Mother!" he gasped and scaled down the tree, running full speed towards the village.

He ran for a short distance when he suddenly stopped cold in his tracks. He had seen something; three men running in his direction. He instantly made a U-turn and sprinted back east. He immediately recognized the men and he knew instinctively he had no other option but to outrun them. But again he knew he did not stand a chance against them that way. Without further thought, he climbed up the nearest tree he could find.

❧   ❧   ❧

Back in the village, the mood was more somber than it had been when Mashaka left.

As usual, the Seer's wife woke up early to milk the cows and let the chicken out of the coop. But when she walked back into the house that morning she noticed that something did not seem right. Usually the Seer would be out in the yard smoking his pipe and demanding breakfast. He would also jokingly berate his wife for her laziness. Usually she would laugh at him and make fun of his insatiable ogre-like appetite.

But he was not smoking his pipe out in the yard that morning. She walked into the house, assuming he was still in bed. It had been a terrible night for him. He spent most of the night tossing and turning, stressed out over the council's decision to throw Mashaka out.

She tiptoed towards his bed and shook him gently. He did not respond.

"Seer! Seer!" she shouted in desperation.

Again, the man did not respond. Unbeknownst to her, the Seer took his last earthly breath during the night.

The elders were the first to his side as was the custom. They talked in undertones as the women wailed outside. Preparations for the Seer's funeral were already afoot. Such a respected elder warranted an elaborate funeral ceremony that could take days. However, the ceremony could not commence until his stave was placed right next to him as custom dictated.

But the stave was nowhere to be seen.

Who could have taken the stave? No man could have dared touch any of the elders' staves. The results of an infraction of such a long held custom would be catastrophic to the offender. Unless of course the Seer gave it to someone; but then who could he have given it to?

"Mashaka!" snarled one elder in disgust. "The old fool must have given the boy the stave last night."

"But we saw him leave the village and he definitely did not have the stave with him," said another elder.

"Or he probably stole it and hid it somewhere," yet another elder added.

The council spokesman, who had not uttered a word yet, broke his silence.

"I know where the stave is." The undertone was cold, matter of fact, and menacing. "And I am gong to get it back!" The last sentence was hardly audible, coming out just under his cold unfeeling breath.

"How do you know where the stave is? And how are you going to get it back?" the medicine man asked in exasperation.

The spokesman slowly turned his head around and faced east. In a determined manner, he stated, "Summon our best speed runners and retrieve the stave right now!" His mouth was twisted in a knowing and wicked smile.

Soon, three speed runners were dispatched to retrieve the stave. They were under orders to retrieve the stave at any expense, even if it meant that they had to take a life.

❦   ❦   ❦

Mashaka climbed up the tree as fast as he could. He looked eagerly through the branches as the three men approached from below the ridge. He sat as still as he could, trying not to move a muscle or make a sound. The men were now very close to his tree and he could hear their every word.

He knew exactly who the men were. He also knew that these were the last people you wanted on your trail. The speed runners were more or less assistants to the council spokesman and they were known for their extraordinary physical attributes. For example, they could run for miles at amazing speeds with absolutely no rest. They were also very skilled fighters who feared no man. But the surplus they possessed in sheer brawn was inversely related to the paucity of their brain capacity. In that area, they were simply deficient. They only took orders from one person—the spokesman, and they did this with blind conviction. They did everything he said and they did it to the letter. He used them for a variety of tasks. For instance, he would use them as messengers to far off villages. Even in the most hostile and dreaded village, their meer presence elicited fear and respect.

Rumor had it that he used them for darker purposes too. It was said that by night, he would send them out to terrorize all those who tried to undermine his position in the village. But most of all the speed runners were known for their viciousness. Once, a village man challenged them to a fight after a small argument. Within minutes the man's body lay on the ground, cut up into several pieces. With pretty much nothing to do but the spokesman's bidding, the runners spent the better part of the day sharpening their machetes and honing their fighting skills. As Mashaka sat trembling up the tree, he could clearly see their killing blades glinting in the morning sun.

"Why do we have to run all this way to get a stupid stave that belonged to a crazy old man anyway?" asked one runner.

"They say it's very powerful. They say it has magical powers and anyone who holds it can put any human being under his control," replied the second runner.

"But do we have to kill the boy just for that? We are not even sure he has it. I do not want to waste my machete's sharpness on a stupid outcast. I spent the whole evening yesterday working on it," the third runner complained.

"Well, we'll find that out when we locate him." That was the second runner.

Mashaka went tense and very quiet. The men were now standing right below his tree.

"I cannot see his trail anymore. He must be hiding somewhere around here," the second runner said.

The men then started scouting the area around the tree. Up the tree, Mashaka held tightly to the stave in his left hand and his travel bag in his right. But the chirping birds on the tree had plans of their own. While hastily climbing up the tree earlier, Mashaka's bag came lose and some of the contents almost fell out. He was now desperately holding pieces of dry food in his right hand as the chirping birds jostled all around him, trying to get to the food. He could not ward them off since this could alert the men below to his presence. One bird finally reached over and tired to grab the food but accidentally pecked his hand with its sharp beak. Instinctively, Mashaka let go. As if in slow motion, he desperately watched the pieces of food descend, bouncing off several branches and finally hitting one of the men right on the head.

Mashaka watched in terror as the man slowly turned his head skyward, locking eyes with him. The man held the gaze for a moment before his face broke into an evil bloodthirsty smile.

"Hey, we have our little man up here," he called out to the other runners.

"Ha-ha-ha, up a tree huh? And how long to you plan on staying up there little man?" the first runner laughed, pointing his machete at Mashaka.

"Boy, you better drop that stave before I dispatch you to your ancestors this minute!" the third runner threatened.

Defiantly, Mashaka shook his head.

"Did you see that? Our brave little man said no," the man laughed.

"He probably wants to put up a little man's fight," the second runner laughed. "Well then, a fight you will get."

It was not long before the men had Mashaka down on the ground, demanding that he give up the stave. But Mashaka would not concede. He held on to the stave with a vice-like grip such that even the three men could not pry it from his hands.

"I am giving you the last warning boy. You either give it up or I will chop it straight off your hand," the first runner warned menacingly, towering over the cowering boy who was now kneeling in the tall grass.

"No, the Seer gave it to me," Mashaka protested.

"Ha-ha-ha, did you hear that? He said the Seer gave it to him. And when did he do that?"

"This morning."

"This morning? Ha! Well boy, I have a surprise for you. The Seer died last night, so you see he could not have given you the stave this morning."

"I don't believe you. He came to me this morning."

"Did you kill him for it?" asked the second runner. "Did you?"

"No!"

The third runner leaned close to Mashaka's ear and bellowed. "Then was it his ghost that gave you the stave?"

They all burst out laughing, pointing at Mashaka mockingly. Meanwhile, the second runner pranced around in circles pretending to be a ghost himself.

"Look at me boy," the first runner said, facing Mashaka and pointing at his prancing colleague. "You see that ghost? I am so scared I am about to wet myself."

"Well Mashaka, listen very carefully," said the third runner. "I am going to turn you into a quick ghost so you can personally apologize to the Seer for stealing his stave!"

With that, he raised his machete in attack. The shiny blade cut through the air and came down straight for Mashaka's head.

In reflex action, Mashaka's hand went up in self-defense.

The machete cut into the stave with a loud metallic clang. A powerful beam of light burst from the stave, shining brightly in the man's face. The blade went flying from his hand as he reached for his eyes. It fell and planted its sharp tip into the ground between Mashaka's legs, missing him by inches. It remained in the ground as the man cried out.

"My eyes! My eyes!" he screamed, grabbing at his eyes and stumbling around blindly.

"Hey, that is not funny," the second runner admonished him.

"Yes, not funny at all," agreed the first runner and added. "What is wrong with you?"

When they finally realized their fellow runner was not fooling, they slowly approached him and uncovered his face. They jumped back at the scene they had just unveiled. They took one last look at him, now kneeling in the grass bawling like a child, looked at Mashaka, and took off running back to the village.

Mashaka jumped to his feet and took off in the opposite direction.

The beam from the stave was so powerful it practically melted the man's face. He remained kneeling in the grass, staring into the empty darkness of blindness with his hands cupped just below his face. In them was a pair of small blood streaked white balls that used to be his eyes. Long strands of burnt flesh and gore extended from his face to his hands.

The speed runner had just experienced the power of the stave, first hand.

CHAPTER 5

Land of Total Darkness

Mashaka was not sure how long he ran. All he knew was he had to run as fast as his legs could carry him. He knew he had to get as far away from the village as possible. Who knows, maybe the council spokesman was sending more runners to catch and kill him. Clutching the stave firmly in his hand, Mashaka felt some renewed energy rush through his system and he ran faster. Occasionally he would hear a rasping sound behind him and at other times he would hear a stomping sound. Although he feared that maybe someone was after him, he did not bother to look around. He figured out it was probably his mind playing tricks on him.

The trees and branches turned into a blur as Mashaka whizzed past them. It is amazing how a person can outdo himself when his life is in danger. The boy ran like a man possessed by a dozen speedy demons. He dashed though the trees, missing huge protruding roots by inches, jumped over fallen trees and stumps and ducked just in time to miss a sharp pointed branch headed straight for his eye. He finally tripped on a thick root and he went flying through the air.

With a loud thud, he landed on a soft grassy patch. He lay there for a long time, dazed and out of breath but otherwise unharmed. He looked up at the tall trees as they stood majestically as if to protect him from his enemies. He remembered what his mother said to him the day before.

"May the spirits of your ancestors travel with you my son," her voice echoed over and again in his mind as he lay on the thick grass. The sun's rays escaped through the leafy branches and playfully hit him on his face. He also remembered the Seer's words that morning. *"You are not alone. You will never be alone."* Suddenly a warm feeling engulfed him and right then he felt he was not alone any more.

Although he felt slightly more cheered by the thoughts, he was nonetheless very hungry and fatigued. All he had with him was the dry food his mother packed for him. He longed for fresh food. He longed for his mother's cooking. The warm porridge she served in the morning; the steaming mounds of the local bread he would dip in a bowl of stewing hot fresh vegetables. The boy wondered if he would ever taste his mother's cooking again. He ate the simple food he had with him and moved on east.

It was hours later when he finally decided to stop and take a rest. The setting sun now stood to the west like a huge orange ball hanging in the evening sky. The orange glow from the sun shone through the trees, illuminating the evening insects dancing above the foliage not too far from where he sat. The frogs were already croaking and the crickets were already chirping. Somewhere high up in the trees Mashaka could hear an early owl hooting in the evening air. Even the mosquitoes were not to be left out as they buzzed in his ear, ducking deftly from his swatting hand. Soon after dark all the nocturnal animals and insects would croak, chirp, howl, buzz, and hoot in unison, as if performing in nature's mass choir.

The setting sun brought in droughts of chilly air, forcing Mashaka to look for a place to spend the night. He also knew he had to get out of the direct light of the setting sun. Children in his village were discouraged from basking in the setting sun. Their parents said it was taboo to do this. They claimed that this sunlight belonged to the people from the otherworld and humans were not supposed to share it with them. The people from the otherworld only came out in the evening to re-energize in the setting sun. Children were warned that if they stayed out too long in the warm rays of the setting sun, the dead would come and snatch them away. Mashaka quickly made for the shadows.

He thought about climbing up a tree and sleeping on a thick leafy branch but once he remembered his encounter with the runners, he shuddered at the mere thought of staying up another tree. He finally found a suitable spot. It was an abandoned termite hole in a giant tree. He snuggled inside the large opening and was soon fast asleep. In the background, the incessant mass choir of animal and insect sounds acted as his unlikely lullaby.

It was the soft rustling sounds that woke him up. He got up very slowly and looked around. All around him were strange people milling around his tree. *Who could they be?* The people looked very strange to his eyes. Although they were all adults, they were not much taller than he was. But that was not even the strangest thing about them. They all wore what looked like long orange gowns that fluttered lightly in the evening air. Mashaka looked closer and realized that these were not gowns. It was the hazy evening air that was absorbing the light from ... his hand shot to his mouth in disbelief. These were the people from the otherworld and they were out enjoying the evening sun. What the parents warned their children about back in the village was true. But the people looked very calm and friendly, not evil the way people described them.

In fact, as the boy sat staring at the spectacle, one of the people, an elderly woman, beckoned him to come over and join them. Mashaka hesitated. The woman floated lightly towards him and in a soft voice asked his name.

"My name is Mashaka," the boy said, his voice sounding eerily distant even to his own ears.

"Then come and join my people. We are out here basking in the evening sun," the woman said invitingly.

"I don't know if I am supposed to do that."

Just then another one of the strange people floated over. She was much younger and she too asked Mashaka to join them. But the boy stood firm. The superstition back in his village was that if you accepted an invitation from dead people they would instantaneously snatch your soul.

It was not long before several of the people were floating in front of Mashaka, begging him to join them. His repeated refusals to their invitations quickly turned on their ire. The orange glow suddenly dimmed into a grayish haze and their kind faces turned into semi-decomposed heads. From the thin red strands that used to be their lips, the people called out to him. Repeatedly and in one ominous voice, the whole group chanted in unison.

"Join us Mashaka, join us Mashaka, join us Mashaka."

"No, I won't!" he shouted back, sliding deeper into the tree. This seemed to anger them even more.

"Join us or perish!" they all shouted in one voice as the old woman reached out to grab him.

Mashaka jumped away, hitting his head soundly on the tree. The pain was so sharp it jolted him from his nightmare. He quickly got up and looked around. It was all dark and there was no one around. It was just a bad dream. Panting and wet from night sweat, he went back to sleep.

When he woke up the next morning the sun was already high. He felt well rested and energetic despite his nightmare. But before he got out of the opening in the tree, he glanced around nervously. *Who knows what lurks in these strange woods?* He knew however he had to make headway and get as far away from the village as he could. He climbed down from the hole in the tree and made for the shallow stream to wash his face. The face staring back at him from the water was worn and gaunt. He ate some of the dry food and washed it down with water from a nearby spring. He continued his journey east.

He trekked about three hours when he suddenly came upon a steep hill. At the top of the hill was a huge and imposing rock wall. The wall stood at least a hundred feet in height and ran for miles on both sides. He could not see any openings in the solid rock formation. Although he thought about scaling the wall, the surface was too smooth to provide any traction. He could not go around the wall either. That would take him hours, even days, and furthermore he did not know how far the rock wall ran. It also meant that he would either have to head north or south. South would take him in the general direction of the village. Heading north meant getting closer to Mount Elgon and the evil lord.

Discouraged, he paced up and down trying to figure out what to do next. Finally the frustration that had been building up inside him took hold. He started hitting the wall while cursing. But a few pebbles kept coming lose each time he hit the rock wall.

Maybe there's a way through the rock. Mashaka scraped feverishly at the wall.

The rock seemed friable and some pebbles kept coming lose. This encouraged him further. Soon, Mashaka had scraped a small hole in the wall. Wisps of a dark smoke-like substance wafted through the small opening in the rock. He wondered what that was. He scraped some more, now using flint that had come loose from the wall. The dark smoke-like substance was now coming out of the hole in thick plumes. But then without warning, part of the wall gave in and Mashaka tumbled right through.

He slid and toppled through a smooth tunnel for what seemed to be an eternity. He desperately reached out and grabbed the smooth rock surface but could not get any traction to break his descend. He finally landed with a thud at the bottom of the tunnel. He groped around in the darkness, trying to make out his whereabouts but he could not see a thing. The place was pitch black. The opening he had just fallen through must have closed somehow. Not even a ray of the powerful sunshine outside penetrated through.

Where could this place be? No it cannot be! The reality dawned on him.

He had descended into the land of total darkness.

No one ever believed the legend. Of course that is why it was a legend. It was one of the popular nighttime tales mothers narrated to their children after the evening meal. The legend told of a land so dark one could almost touch the darkness itself. The darkness was so thick that if one was to capture it and bring it into the light, it would waft in the air like dark smoke. This is what Mashaka saw coming through the rock wall earlier.

So the legend was true.

Mashaka stood up slowly. He needed light. Then he remembered the stave. Earlier yesterday the stave shone bright when he rubbed it. But he could not find it. He probably lost it while falling into the darkness. In a mad panic, he groped around in the darkness hoping to find the stave. All he found were stones and pebbles. He then grabbed something that did not feel like stone. It felt smooth and slippery. He froze, still holding the thing in his hand. He nearly lost his balance when the thing came to life with a screech, wiggling free from his hands and slithering away into the dark rocks.

Mashaka fell back, still groping in the darkness. He could not see a thing. He finally located his stave a few feet away from where he landed. He quickly rubbed it and with the familiar purr, the stave came to life with its golden glow.

Now he could see his surroundings. The rocks looked different inside. They were all black as though they were covered with soot. But this was not soot he was looking at. It was the darkness, which through the years clung fast to the rocks, permanently painting them black.

The glow from the stave revealed luminous wall paintings reflecting back through the dark. Mashaka moved closer to study the paintings. The life-sized paintings looked almost alive. The intricate artistry showed every detail of the human faces. Even the clothes were carefully painted in the very colors they would have had in real life. But a closer look revealed that the faces on the wall were frozen in eternal screams while others were contorted in agony. Even more frightening was the fact that the people in the paintings looked as if they were trying to hold on to something from outside the rock wall. Their arms were extended in a desperate grabbing manner while others shielded their faces defensively.

Not making any sense of that, Mashaka pointed his glowing stave a little bit farther and discovered more paintings. But these were simpler and they did not have the refined artistry of the other paintings. These must have been drawn a long time ago because they depicted animals that were long extinct. They depicted strange creatures chasing humans. The creatures on the wall had the body of a snake yet they had large sharp edged wings like those of a bat. While they had sharp beaks like eagles, they also had short protruding clawed legs.

Mashaka peered at the drawings even closer. *Could these be the legendary flying snakes?*

Legend had it that these creatures existed millions of years ago. While they could retract their claws and slither like snakes, they could also unfurl their wings and fly like birds. This is what made them very dangerous. They would attack their victims from above, breaking their heads open with their sharp beaks then carrying them off to their nests high in the mountains.

In order to protect themselves from these flying predators, people in those dangerous times had to walk around carrying grinding stones on their heads. When the creatures came swooping down for the kill, they would simply hit the stones and the impact would kill them instantly.

Mashaka was so keen studying the drawing that he failed to notice the protruding bones beneath. He stepped on what he thought was a round stone, lost his balance and went crashing to the ground. An avalanche of soft rocks and pebbles followed and momentarily pinned him down. He finally struggled to his knees and pointed the glowing stave around.

He jumped to his feet with a stifled scream, not believing what lay in front of him. These were not rocks and pebbles. They were human skulls and bones. He looked around nervously. The place was full of bones. Not just human bones, but animal bones too. He wondered who would live to die in this type of darkness, with their livestock too.

Then he remembered.

The legend of the flying snakes continued to state that after the snakes realized they could not kill the humans who now carried stones on their heads, they devised a new way to hunt their prey. They started hunting in packs. Using their clawed legs, they crawled and ambushed unsuspecting victims on the ground and engaged them in a chase. As soon as the victims dropped their protective head stones their flying compatriots would come down for the kill.

There was only one way to escape—run into the rocks and hide there. The humans gathered all their livestock and made for the protective rocks. This was a fatal error, for during the trek to the rocks they exposed themselves and the flying predators took full advantage. Those who made it to the rocks were trapped inside. They could no longer venture outside because the predators lay in wait, circling the rocks for weeks. Trapped inside their rocky confines, the humans and their livestock lacked food and water. After consuming the livestock they carried into the rocks, the humans perished, one by one.

What Mashaka was staring at was the grotesque evidence of the ancient tragedy of the flying snakes. Nobody knew what happened to the snakes after that.

They boy walked farther, still studying the drawings and paintings on the wall. But then something strange happened. Whenever he moved the stave close to the wall, the luminous life-sized paintings seemed to move. He assumed it was his eyes playing tricks on him. He stood back and rubbed his eyes and took another look. Indeed, the figures moved some more.

Farther down was a larger painting of a mysterious man. Mashaka moved the stave closer to study the figure. He looked like a great chief or something. His ceremonial attire and elaborate headgear indicated he was no ordinary villager. But then Mashaka made the mistake of shining his stave too close to the painting and it too seemed to move.

It cannot be! Mashaka gasped and stepped back from the wall. But his curiosity got the better of him. He shined his stave on the figure one more time. The figure moved once again, this time much more noticeably. Frightened, Mashaka stepped back. But it was too late. With cracking and breaking sounds, the figure wiggled and pushed its way out of the rock wall and a man stood before Mashaka.

The stave had just brought an ancient rock painting to life.

Speechless, Mashaka stepped back defensively. "Who are you?"

"Who am I? You don't know who I am?" the man asked in reply.

Mashaka shook his head, too scared to talk.

"I was once a great leader, a great leader of men. But that is a long time ago. A long, long, time ago."

"You just emerged from the rocks!" Mashaka gasped, trying to gather his wits. Meanwhile, his hand was frozen in place, pointing at the spot the man had just emerged from.

"Yes I did."

"But ... but ... how?"

"Easy, you just walk out of the rock wall," he said and laughed softly. But then his mood changed and he took a long pause and kept quiet, as if lost in deep thought.

"Did the flying snakes chase you in here?" Mashaka inquired.

The man nodded.

"So you must have starved to death like them," Mashaka said, pointing at the skulls and bones.

"No. We did not starve to death. We had enough food and water to last us a long time."

"So how did these people die? Why didn't they try to escape?"

"Escape? You cannot escape this place. Anyone who walks in here is trapped forever."

Mashaka gasped at the dreadful prediction. After a long pause, the man explained what happened.

After the man and his people ran into the rocks, the flying snakes staked out the place for a few days but eventually left. But fearing a surprise attack, the people refused to go outside and stayed in for a few more days. After all they had enough supplies to last them a while. It was during this time that they drew the simple images of the flying snakes on the rock wall.

"Did they also do the other paintings?" Mashaka interrupted the man.

"Those are not paintings!" he snapped angrily.

Mashaka was apologetic. "I am sorry, but they looked like ..."

It was on the eighth day that it happened. The leader sent a reconnaissance team to scout the area for flying snakes. The team returned and reported that the snakes were nowhere to be seen. They probably found new hunting grounds.

The people rejoiced and quickly packed their belongings, ready to leave the dark confines of the rocks. That is when something inexplicable happened. The darkness suddenly seemed to grow thicker and the place became colder. In fact, the darkness grew so thick and heavy people started choking on it. What started out as a slight wind soon picked up and turned into a powerful whirlwind. The wind tossed the helpless people around in the darkness. Mothers lost grip of their babies as grown men shot through the air like missiles. But the wind did not emerge from outside. It seemed to have come directly from the somewhere within the rocks.

In a mad and desperate stampede, the people ran for the one opening through the rock wall. However, before anyone could escape, a pile of rocks came crashing down, covering their only escape route.

They were all trapped inside.

It was at that moment that they appeared—the creatures from the dark. The ghostly creatures emerged from the rock wall, glowing menacingly in the choking darkness. They were tall, thin, and luminous. Frequently they would let out high pitched screams that seemed to split right through everyone's head. Those who did not cover their ears in time had their eardrums explode instantly. Soon the creatures pinned the people against one side of the wall—the side with the rock paintings.

These were the *Gizas*, the keepers of the darkness. They lived deep inside the rocks and only came out whenever their dark peace was disturbed by trespassing strangers who brought in light. They hated light with a passion and would do anything to extinguish it.

Strangely though, they did not kill their victims physically. They simply snatched their souls and took them deep inside the rocks, leaving the mortal flesh to decompose on the outside. What Mashaka saw earlier on the rock wall were not actual paintings. These were representations of the souls of the poor people the *Gizas* forced into the rocks. This also explains their agonized countenances. The creatures forced the fighting victims to their eternal grave. They would forever be trapped inside the rock wall.

This is what actually happened to the leader and his people.

"Did you see the *Pepos*?" the man asked.

"The who?"

"The *Pepos*. The slitherers of the dark. It is them who carry the warning to the *Gizas*."

Mashaka then remembered the thing that slipped from his hands earlier when he was groping around for the stave in the darkness.

"They send the warning to the *Gizas*?" Mashaka said quietly, probably to himself. "Yes, I saw one. In fact I held it in my hands."

"Then you have to find a way to get out of here fast. The *Gizas* must have been warned of your presence."

"But how do I get out of here?"

"Your stave, it brought me to life. It has the power of bringing things to life. Draw a door in the wall and your stave will bring it to life. But you have to be quick. They will be here soon."

With those words, the air grew cold and the wind picked up in the darkness. Mashaka scrambled for a piece of bone and desperately started scratching a door on the wall.

"Faster!" commanded the man.

"I am trying," replied Mashaka, dropping the bone.

He groped in the darkness for another piece. The wind picked up some more, now producing menacing howling noises. Mashaka drew feverishly as the noises grew louder. The *Gizas* were approaching fast.

"They are coming, you have to hurry!"

There was an ear piercing scream accompanied by menacing howls and sounds of labored breathing. Then the whole place started shaking in tremors. The wind picked up even more and the noises drew closer. Mashaka quickly finished drawing the door and desperately pointed the stave at the figure.

The noises were getting very close.

"Please open…. please," he begged.

The place grew colder as the wind churned, turning into a powerful whirlwind. The darkness seemed to thicken even more. Mashaka could now feel the darkness filling his lungs and throat as the *Gizas* approached. They were now so close he could actually see them through the dark. The tall thin creatures looked like they were wearing long dark robes made from the darkness itself. He could tell that by how their dark robes glowed luminously at the edges. The pointed hats they wore only added to their frightening presentation. At their feet were hundreds of *Pepos*, coiling in a boiling mass in the darkness. As they slithered towards Mashaka and the man, the

Pepos produced a constant hiss but unlike a snake's. Their's sounded hollowed, as if it was coming from an echoing enclosure.

The door Mashaka drew on the wall now glowed luminously in the dark. It was coming to life at last.

"You have to leave ..."

The man did not finish the sentence. The *Gizas* were already there. Mashaka could not believe the sight. The keepers glowed in the dark, floating menacingly as they engulfed the screaming man and pushed him back into the wall. Having returned the man into the wall, the *Gizas* now turned their attention to Mashaka. They floated towards the boy rapidly. The ones closest to the boy leapt forth to grab him.

Just in time, Mashaka jumped at the door, flew straight through it and landed on a grassy patch beyond the rocks. He lay there dazed, watching as rocks piled up to close the opening he had just jumped from.

Plumes of darkness escaped through the opening, flowing in the air and disappearing into the powerful sunshine.

CHAPTER 6

Land of the Living Statues

Mashaka remained on his knees, his eyes still fixed on the rock wall as the opening he had just jumped from slowly filled up. The last puffs of darkness wafted skyward only to be absorbed by the powerful sunlight. He rubbed his eyes as they slowly adjusted to the powerful glare of the midday sun. He felt sorry for the people trapped inside the rock wall. Probably one day he would come back and rescue them from their bondage. But right now he had a journey to complete. He struggled to his feet and strode east through the rocky terrain.

The sun burned mercilessly on him and occasionally he would take shelter in the shade of a large rock. As he rested, he studied the rocky terrain around him. The whole place was covered by a thick carpet of dark green grass. He had never seen grass that looked healthier or greener. Huge outcrops of smooth shiny white rocks stood firmly on the grassy ground and seemed to go on for miles all around. The huge boulders protruded from the ground as if to announce their imposing presence to all passers by. But Mashaka also noticed that the place was very quiet. It was so quiet even the forceful wind blowing in his face did so without making any sound. It seemed as though the wind was afraid of making any noise. No birds flew overhead, no lizards darted around the rocks, and even though there was plenty of grass, no grasshoppers jumped in it.

Only burial grounds are this quiet. But he could not see any signs of graves or any other burial symbols. Confused at the strange sight, he got up and walked farther east.

He had not walked much farther ahead when he had the strange feeling that he was being watched. He glanced around nervously but there was no one around. The place was very quiet and if someone was trailing him he would definitely have heard a footstep. Not sure if it was just his mind playing tricks on him, Mashaka decided to scout the area and so he took a closer look at the rock outcrops. Some of them had very strange markings etched on them. But the more he looked and concentrated on the markings, the more they seemed to fade into the rock surface. It was as if they were shying away from him.

It's probably just my eyes. He walked around and found another rock with similar markings. This time he tried to feel them with his fingers. No sooner did his fingers touch the rock than the markings jumped away, scattering away on the rocky surface. His jaw fell open in awe. Excitedly, he jumped from rock to rock, touching the markings and laughing as they jumped in reaction. He was so engrossed in his new fun activity he was no longer paying attention to the types of markings he was touching. He did not even have the faintest inkling what these markings represented.

The next rock he touched did not have regular markings on it. It had small etchings that looked like miniature imps.

Mashaka's fingers were just a fraction of an inch away from the rock when he realized what he was about to touch. His knew right then that he needed to pull his fingers away. But his reaction was a wee bit too slow. The moment his fingers touched the markings the whole rock came to life.

First came the bites. The impish figures screamed as they dug their sharp little teeth into his fingers. Mashaka tried to pull his hand away but the determined demons held fast to his fingers. He struggled to pull himself free but the imps, showcasing a feat of strength well beyond their miniature size, actually managed to pull his hand farther into the rock. Now Mashaka had good reason to get very, very, worried. The imps had his whole hand inside the rock. He looked on helplessly as his arm disappeared into the rock, inch by inch. Mustering all the strength he could, Mashaka pulled his arm away. The arm came free and sent the rock splintering into small pieces. He fell to the ground, nursing his scratched arm. Perhaps that was not the wisest thing to do in that situation. Standing right at his feet was an army of stone imps, angry and ready for attack. Mashaka scuttled back but the army of miniature demons advanced, growling and muttering in a strange tongue. This was the language of the stones; a tongue Mashaka had no prior knowledge of. Grabbing the stave and his leather bag, Mashaka took off. The imps followed in hot pursuit.

He must have underestimated their speed for soon they had him surrounded. Panting, the boy looked down at his feet as the little army pointed dozens of sharp miniature stone spears at him. All this time they were talking in a language he did not understand. He did not have to ponder the linguistic barrier for long. The imps jumped on him in attack. Within no time he was skipping up and down in pain as the imps stung his feet with their spears. He kicked out while simultaneously throwing the little demons off his clothes. But his assailants were relentless. They soon had him down and pinned against a rock. They were about to jump on him again when he instinctively held out his stave. But this time the stave did not light up in a powerful beam. It just stopped the demons short, simple as that. They froze in their step, stony eyes fixed on the stave. With their tiny mouths open in fear, they slowly retraced their tiny steps. Sensing the fear, Mashaka shoved the stave towards the imps. With a chorus of painful shrieks, the demons jumped back and sprinted towards the nearest rock. Mashaka watched in amazement as the imps jumped into the rock. One by one they disappeared into the rock's surface, turning into the harmless and lifeless etchings they had been before he touched them.

Mashaka knew that he had to get out of the vicinity quickly. He jumped to his feet and sprinted eastward. His adrenaline took him farther and farther away from the attacking imps but soon his legs gave away and he had to take a rest. It was not long after that the sun was setting in the west and the darkness of night gradually took over.

The night was very quiet. There were no crickets chirping, no owls hooting, and no frogs croaking. It was just the wind howling through the empty night air. Mashaka could not help notice that while the wind made the howling noise at night, it blew very quietly during the day. Up above in the sky the half moon shone eerily over the rocky terrain, adding to the mysticism of the place.

Mashaka held tightly to the stave. When the Seer told him the stave was very powerful Mashaka did not realize how powerful it really was. He wondered if whatever it was the Rainmakers would give him to fight the evil lord would match the stave's power.

As he walked through the stony ground in the moonlight, Mashaka's thoughts went back to the evil lord. No one had given him any answers yet. The Seer promised him the answers would come to him when he was ready. He longed to know about his real father. His stepfather had been good to him though. He had not treated him any different from his stepsiblings. But he still yearned to know who his real father was. The village too accepted him as one of their own. Well, that was until the *Damus* attacked. He wondered if the evil lord still had his sights on him. What if he sends his sentinels to get him in the wilderness? All he had was the stave—and the bracelet.

"Yes! The bracelet!" he shouted.

He had forgotten all abut the bracelet. The Seer said that if he wanted to get in touch with him, all he had to do was hold the bracelet and concentrate. He lifted his wrist to his face and peered at the bracelet. It glinted softly in the moonlight, as if inviting him to use it. He took it off his wrist, held it in his palms, and closed his eyes.

"Seer, Seer," he called out.

But nothing happened.

"Seer, can you hear me?" he tried again.

This time he felt the same tingling sensation he felt when he first put the bracelet on his wrist. The bracelet now glowed in the moonlight, giving a luminescent radiance in his palms.

"Massshaka!" a voice whispered out sharply.

He turned around. "Seer, is that you?"

"Yes Mashaka, it is me," the Seer replied.

"Well, I cannot see you, where are you?"

"I can see you my son, but you cannot see me."

'Where are you speaking from Seer?"

"I am in the netherworld my son."

"But I thought when you die you go to be with your ancestors?"

"My son, my soul cannot rest until you have completed this journey. It is important that you reach the land of the Rainmakers."

"Can you see the village from where you are?"

"Yes my son, I can."

"Then how's my mother doing?" Mashaka was anxious.

"My son, she misses you deeply. But if you finish this journey, you will be reunited with her very soon," the Seer replied encouragingly.

"How much longer do I have to go before I reach the land of the Rainmakers?"

"Son, you ask too many questions," the Seer chided. "That is not important. What's important is that we destroy the evil lord before he takes over the world and spreads evil and death across the whole universe."

Mashaka nodded his head silently.

"Now my son, you have to get some sleep and get the energy to keep on going east."

"Yes Seer."

The luminance from the bracelet faded and Mashaka put it back on his wrist. By this time the wind had picked up some more and the night was growing colder by the minute. Mashaka decided not to go any farther and take a rest. He found shelter in a cluster of rocks and soon fell asleep, spent and tired after an eventful day.

He woke up the next morning to the sound of strange chattering noises coming from behind him. He glanced around but could not see anybody. Memories from the day before sent his eyes shooting to his feet. But there were no stony imps standing by his feet ready for attack. He rose slowly, still holding the stave and peeped around the rocks. But the place was empty. He carefully tiptoed around the rocks but he still did not see anything. He assumed it was his imagination playing tricks on him. Probably having been out in the wilderness alone for so long had made him go crazy.

He stretched out and decided to look around the rocks some more. He found himself in the middle of two rows of gigantic statues carved out in a corridor-like formation. The statues stood high and majestic as if to convey the power of whoever they were fashioned after. They seemed to depict fierce warriors. They were probably great fighters from the olden days. Mashaka scanned the great statues in awe and amazement.

At the end the corridor of the statues were some rock outcrops that seemed to have figures engraved on them. Cautiously, Mashaka approached them. They looked like human faces and Mashaka moved closer to examine them. This time he kept his fingers clear off the rocks. The engravings were artfully done with such detail he could see all the facial features only a skilled sculptor could produce.

Memories of the rock paintings in the land of total darkness and the imp attack flashed through his mind and he instinctively stepped back. The first time he stared at rocks this hard, the rocks came to life. The second time he did that, demons chased him down. But these particular engravings did not look sinister. In fact, the faces looked calm and inviting. He moved closer.

Mashaka studied the faces closely. They seemed to depict warriors, just like the statues did. He wondered why someone would engrave warrior faces with eyes closed. Probably it was some kind of burial ground for men who fell in battle a long time ago. Just about when he was about to move to the next engraving, something moved. Surprised, Mashaka peered closer. That was another mistake he was about to commit. With a cracking sound, the engraving opened its eyes and stared right at him. Mashaka jumped back, bracing himself against a rock behind him.

"Watch out you fool!" shouted a high pitched voice behind him. Mashaka jumped around and came face to face with another open eyed engraving.

"Ha-ha-ha, what a coward," said a deep voice behind him.

He turned around to see the engraving that had just opened its eyes laughing at him.

"You … you … you talk," Mashaka stammered in surprise.

"Of course we do," it replied.

"But … but … how?" Mashaka asked, feeling cornered between the talking rocks.

"Because we have mouths, you idiot!" said the other engraving.

Laughter burst out from all around him. Mashaka glanced around and saw faces looking at him from all the rocks around him.

"Let the boy be Sura," answered the deep-voiced engraving.

"Sura?" Mashaka repeated.

"Did somebody just call my name?" Sura asked. This was the engraving he bumped into.

"Shut up Sura! Don't give the boy any more trouble," said the other engraving.

"Trouble? I didn't give him any trouble, Sanamu. Matter of fact, it is him who bumped into me. If you ask me, it's him who is giving me trouble," Sura protested.

"So what brings you here young boy?" Sanamu asked.

"I was heading east."

"Heading east—Mmh," replied Sanamu.

"You look lost," Sura said.

"Are you lost?" Sanamu asked.

"No, I am not lost."

"Do you know where you are?" Sura asked

Mashaka shook his head. "Not really."

"Tell him where he is," said Sura to Sanamu.

"You are standing in the land of the living statues," Sanamu explained slowly.

"Living statues ... you mean ... I can't believe this!"

"And what's your name young boy?" asked Sura

"I am Mashaka. I am traveling from Amani."

"Amani ... mhh ... they had good warriors back in the days," said Sanamu.

"And we also had a good time beating the daylights out of them, ha-ha-ha," mocked Sura.

"Come on Sura, that is a long, long, time ago," said Sanamu.

"You were once great warriors?" asked Mashaka.

"Yes we were," both Sura and Sanamu relied in unison.

"So what happened? Are you trapped inside these rocks?"

"I would not call it trapped inside the rocks. I call it resting in the rocks. This is our final resting place. In our day, all great warriors were not buried in the ground. We believed that even after death, your warrior spirit still lived on," Sanamu explained.

"Like we do," Sura interrupted, much to Sanamu's displeasure

"Shut up Sura!"

"Okay, okay, I will keep quiet."

Sanamu continued, with Sura still grumbling in the background.

"You see if they buried you in the ground, your spirit would be stifled forever. As a warrior, you have an eternal obligation to guard your people and your ancestral land. That is what we do to this day. We still protect the land of our forefathers."

"So that means all the warriors had their faces engraved into the rocks?" asked Mashaka.

"Well, not exactly. Only the brave ones received the honor of an engraving. Their bodies were first cremated then their faces were engraved on the rocks. Cowards who turned their backs to the enemy and fled were interred into the ground, never to be honored again," Sanamu explained.

"This is amazing," said Mashaka, turning to Sura. "So you were a great warrior too?"

"Well, let's just say I was not put into the ground."

Sensing Sura's evasiveness, Mashaka persisted. "If you were not a great warrior, then how come you were engraved on the rocks?"

"Stop asking too many silly questions young boy. Aren't you supposed to be heading east or something like that?"

"Don't mind him. He was the chief's court jester. And he was too short to be a warrior anyway," Sanamu offered.

"I wasn't too short! They did not have spears in my size," Sura defended himself.

"Well," said Sanamu, "he helped us a lot in battle. He had a way of using his humor to bring a smile even to a mortally wounded warrior. We won a lot of battles because of him. That is why he deserves a spot among the rocks of the fallen warriors."

"But how did you reach the burial grounds?" Sura asked. "Weren't the guardian spirits supposed to stop you?"

"You mean those stupid little imps?" Mashaka spat in disgust.

"Watch what you call those who guard these sacred burial grounds!" Sanamu boomed at him. All the faces chorused their disapproval of Mashaka's statement.

"I am sorry, I did not mean to offend your guardians but ..." The rest of his sentence was drowned by a powerful thud.

"Uh-oh, here they come again," said Sura.

The ground shook with another powerful thud.

"Who are coming?" asked Mashaka.

"Oh, I see you have not met them," Sanamu said.

"Met who?" Mashaka asked as the thuds grew louder, now coming with higher frequency. "Who are you talking about?" Mashaka asked, wishing he had not ventured into this mysterious rocky terrain.

The thuds were louder and getting very close.

"You better take shelter behind the rocks young boy," Sanamu warned him.

Mashaka darted behind some rocks, just in time as two gigantic statutes appeared.

"Why don't they ever learn," lamented Sura.

"Dumb, dumb, dumb," boomed Sanamu.

As the two statues approached, Mashaka could tell they were engaged in some kind of struggle. He watched speechlessly as the two statues continued their fierce fight. They produced menacing guttural noises as they landed powerful blows on each other. As soon as they approached the burial ground, all the engraved faces erupted in a chorus of taunting and cheering.

"You hit like a girl!" Sura shouted at one of the statues.

"I will crush you, you little humor monger!" the statue roared back in a deep angry voice.

"Let him be, it is me you are fighting," the other statue challenged.

As the fight raged on, huge pieces of stone came raining down all over the place, some missing Mashaka by inches. He ducked from rock to rock in order to escape, not just the warring giants, but the rocks flying down all around him. The engravings cheered on, urging the fighting statutes into a more fierce engagement. The fighting lasted for a while as the two statues passed just yards away from Mashaka's hiding spot, taking their fight past the burial grounds and over the horizon.

"Who are those, Sanamu?" Mashaka was breathless.

"Those were the two sons of the last chief, Maga the Great."

"Maga the Great!" Mashaka cut in "I have heard about him."

"Well, before he died, the chief did not name his heir and both sons did not want to share the chiefdom," Sanamu continued.

"So they are still fighting over the chiefdom?"

"No exactly. After a bitter struggle for the chiefdom, the younger son lost. He took his followers and established his own chiefdom. He vowed vengeance on his brother, who in turn put a price on his head."

"So they killed each other?" Mashaka stated anxiously.

"Boy, will you just shut up and listen!" That was Sura.

"Let the boy be Sura!" replied Sanamu and continued. "No, they did not kill each other. When the chiefdom split, it weakened and could not defend itself so it fell to conquerors. It was a fierce battle and many of our people died. As usual, the survivors engraved the fallen warriors on the rocks. Then as tradition dictated, they carved out two statues to represent the two rival chiefs. But before cremating their bodies they put their hearts inside the statues. Soon after the statues came to life and they have been fighting ever since."

"So where is Maga the Great's statue?"

"He does not have a statue," explained Sanamu.

"But why?" Mashaka asked, perplexed that such a great leader would not be honored with a statue.

"You see Maga the Great had supernatural powers that nobody could figure out. No man's spear or machete could kill him. Many tried but to no avail. No enemy or traitor could touch him. His skin was as strong as iron. Spears, machetes, and knives would simply bounce off his massive frame. No one knew how to kill him, and that is why he ruled for as long as he did. He outlived generations of his enemies."

"Then how did he die?"

"He did not actually die. When his enemies could not use spears and machetes to kill him, they infiltrated his ranks with traitors and spies and tried to poison him. To their amazement, even the poison could not bring Maga the Great down."

"He must have descended from the gods," Mashaka thought out aloud.

"Nobody knew where he came from. Some said he was the manifestation of nature while others said he was a spirit from high above. Nobody knew where he came from or where he got his powers from."

"I wish I lived in those times," Mashaka whispered.

"Well, finally his enemies came up with a new plot. They sent out word that they were ready for a truce, and to show their good faith, they sent him a new bride. But she was really not a bride. She was a spy. They sent her to find out where Maga got his powers from. She stayed with Maga and begot him two sons, the ones who fight to this day."

"So his new bride killed him right?"

"No, but she finally figured out the source of his power. His power lay in his shadow, for in the dark, when there was no light, he became weak. His new wife quickly gave word to his enemies. In the next battle his enemies repeatedly thrust their machetes and spears into his shadow. Each time they thrust their weapons into his shadow, blood would spurt and gush from his body. They did not stop the attack until he collapsed. Then the most amazing thing happened."

"What happened?"

Sanamu paused for a while, as if in deep thought.

"As he lay dying, his enemies, still in awe and fear, stood at a distance. They watched as his body disintegrated into the ground. It was as if he never existed. Even his spear, his machete, and his shield just melted into the ground. And that is why there was no body to cremate, and hence no statue. People believed that he must have come back in a different form and carving a statue would anger him and cause him to bring his wrath upon the land."

Mashaka was speechless.

"If you are heading east then I advice you be on your way before the brothers come fighting again," said Sanamu.

"Yes, I think I should be leaving."

"And send my greetings to the people of Amani," said Sura in his high pitched comical voice.

"Do you think anyone in Amani knows you Sura?" asked Sanamu.

"Everybody knows me. I am the great Sura."

"Great? Great for what?" laughed Sanamu.

Sura and Sanamu continued bantering back and forth as Mashaka headed east. He occasionally looked back, still in shock at what he had just witnessed. No one back in Amani would believe him. He felt a little giddy just thinking what a thrill he would have relating all his adventures to the people in the village. In his mind, he pictured all his friends staring at him in open-mouthed awe as he told them about the imps, the talking faces, the fighting statues, and about Maga the Great.

But that would only happen if he made it back home. He knew had to accomplish his mission. He had to get to the land of the Rainmakers.

With renewed determination, Mashaka strode east.

CHAPTER 7

Land of the One-Eyed Ogres

It was so long since Mashaka left the village that he had lost the count of days. He felt lonely and forsaken, wandering out in the wilderness all by himself. Who wouldn't? In a flash, everything was taken away from him. The village, the only place he called home; his mother, who knows if he would ever see her again; his friends, who he wished would share in his adventures; his siblings, who he missed terribly. *And all that for what?*

But the Seer's voce kept echoing in his mind. *"The answers will come to you with time."*

It was days since he encountered the living statues. In his mind he could still hear Sura and Sanamu going off at each other, chattering back and forth for eternity. He could hear Sura, chattering away in his comically high-pitched voice and Sanamu, confident in his deep and authoritative tone. Would his name ever be remembered for ages after he was gone from this world? Would anyone ever carve out his likeliness in stone for his good deeds? Would he be forever epitomized in lore, myth, and song like some of his ancestors? Or would he vanish from the face of the earth, forever forgotten like yesterday's rain? Or probably he would live to be a great village elder like the Seer. These questions burned inside Mashaka's mind as his tired feet took him farther and farther east.

The place he was traversing now was eerily quiet. It was almost as quiet as the burial grounds in land of the living statues, almost as cold as the land of total darkness. He shuddered whenever he remembered how close he came to perishing at the hands of the *Gizas*, the keepers of the darkness. The evening air felt unusually cold all around, making Mashaka wonder if his rough sisal thread cloak would keep him warm throughout the night. As the sun set in the west, temperatures fell precipitously low and Mashaka was soon shivering in the bitter evening cold. He had to find shelter somewhere quickly.

His trained eyes peered through the darkness to see if there was any warm enclave he could call home for the night. The whole place seemed entirely empty. There where no gigantic trees with huge holes that termite colonies had dug out. Neither were there any rock formations with caves in which to hide in from the cold. As he walked up a small hill, Mashaka saw what he thought was light of some kind shining in the horizon. He peered harder and true enough it looked like the light was coming from a house. He quickened his step, hoping some benevolent soul would open the door and allow him to rest for the night.

As he drew closer, he could see that indeed the light came from a house. Energized with renewed hope, he walked faster towards it. He had just crossed a small stream about two hundred yards away from the house when he had a crackling sound behind him. He froze in his step. The last time he was followed was when the speed runners were sent to retrieve the stave from him. Mashaka held firmly to the stave and took one step forward. Again, he heard the crackling of a footstep behind him. He turned around but it was too dark to see anything. He took another step forward and heard yet another crackling sound. He knew someone was trailing him and whoever it was, he was matching him footstep for footstep.

But who could it be? Mashaka shuddered at the prospects.

Although his pursuer did not make a sound, Mashaka instinctively knew he was not too far behind. With his lips quivering in fear, his heart racing faster than a kite in the sky and his stomach sinking into an endless abyss, Mashaka took one dreadful step after another. He did not know which one would be his last. Each time he took a step, whoever was behind him took one too.

Had the runners followed him this far? Had the evil lord finally pinpointed his whereabouts and was now sending his evil sentinels to finish off the poor boy? Probably it was a bandit who was out ambushing unsuspecting travelers.

Mashaka was too scared even to rub on his stave for light. Probably if he kept in the dark the intruder would not know his position. Against his better judgment, Mashaka quietly reached for his stave and rubbed it. Just at that moment an ear piercing shriek cut through the night air as his pursuer leaped right over him, somersaulted over his head and landed right in front of him. The pursuer was now staring at him from behind the glowing stave. The tall sinewy man who wore only a small loin cloth around his waist now stood facing Mashaka. The man held his arms in the air in a grabbing manner as if to imitate an attacking ogre. His face was covered by a frightful mask through which Mashaka could see his bloodshot eyes. From the small opening in the mask, Mashaka could also see his mouth. It was open in a silent scream. He slowly advanced towards Mashaka, stamping his feet on the ground, one after the other. Instinctively, Mashaka reached for his machete. With another ear piercing shriek, the man jumped over Mashaka, landed with almost no sound behind him and faded into the darkness. Mashaka took off running for the house.

He ran up to the house panting and desperately banged on the door. Had he been in a more composed disposition, he would have noticed the strange architecture of the house. Although it looked like a typical house similar to those built back in Amani, this one seemed much larger and taller. But Mashaka was so desperate to get into the house all he could do was bang on the massive door even harder.

"Who's there?" called a woman's voice from inside.

"Please open, someone's chasing me."

The massive door swung open and there stood a woman who peered at Mashaka in a strange way.

"Someone … someone tried to …" Mashaka stammered.

"Don't you worry my son, you are safe in my home. Now come in before the cold turns you into rock."

Hastily but timidly, Mashaka stepped inside the house.

"Come in and sit by the fire. You need to warm your blood or otherwise your heart will turn into stone," the woman offered.

"Thank you," Mashaka said, snuggling by the gigantic fireplace.

The warm fire crackled lively, sending bright sparks flying into the air. The harmless sparks reached midway into the air only to die out and turn into ashes that landed on Mashaka's feet.

"What is your name, my boy?" the woman inquired.

"Mashaka."

"And from where do you travel?"

"I am traveling from Amani."

"That is a far off village. May I ask for what purpose you wonder so far away from home?"

"I am traveling to the land of the Rainmakers."

The woman turned around sharply. "The land of the Rainmakers? For what purpose do you travel to the land of the Rainmakers?"

"I … I am seeking some rare medicine for my ailing mother," Mashaka lied.

"I see," replied the woman. "Here, have some porridge. It will warm your stomach up."

"Thank you," Mashaka said, eagerly reaching out for the bowl of hot porridge.

"And what is that you have in your hand?" The woman was looking at the stave.

"Oh this, it is just my traveling bag," Mashaka replied, knowing fully well the woman was asking about the stave.

But the woman did not fall for the ruse. "Not the bag. I am talking abut the thing you carry in your other hand."

"This is just something I carried for protection. It is nothing really," Mashaka replied, glancing warily at the stave as he laid it on the ground. He had not yet let go of the stave until the moment the woman handed him the bowl of porridge. Customarily, it was considered disrespectful to receive things from older people with a single hand. You always held out both hands whenever an older person handed something to you.

"Do you live here alone?" Mashaka tried to change the topic.

"No, I live with my husband, Jitu. He is out hunting but he will be home anytime."

"Where is this place?" Mashaka asked as he sipped the hot porridge.

"This is the land of *Macho Moja.*"

"Do you have bandits in your town?"

"No, why do you ask?"

"Someone tried to attack me."

"But you look unharmed Mashaka. Tired, but unharmed," the woman said, studying Mashaka some more.

"Well, he did not attack me but probably he was just trying to scare me or something."

"Oh, it's him again," the woman sighed under her breath.

"Who's him?"

"It's just a prankster. That is Chawi. He does that often. Now don't worry about that lunatic. I hear my husband approaching. Soon I will have a hot meal ready for both of you."

From a distance, a man approached the house singing and whistling. Soon there was a loud knock on the door. The man walked in and took a long look at Mashaka.

"Who do we have here tonight?" he asked, his voice booming from across the room.

"This is Mashaka. He travels from Amani and he is heading to the land of the Rainmakers," the woman explained.

"The land of the Rainmakers?" the man frowned quizzically. He looked at Mashaka in the same strange way his wife had done earlier. "Nobody goes to the land of the Rainmakers. What life and death matter takes you to the land of the Rainmakers?"

"His mother has a serous ailment and the boy has to get medicine for her," she told her husband.

"It must be a very serious ailment for you to need medicine from the land of the Rainmakers."

"Food is ready. Let's eat before it gets cold. There is nothing as abusive to the palate as a plate of cold food," the woman called out.

It was days since Mashaka tasted a decent meal. He'd survived on the dry food his mother packed for him. He had been very frugal with his consumption, since he did not know how long his journey would take. He supplemented his meager rations with wild fruits and berries, washing that down with water from the abundant springs that dotted the land. Although he'd tried his hand at hunting with his friends back in the village, he was afraid to light a fire out in the open in case someone spotted him. It felt good eating a warm meal and Mashaka swallowed chunks of the food his hosts put before him. After gorging himself full, Mashaka asked to be excused early. The woman laid out a simple bed for him and no sooner had he placed his head down than Mashaka fell into a deep sleep.

He woke up later to the sound of heavy breathing. Without moving a limb, Mashaka opened his eyes slowly. But he could not see anything. All he could hear was some kind of argument his hosts were having in the next room. But there was something different in their voices. Although it sounded as though they were talking in whispers, their voices were loud enough for Mashaka to hear each and every word they spoke.

"You think he is the right one?" whispered the woman.

"I don't know. You can never be sure until you do it," answered the man.

"No we cannot do it. We promised the Seer."

"But I still have the hunger. Until I taste it, the hunger will keep burning inside me."

"But he is just a young boy," the woman pleaded.

"Yes! That means he is juicier and easier to chew. The last time I ate a grown human I chipped one of my teeth chewing on his old bones."

"But that is a long time ago. We are different now. The Seer made us different."

"But where is the Seer? He promised he would return but he never did!" the man whispered back angrily.

"I think he did."

"Woman, what are you talking about?"

"Did you take a close look at him?"

"Ha-ha-ha. You mean to tell me that the Seer came back in that little boy's body? Woman, have you taken leave of your senses?"

"I don't know. But we must resist the temptation. Plus the boy carries the Seer's stave. And you know very few men have come this far. It must be the Seer."

"You did not tell me he carries the Seer's stave!"

"Yes he does. Come, let's take a look."

Mashaka froze, pretending to be fast asleep. He peered through the slits of his eyes as the couple emerged from the other room. He almost fainted in shock at what he saw. The man and the woman now stood at least five times taller and bigger than they had been before. Instead of their regular clothes, they now wore animal skins around their gigantic bodies. A thick twisted band that looked like it was made from human skin wound around their huge protruding bellies. As they approached Mashaka, their footsteps thundered and shook the ground as their massive feet crushed the ground beneath them. They reached Mashaka's bed and peered close to take a look at the stave he had placed next to him.

Their faces were no longer human. For starters, they did not have two, but one eye each. The lone eye stood prominently in the middle of the forehead. It was located just above a humongous flapping nose that opened and closed with every labored breath they took. The hair growing inside their nostrils must have been thicker than a young child's. Their heads were covered sparsely with spike-like strands of hair that made their scalps look like porcupines. Inside their mouths were sets of large countless horse teeth that were so jagged they send chills down Mashaka's spine. Whenever they opened their frightful maws to speak, an offensive odor would emit and streams of sticky saliva would drip down their chins. Their huge paw-like hands looked like appendages sent straight from hell to torment Mashaka eyes. These were covered by an unsightly prickly fur that jutted out in bunches from the thick wrinkled hide covering their arms.

The man reached out and examined the stave that lay just inches from Mashaka's face. He then turned to the woman in disbelief.

"It's him," he mouthed to her.

With that, the couple stood up and embraced. A halo-like luminance then engulfed them. Still standing, they convulsed violently as their bodies shook against each other in powerful spasms. With cracking and popping sounds, their bodies started shrinking right in front of Mashaka. Finally, back to their human form, the couple collapsed in a heap. They had spent all their energy in the reverse transformation process.

It was too much for Mashaka to take. His eyes rolled deep into his forehead and he fainted. He came back to his senses much later to the voice of the woman trying to wake him up.

"Mashaka, Mashaka, wake up. The sun is up and you need to be on your way," she called out to him.

Mashaka jumped from the bed in fear. He stared at the woman, expecting the worst, but she looked normal. She also acted as if nothing happened the night before. Was it just a dream? Could these people be the one of the one-eyed ogres he'd heard so much about? Mashaka searched his head for answers. But then why had they not eaten him already? Legend had it that no man had successfully gone through the land of the one-eyed ogres. Not only did they relish human flesh, these monsters were also known to be clever shape shifters. They could easily take on human bodies, mingle with humans and capture the foolish victims who fell for their guise.

There was a popular story of a beautiful girl who fell in love with a handsome young stranger. Against her parents' warnings, she insisted on marrying the mysterious man. As tradition dictated, the bride had to leave her parents' home to live with her new husband in his village. But nobody knew where the man came from and he did not divulge any information about his origins either. All that her people knew was the man and his entourage possessed an insatiable appetite. No matter how much food they were served, the greedy party would quickly gobble it down and demand more. It was only after newlyweds left for the man's home that the truth about him came out. The bride's younger handicapped sister had tried to warn everybody about the strange man earlier. But people, including her sister, accused her of jealousy and envy. The girl then decided to do her own sleuthing, so she followed the departing bridal party secretly. Midway through their journey to the unknown, the man and his group revealed their true identity. The sister watched in horror as the man and his entourage transformed into the dreaded one-eyed ogres. They proceeded to consume the bride and her bridesmaids in a bloody human gore fest. The strange man and his group were never seen again.

"Here, have some breakfast," the woman offered. "My husband will escort you through the Forest of the Damned. That is the quickest way east and you cannot go through that forest alone."

"The Forest of the Damned?" Mashaka asked in puzzlement.

"Yes, it's an evil forest. Many people were killed and thrown into that forest and the trees are now possessed by their spirits. They attack anyone who tries to pass through. But don't worry. No one will harm you if my husband accompanies you."

"Is the boy ready to go his way?" the husband's voice boomed from outside.

"Yes he is," called the woman. "Here, Mashaka, I have packed more food for you. This will last you a few more days."

After saying his goodbyes, Mashaka headed for the forest, accompanied by Jitu, the woman's husband. The woman watched as Mashaka and her husband walked away, getting closer and closer to the Forest of the Damned.

"I knew you would come back Seer. I knew you would," she said to herself, clutching her chin with both hands, tears of joy and relief streaming down her cheeks.

As they walked towards the forest, Mashaka's mind kept going back to the events from the previous night. *Had it been a dream?* With all that was happening to him lately, nothing seemed too strange for fiction. If indeed the man and the woman were man eating one-eyed ogres, then probably the man would kill him in the forest. Perhaps it was best to run before the man attacked. Probably he should run once they reached the edge of the forest so he could climb a tall tree or hide in the thick foliage. But just when they reached the edge of the forest, the man turned around and faced Mashaka. He took a long look at the boy, who stood speechless before him.

"Now I want you to listen very, very, carefully," the man bellowed. "That forest is very dangerous, and you are a stranger to our land. You have to remain still and very silent no matter what happens. Do you hear me?"

Mashaka nodded his head, speechless.

"The forest does not like to be disturbed. If you stay silent it might let you be, but if you disturb it, you might not make it to the other end."

With that, Mashaka abandoned his escape plans.

The forest was cold, dark, and eerie. The trees stood tall and majestic and their thick leafless branches blocked most of the sunshine from reaching the ground. The trees were covered by a strange type of bark uncannily similar to human skin. The branches hung limp like tentacles and they menacingly swayed in the air. But there was no wind blowing in the forest. The branches were actually swaying on their own accord. The forest floor had no foliage on it. Not even a single plant grew on it. It was just the trees and a hazy green fog floating ominously up to Mashaka's knees. Inside the low lying fog were mysterious open-mouthed ogre faces staring as the two made across the forest. The haze hung so thick Mashaka and the man were practically plodding through it.

"Stop!" the man ordered. "Don't move."

They stood still.

In awe, Mashaka watched as the forest came to life. The trees started shaking and swaying with vigor as the branches rose and fell through the air on their own will. They slithered and wafted like snakes, coming straight for Mashaka and the man. Some branches stopped right in front of Mashaka and strange reddened eyes popped out and stared him down. The branches then rubbed softly on his head, shoulders, and back as if they were trying to acclimatize to his scent—just like a dog does to a stranger. They went ahead and examined the man, and as if acknowledging his presence, the strange eyes shut and the branches retreated back into the trees they had just emerged from.

The man looked back at Mashaka and nodded sideways, signaling that they should continue their journey.

Mashaka was too afraid to look to the side so he kept his gaze straight ahead, anxious to get out of the forest. But just a few steps ahead, a huge tree bellowed and bent down to block their way. As it came down, the man quickly pushed Mashaka back. The boy, who was now trembling visibly, tried to say something. The man quickly reached out and covered the boy's mouth, signaling him to keep quiet. The huge tree truck now lay across their path. Even the hazy fog seemed to be afraid of it. The foggy faces screamed in fear and darted away as the huge trunk hit the ground softly. With audible gasps, the other trees followed suit and swayed away from the trunk. Then amazingly, the part of the trunk that now lay on the barren forest floor melted into a pool of sticky green fluid. The pool then started bubbling and boiling on its own as it transformed into the face of a one-eyed ogre. From its bubbling liquid mouth, it gurgled out its words.

"Who dares to cross my forest today?"

"It is me Jitu."

"And who is your companion, Jitu?"

"This is Mashaka. He travels from a far off village."

"And what business brings him to the land of the one-eyed ogres?"

"He travels to the land of the Rainmakers."

"To the land of the Rainmakers? What trouble takes him to a land so strange and remote?"

"His mother ails terribly and he travels in search of medicine for her."

"But how do you know he is not dangerous?"

"He is a good boy. He is a friend of mine."

"Jitu, you were always so gullible. How can you trust a human being?"

"This boy has been sent our way by a very powerful man."

"And may I inquire who this powerful man is? Do I happen to know him?"

"He is the Seer. The same man who healed me off the evil affliction."

"The Seer sent the boy? Oh, how I wish I could meet the Seer," the face gurgled. "I have heard so much about the man. If the boy comes in the name of the Seer, then he is a friend of the forest. You can pass now."

The tree then magically solidified back to its original form and let them through. As they marched on, even the fog now parted respectfully to let them by. It was not long before they finally emerged through the other side of the forest, and

Mashaka, now trembling in both fear and relief, inquired about it.

"That was *Miti*, the great spirit of the forest. He lies in guard to protect the forest from any marauders."

"And what about the rest of the trees?"

"There in the forest lies the spirits of my people. My brothers, my sisters, my parents, my friends, my ancestors ..." The man could not finish as he choked with emotion.

"Your family was killed and thrown into the evil forest?"

"Yes they were killed, but not in that way. I am the last in a long line of Jitus, the one-eyed ogres. We were once human beings like everybody else. Then one day came the mysterious ones. It happened one night during a terrible storm. It came to be called the night of the infants' rain. They must have fallen down to earth with the night rain. All around where little male infants hanging from the trees, while others lay on the dewy morning grass. Some of them had succumbed to the cold but most of them were strong and survived both the storm and the bitter cold. My people are kindhearted. They did not reject the needy. They helped the needy. Always! So they took these children into their care."

The words rang deep inside Mashaka's heart. The people of Amani did not reject the needy either. They took in his destitute mother and cared for her. They even accepted him as one of their own. Just like the Jitu people did to the little children so long ago. Mashaka looked up at the grieving man's face with new respect. They were just the same after all.

"All we know is that these children grew up rapidly to become strong handsome men. They were irresistible to the women. Soon they mated with the women, and from their union came a new human-like species—the Jitus; gigantic men and women who possessed tremendous physical power. They were so powerful they could easily uproot a mature tree straight off the ground and snap it into two. But that was not all. They were also powerful shape shifters, and they could easily transform themselves into one-eyed ogres."

So it was true. It was not a dream after all.

"It was in this new and altered state that they were most dangerous. They wrecked havoc upon the land. Now don't get me wrong, not all ogres were violent, but some of them were. These were the rogues, also called the *Korofi* ogres. They would not let a human live, just as they would not leave a tree standing. They even consumed their human parents and any human being who was left. Soon no people were left, just the ogres. They ate whole animals like it was nothing. Then the plague hit."

"The plague?"

"Nobody knows where it came from. Probably it was a curse from the humans they consumed so mercilessly. Probably it was a curse from nature, which they terrorized for so long. Probably it was just an accident. But it wiped out most of the ogres. One by one they died, and we dumped them into the forest. We feared the disease was contagious so we got rid of any sick ogres too. It was terrible, hearing their moans and cries as they lay dying in the forest. But most of them did not die—the evil ones at least. Their spirits, in an effort to remain eternally alive, possessed the forest. That is why it is called the Forest of the Damned. Soon there was no one left but me and my wife."

"How come you two did not die?"

"We almost did. We were lying on our deathbed waiting for death to take us when a mysterious man showed up at our door. He said his name was the Seer. He also said he had powers to heal both of us off the plague. But before he did that, he made us promise that we would never transform into ogres ever again, and we would never harm another human. We agreed and he healed us. We are forever indebted to him."

"He is a good man."

"Yes he is. You carry his stave don't you?" said the man, looking down at Mashaka.

"Yes I do. But what about Chawi, he tried to attack me last night?"

"Son, there are things that even grown men cannot comprehend. Deep inside I am still an ogre. I have to quench the spirit and the urges that come with that one way or another. I am sure you have night runners in Amani."

"Yes we have them."

Jitu was refereeing to those individuals possessed by forces well beyond their control. While these forces were really benign, they never left a person at rest until they were dispensed off in one way or another. Some people fell sick with mysterious maladies while others experienced periodical instances of lunacy. Another manifestation would be possessed people who stutter in times of a full moon. Although no one had ever seen this, people rumored that some possessed people actually turned into bloodhounds and bayed at the moon incessantly.

A majority however, resorted to night running as a way of dispensing off these forces. They would on occasion run wild in the night, scaring night travelers but really doing them no harm. In fact, even when captured, no one really punished a night runner. Brave victims would normally turn on the night runners and chase them out of the vicinity instead. When faced with a charging victim, a night runner usually succumbed and ran away.

However, they had to abide by certain unspoken rules. They were not supposed to run outside the confines of their home village. A night runner's life was in peril if he or she attempted to run in a strange village. If captured in that situation, runners would be tied at stake until morning. This would spell doom for them because the morning sun was not supposed to shine on them before they returned home. If that happened, the morning sun would suck out all the melanin from their skin. The night runners would first turn as pale as a cloud then mysteriously fall sick and wither away within days. There was no cure for a night runner's disease so no one dared to break the rules.

But at the same time it was not uncommon to hear stories of a night runner who broke the rules and attacked his victim in a strange village. When identified, this same runner would mysteriously vanish, never to be seen again. Rumor had it that the victim's family would capture and torture him slowly and finally dismember his body. They would then dispose off the parts in different locations in order to get rid of the forces that existed inside him.

"So why do you head to the land of the Rainmakers?" the man, obviously embarrassed, tried to steer the topic of conversation away from night running.

"To get medicine for my ailing mother," Mashaka lied again.

"Listen. You can trust me with the truth."

"I head to the land of the Rainmakers to get the answer to destroy the evil lord."

"And how do you plan to kill such a powerful force?"

"I don't know. But the Seer said I must. Plus if I don't destroy the evil lord he will destroy the whole world. Furthermore, I will not be allowed back to my village. That means I will never get to see my mother, my friends, or my siblings ever again."

"Then I think it's time you headed east to the land of the Rainmakers."

Mashaka shook the man's hand in farewell and headed east. He occasionally turned back to look as the man disappeared back into the Forest of the Damned.

CHAPTER 8

Escape from Gereza

Mashaka felt a strange sense of relief walking away from the Forest of the Damned. He was glad to be out of there but again he didn't know what awaited him on his journey. He kept wondering if anyone would believe his adventures once he got back home; especially the one about the Forest of the Damned. How was he going to explain a forest possessed by evil spirits? Evil spirits possessed people and sometimes animals, but forests? They would probably laugh at him and call him crazy. Just the way they laughed at the Seer—initially that is.

Mashaka heard that nobody believed the Seer when he first talked about the evil lord and a child born of mysterious conception. The people of the village assumed he was just a demented old man with an active imagination. But then his mother was found on the outskirts of the village. Even then, people still doubted the Seer's words. After all what was so strange about a villager getting thrown out? It was common for villagers to banish people for good. Rapists were thrown out. Habitual thieves, especially those who pilfered from the indigent were thrown out. Murderers where banished from their villages too. Many people theorized that the situation with Mashaka's mother was a typical case of banishment. They assumed that the simple reason for that was the apparent shame she brought upon her father.

It was only after the *Vuas* attacked the day Mashaka was born that the Seer won a few converts. It was only then that people started paying more attention to his words. But then fifteen years passed and nothing happened. Human memory, as fleeting as it is, fades quickly. Within no time people forgot the Seer's warnings. It was only after the *Damus* showed up again that people started to heed his warnings again.

But all that did not matter. After all, Mashaka was eventually thrown out of the village. The only way to redeem himself and gain acceptance back was to do what the Seer instructed—reach the land of the Rainmakers and get the answer to the destruction of the evil lord.

Mashaka wondered whether the Seer himself had been to the land of the Rainmakers. At least he reached the land of the one-eyed ogres. *But why did he come so far?* And why was he so secretive about the answers Mashaka so desperately needed? These questions would haunt the boy for the rest of his journey.

The Seer was as mysterious as a strange voice in the dark. No one really knew of his origins and he far outlived everyone in the village. Rumor had it that he was probably the first resident of the village. But it was his strange life that actually fueled the mysticism that embodied him. For example, Mashaka heard that the man once disappeared into the wilderness for fourteen years. They added that it was during this sojourn that he became a changed man. Somehow somewhere in the wilderness, he received supernatural powers. He could now perceive things normal human beings could not. He even gained great knowledge in herbal medicines and strange languages. They said he could communicate with animals and that he knew the language of the birds. But it was the supposed supernatural powers he possessed that people talked about the most.

They said he could foretell the future. They also said he could read peoples' minds upfront. In fact, it was exactly for these two reasons that he earned the title of the Seer. Some people claimed to have seen him remain dry in a rainstorm. Others said he could hold his hand inside a hot flame with no effect on his skin. But the Seer himself was a very modest and humble man. Even if he possessed these so called powers, he was not the kind of person to flaunt. He let his actions speak for themselves and that made him an even larger enigma to the villagers.

Probably I should use the bracelet and confront him about the answers to all my questions. But Mashaka quickly answered himself. *But he said the answers will come when I am ready. Probably I am just not yet ready for them.*

Did the Seer know who his father was?

What happened to his father?

Why had his father not come looking for him all these years?

Why hadn't his mother ever mentioned his father?

Or was he dead?

These questions ran through the young boy's mind as he went on his journey, pushing deeper and deeper east.

He was almost running out of the meager food the woman in the land of the one-eyed ogres packed for him when he finally reached the outskirts of a large city. It was the largest settlement the boy had ever seen. It stood majestically on top two hills protected by massive and imposing stone walls. A long flight of rough stone steps led up to a massive wooden gate. The fields outside the town where covered with crops of all kinds and from afar, Mashaka could see people working the fields.

He slowly approached the town, unsure exactly what type of people he was bound to run into. As he drew nearer, he met some of the town's people tending to their crops. He approached one old man and inquired about the city.

"This is the city of Gereza, and where are you from?"

"I am from Amani."

"Amani, I have never heard of such a place. It must be a very far off land," the man replied, looking at Mashaka quizzically. "So what brings you to Gereza?"

"I am traveling east to the land of the Rainmakers."

"To the land of the Rainmakers? What business takes you to the land of the Rainmakers?"

"My mother has a serious ailment and I need to get medicine for her," Mashaka lied one more time.

"Then you must love your mother very much for that is a long and dangerous journey you are making," the man said, showing genuine concern for the boy. "Well, welcome to Gereza."

"Thank you," Mashaka said and walked towards the huge city gates.

At the gates he had to go through a check point where armed guards grilled him on the purpose of his visit.

"You are traveling to the land of the Rainmakers?" asked one burly guard.

"Yes, my mother ails seriously and I have to get medicine for her."

"They have medicine men all over the land, why make such a long trip to the land of the Rainmakers?" another guard asked, not convinced by Mashaka's response.

"No … no … it is true …"

"Ha! You are lying!" the burly guard snapped. "We have been getting a lot of reports about spies trying to get through the city walls. Are you a spy?"

"No, no I am not a spy. I am just an innocent traveler."

"We will see about that. Take him to the station!" the man ordered.

Mashaka was roughly escorted to the guard station just inside the city. Even though they put him through hours of interrogation, the guards still remained unconvinced about his innocence.

"Take him to the high priest. He will tell if the boy is a spy," his interrogator commanded.

Mashaka was led farther into the city to meet the high priest. The high priest's temple stood at the top of one of the hills he'd seen from afar and Mashaka and the guard had to climb numerous stairs to get to it. The massive doors to the temple were guarded by more armed men. After his escort explained the situation to the temple guards, Mashaka was finally led inside.

He entered a huge hall lit by powerful flaming torches hanging midway on the wall. Along the walls stood statues depicting different people garbed in religious attire. Each held out a globe, probably symbolizing the earth. In the middle of the hall lay a long thick carpet that seemed to run for miles, ending at a huge throne on which sat the high priest.

He was a tall intimidating man whose sharp eyes seemed to penetrate the very core of any person he talked to. He was dressed in his ceremonial attire that consistent of an immaculate flowing robe that ostentatiously sparkled with numerous jewels. On his head was an elaborate thick leather band with more jewels encrusted into it. Above his forehead was a tall ostrich plume that wavered softly anytime he moved his head.

"Who comes in when I am about to go to my evening prayers?" his voice boomed across the hall.

"Your holiness, this boy travels from a far off land and we think he is a spy come to steal secrets from our city," the temple guard said.

"Bring him forth, now!"

The temple guard nudged Mashaka forward using his long spear. Mashaka stumbled towards the high priest.

"So you are a spy come to steal our secrets?" the high priest hissed at Mashaka, who now stood at the foot of the throne.

"No ... I ... I ..." Mashaka could not muster the words to continue.

"You shall speak to the high priest on your knees. Now!" the man commanded, pointing to the ground.

Mashaka went down on his knees.

"You know what we do with spies around here? We throw them in jail ... forever!" the high priest hissed some more. "From where do you travel?"

"I come from Amani."

"Amani ... Mmh," the high priest stopped to ponder for a moment, as if trying jog his memory.

"And what is that stick you carry?" he asked, looking curiously at the stave.

"It is a ceremonial stave given to me by an old man in Amani."

"Bring it closer."

The high priest leaned over and took a closer look at the stave. He jumped back in surprise, cringing in his throne and reacting as if he had seen an apparition.

"Guard, take this boy out of my sight now! Get him away from me!"

"Yes your holiness," the guard said as he quickly jumped on Mashaka, hauling him roughly across the hall. The high priest jumped from his throne and followed them, still berating Mashaka.

"You, I know you, I know you," he hissed even louder. "I know what you want. I know what you want."

Mashaka turned his head back in fear and disbelief. How did the high priest know him? He had never been to this city before.

"Throw him in prison with the rest of the scum. I will deal with him tomorrow," the high priest hissed as Mashaka was transported to the prison located on the other side of the city.

As Mashaka was escorted roughly across the city, people stopped to look, wondering who the young boy was and what he might have done. Mashaka was hurried past the prison gates, down a steep flight of moldy stairs and into the dark confines of the city prison. The guards finally shoved him into one of the cave-like enclosures that made the prison cells. The heavy metal bars clanged with a bang as the guards closed the door on him.

He crouched in the semi-darkness, still trying to grasp what had just happened to him.

He glanced around his cell nervously. The floor was dirty and full of debris. In the corner, he could see shackles joined to a thick chain anchored to the floor. In the dim light of the cell Mashaka could make out strange stains on the wall. On further examination the stains turned out to be dried blood, probably from a tortured prisoner. As if to confirm Mashaka's suspicions, an agonized scream rang out from one end of the cells. He could also hear thudding sounds accompanying the agonized screams. Mashaka dashed to the door and peeped through the metal bars but he could not see anything.

Just then he heard heavy footsteps and the low moaning sounds like those of a wounded man. Mashaka ducked into the shadows. The footsteps drew closer and from his hiding spot he could see the sandaled feet of the prison guards as they dragged a bleeding man across the stony ground. They proceeded to dump him in the cell opposite his. As they banged the metal doors shut, the guards shouted insults at the prisoner, sending him all kinds of threats.

"You will speak finally," shouted one guard.

"Yes, we will break you down," shouted another.

"You think you are a great warrior? Let's see how you will handle what I have in store for you tomorrow, traitor!" taunted the first guard.

"Ha-ha-ha," the second guard laughed as they both spat on the man and walked back down the hall. The whole place echoed with their sadistic laughter.

The wounded man lay motionless on the dirty floor for several minutes before he slowly and laboriously tried to haul himself up. But it took several attempts for him to even get on all fours. He looked like he had undergone severe torture. As he coughed and gagged, blood spattered from his mouth and he used his dirty clothing to wipe it off. He finally got to his knees and while supporting himself on the metal bars, he peeped outside his cell.

Mashaka slowly emerged from within the shadows and peered at the man, speechless.

"What are you looking at young boy?" his gruff voice sounded from across the hallway.

"Nothing," said Mashaka, moving back into the shadows.

"Wait!" said the man in a low voice. "What is that you have with you?"

"This is just my travel bag. I have some dried food if you want," Mashaka offered.

"I am not talking about your damned food. I am talking about the stave. Where did you get that?"

"It was given to me," Mashaka answered, wondering why the man would be interested in the stave.

"By who?"

"A friend."

"The Seer!" the man said in disbelief. "The Seer gave you the stave?"

"Yes ... do you know the Seer?" Mashaka asked, now hanging desperately to the metal bars.

"Of course I know the Seer. You are traveling to the land of the Rainmakers aren't you?" the man asked, his eyes brightening up in amazement.

"Yes!" Mashaka exclaimed in utter astonishment.

"Then I advice that you leave this place today, otherwise your life will be in real danger."

"My life in danger, but why?"

"Because the high priest cannot have you go into the land of the Rainmakers. You have to leave tonight."

"But how can I leave this place? I cannot break through these metal bars."

"Look here young boy ..." The man stopped short as footsteps approached from the end of the hallway.

"Who is talking?" a guard shouted, approaching Mashaka's cell. "Prisoners are not allowed to speak unless spoken to! You, great warrior, did I hear you speak?"

The guard was now standing right across from Mashaka's cell. The boy was cowering in shadows.

"No," answered the man.

"What, are you scared to admit the truth?" the guard mocked, laughing sarcastically. "Great warrior indeed."

"I am not afraid of any man," the man shot back at the guard.

"Well, you better keep it down," the guard said as he returned to his station.

"Hey, hey," the man called out to Mashaka in an undertone. "Listen. Tonight is the celebration of the first harvest. The people of Gereza have to thank their ancestors for a good harvest this year. They will be drinking and eating. Late in the night all the guards will be drunk and asleep. We have to get you out of here then. Do you hear me?"

Mashaka nodded in agreement, totally baffled by the man's kindness.

"Now sit back and act like nothing happened between us. I will give you a signal when the right time comes."

The celebration of the first harvest, or the feast of *Karamu* as it was called in Gereza, was the biggest celebration of the year. This was the time the city's people gave thanks to their ancestors for a bountiful harvest. Having been through many lean years, this year's harvest was something to celebrate for.

The harvest had far out done any other in memorable history and there would be more than enough to feed the people for a long time. It was time to give thanks to the ancestors for their benevolence and the people of Gereza did not spare any resources or energies in showing their appreciation.

The high priest, who was also the city's chief administrator, kicked off the week long festivities after the evening prayers. Since it was believed that he was the sole link between the human and spirit world, he had to be as pure as possible before he led the celebration. He had to spend days fasting and meditating in order to purify his spirit. But in his case no amount of fasting or meditation could cleanse his sprit. For as any man who makes a pact with the devil knows, there is always payback time. For this particular high priest, pay back was long overdue.

The city had been on the verge of collapse after long years of drought and famine. Weakened by hunger, the people of Gereza succumbed to disease and malnutrition. Over the years the enemies of Gereza enviously eyed the city's prosperity. Each year saw the city grow to greater heights. The army of Gereza was strong and on countless occasions defended the city from attack. But the drought weakened the system and brought the great city of Gereza to its knees.

Sick and hungry, the people of Gereza camped outside the high priest's temple and begged for help. Day in and day out the sick succumbed to disease and hunger as the high priest watched helplessly. The burial grounds soon filled up. Even the grave diggers were too weak to dig anymore. Then word reached the city that invaders were planning to conquer and overrun it once and for all. It was too much for the high priest to take. In desperation, he decided to do the one thing he thought would save the city. He made the treacherous journey to Mount Elgon and made a dark pact with the evil lord. In exchange for the city's salvation, the high priest agreed to give up his soul to the evil lord. This was a one time deal neither of them could undo. His soul forever belonged to the evil lord both in life and death. This also meant that from then henceforth, he would be the evil lord's vassal, doing his evil bidding anytime he so desired.

On his return, the rewards from the dark pact were almost immediate. Rejuvenating showers of rain fell for days. The parched and arid soil quenched its decade long thirst as it soaked up the long awaited rain. Plants sprouted from the newly moist ground almost overnight. The diseases afflicting the people of Gereza seemed to disappear in a matter of days. Once again the rivers filled to the brim with life sustaining water. Needless to say, the dark cloud of desperation that hovered over the city for years lifted. It was as if the whole city had undergone a ritualistic catharsis. On the horizon, a new era of prosperity awaited the residents of Gereza.

But the people did not know the source of their new bounty. All they knew was that they woke up everyday to see their city grow bigger and stronger. The army of Gereza almost doubled in strength and number. The city expanded to limits that beat the imagination of even the most prospecting resident. The only things that mattered to the people of Gereza were; their stomachs were full, their bodies were healthy, and they lived in the safest city known to mankind at that time. What more could they ask for? There was only one thing they knew they had to do; give their total allegiance and loyalty to the man who saved them from the jagged maw of peril. The people showered the high priest with praise and admiration. The city held him in a manner only reserved for the most sacred entities.

But the high priest knew very well where his new allegiance lay. He also knew he was forever bound to the whims of the one who resuscitated his city. It was not surprising therefore that the evil lord warned the high priest to keep an eye out for anyone heading east to the land of the Rainmakers. Anyone arrested under those circumstances was to be held in prison and delivered straight to the evil lord himself.

Mashaka had to get out of the city as soon as possible.

From his cell, Mashaka could hear the celebration going on outside. He could hear people singing and shouting, children playing and squealing in joy, and ceremonial horns blowing. Inside the prison, the guards would frequently make their rounds to make sure all prisoners were locked up in place. But as the night wore on the frequency by which the guards came by lengthened. Every time a guard came by he would stagger on his feet and whenever he spoke he would reek of alcohol.

"Hey, hey," called the man across Mashaka's cell. "We have to make our move soon. Listen very carefully."

The man went ahead and laid out the escape plan.

When the next guard came staggering down the hall, Mashaka watched and waited quietly from the shadows until the man was right outside his cell. He then extended out his stave, on which the guard tripped, falling to the ground in a heap. The drunken guard remained on the floor, too inebriated to move. His alcohol flask lay by his side and the liquid seeped out slowly, forming a tiny rivulet that flowed into Mashaka's cell.

"Quick, reach for his keys," the man commanded.

Mashaka strained against the metal bars to reach for the guard's keys but he was just a few inches short.

"You have to do it now, someone is approaching," the man said desperately.

With on last heave of determination, Mashaka got hold of the keys and yanked them off the guard's belt. Just then another guard came staggering down the hall, calling out to his comrade.

"There you are you old goat. Get up! I have more beer for us. Who says you cannot have fun on the job?" the guard said as he hauled his comrade away.

"Now open the door, and do it quietly."

Shaking, Mashaka fumbled with the keys as he tried to work the simple lock from inside the cell. He was so nervous he dropped the keys several times. Just when he had the key inside the lock ready to open the door, he heard more footsteps approaching. He quickly ducked into the shadows, leaving the keys hanging on the door. The man across from his cell fell to his knees, covered his head in anguish and cursed bitterly. He knew they had come so close.

Or had they?

"Askari! Askari! Where are you?" the guard shouted, looking for his colleagues.

To Mashaka, everything started to happen as if in slow motion. His heart sunk as he watched the guard pass right outside his door. The man was so close his fingers brushed the keys slightly as the hung on the door. The keys chimed gently as the man called out.

"Askari, can you hear me?" the guard called as he disappeared towards the opposite end of the hall, looking for his comrades.

"Now do it!" the man hissed from across the hallway.

Mashaka turned the key and the lock gave. He opened the door slowly and tiptoed into the hallway.

"Open my door quick!" the man whispered sharply.

Mashaka rushed across and opened the man's cell door. Free from bondage, they made a hasty exit through the unguarded entrance—but not before the man grabbed the guard's beer flask and chugged the remaining alcohol.

"We have to move," Mashaka urged the man as he gulped the beer noisily.

The man dropped the flask. "What a waste of good beer. Let's go."

Outside the prison, the streets were teeming merrily with revelers as they went about their boisterous celebration. Everybody was dressed in fancy and colorful clothes and their faces were painted in all types of shades too. Children ducked in and out of the crowd as their parents called out to them. Dancers performed in the streets and acrobats displayed their skills on tightropes. All around was joy and fanfare.

Mashaka and the man mingled into the crowd.

"This way," the man said as they ducked into a side street.

They hastily walked through the narrow back alleys of the city, making for the back wall. But they had to duck into the shadows several times to avoid the patrolling guards.

"Where are we going?" Mashaka asked.

"We are going to the back wall. There is a sewage tunnel that opens up through the city wall into the burial grounds. We have to get to the river quickly."

"We will go through the burial grounds? Is there no other way to get to the river?" Mashaka asked worriedly. He was not very enthused by the prospect of crossing the burial grounds.

"Don't be afraid. Furthermore, that is the only escape route we have. Unless of course you want to go through the city gates."

Mashaka shrugged his shoulders and went along with the idea. It was not long before both were running through the smelly tunnel and into the burial grounds outside. The man, who seemed to have bled profusely from the torture, was losing strength rapidly.

"Are you okay?" Mashaka inquired.

"Yes I am okay. We have to reach the river," the man said, panting hard with blood spattering from his mouth.

"Who are you and why are you doing this for me?" Mashaka asked, still not sure about the man's intentions.

"My name is Moran, the best warrior Gereza ever had. I did not agree with high priest's decision to sell out to the evil lord so I resigned from his army. The only way you leave the army is through death. Deserters are thrown in prison and tortured for the rest of their lives."

"But how did you know the Seer?"

"He came to me in a dream and showed me a vision. It was the future of my city under the rule of the evil lord. It was horrible! I cannot allow that to happen to my people. Never! You have to get to the land of the Rainmakers and stop this evil. Now let's hurry."

The burial grounds were located inside a thick wooded area not far from the city walls. Mashaka and Moran dashed through the trees, making for the river that ran not too far ahead. The place was eerily quiet and it reminded Mashaka of the Forest of the Damned. The wind howled through the trees and occasionally Mashaka thought he heard voices in it. The wind intensified midway through the burial grounds, shaking the trees violently and sending thick braches falling all around them. So now, not only did they have to make haste for the river, they had to run in a zigzag pattern to avoid the falling branches. The wounded man was heaving in pain but with the determination only a warrior of his stature could muster, he kept his step.

It was not long after they were deep into the wooded burial grounds that Mashaka lost his footing and went crashing face fast into the ground, losing his grip on the stave. He fell into a very soft, wet, and fluffy spot. Shocked but unharmed, he quickly struggled to get up. But the ground underneath him gave in. Soon, huge chunks of the earth were falling into a hole on his left side. He scrambled to his feet but slipped once more. He held on to the edge of the hole desperately while his lower body hung precipitously over a huge dark abyss.

"Hold on to my hand," Moran shouted to him.

Mashaka reached out and grabbed the man's hand.

"What is that hole?" he asked, desperately clinging to the man's hand.

"That is the *Shimo La Mauti*. The pit of the undead," the man replied as he tried to pull Mashaka out of the pit.

He had almost pulled the boy out of the pit when suddenly and without warning, loud moans and cries erupted from deep inside the huge dark hole. Mashaka fought to keep his grip on the man's hand, not knowing what it was that was producing the frightful sounds. He finally put one leg on the edge, but just when he was about to swing his other leg from the pit, several ghostly appendages shot from the dark hole and grabbed it. The hands that grabbed his leg where a sight to behold. To begin with they were thick, round, and long. Their strange texture made them look as though they were made from some form of sticky mud that came from a type of deep red soil. They wound themselves around Mashaka's legs but due to their slippery composition, they slipped back into the pit. But more hands shot up instantaneously, pulling him down some more. Meanwhile, the ghostly moans turned into very audible cries. The voices were painfully calling out one name—Mashaka.

It was not long before the mysterious hands had Mashaka chest deep into the pit. Moran stared at the spectacle in disbelief but all this time he never let go of Mashaka's hand. He knew exactly who the mysterious hands belonged to. In the vision, the Seer showed him who they were. These were the hands of the *Mauti*; the hands of the damned, the hands of the undead. The hands belonged to the people from whom the high priest harvested souls. He harvested the souls as a sacrifice to appease the evil lord. These were innocent men, women, and children, given away as part of the dark pact the high priest made with the evil one.

The sacrifice was probably the most horrendous act anyone in Gereza could commit, let alone the high priest himself. These people were sacrificed in the most heinous manner. The high priest would first starve them to the brink of death. When they were on the verge of dying, he would personally force-feed them a type of red soil only found in deep graves. But this was no ordinary grave soil. Ordinary grave soil was also known as the forbidden and cursed soil. This type of soil came into contact with only two types of people; the dead, and the grave diggers who fashioned their eternal abode. This was the same soil the high priest carried with him from Mount Elgon. It was also the very soil upon which he shed his blood to seal the dark pact he made with the evil lord. The evil lord took the cursed soil and vilified it even further. The resulting product contained malevolent properties beyond imagination. Its dark potency would soon befall the hapless victims on whom it was used upon.

After consuming the ultra-potent soil, it would then start boiling over then spread throughout the victims' veins like fast acting venom. Within minutes, their bodies would fill with the poison, forcing the soil to spill out from their skin pores, eyes, mouths, and noses. Still alive, the high priest would have them deposited into the pit of the undead. Here, the cursed soil would start eating the victims from inside. It took only but a few days for it to consume them completely. It was at this point that their tortured souls departed from their bodies, to be snatched forever by the evil lord. The soulless bodies left in the pit faced an eternity of a semi-dead state of purgatory. They could not join the spirit world because they were not dead. But at the same time, without their souls, they could never be human again. The hands from purgatory did not mean Mashaka any harm. To them, he was exactly what a floating straw would seem to a drowning man. They were just fighting to have their souls back.

"Here, take the stave, quick!" Moran called out to Mashaka.

Now grasping Mashaka by one hand, Moran quickly reached for the stave and handed it to the boy. No sooner did Mashaka touch the stave than the hands from purgatory let him go. Mashaka quickly scrambled to safe ground.

"What happened to them?" Mashaka asked in fear, peering at the pit from a safe distance.

"The stave freed them from the pit of the undead. Its powers reclaimed their souls. They are now free forever."

"How did you know all that?"

"The Seer showed that to me too."

The cries coming from the pit stopped the moment Mashaka touched the stave. The rough wind blowing thick branches to the ground also ceased at the very moment. Nothing but calm descended upon the entire burial ground. A luminous mist lifted from the depths of the pit of the undead as the spirits of the sacrificed people rose into the sky. The stave had just granted them the freedom that for years, they longed and thirsted for. They were now liberated to roam the land of the spirits, free at last.

"Now we have to get to the river. Come on," Moran said.

They crossed the eerie burial ground quickly and soon made it to the river. Although the riverbank was dotted with several guard boats, there were no river guards in sight. Just like the prison guards, these too had consumed their fair share of alcohol and had momentarily left their positions. Mashaka and Moran approached the boats slowly.

"Shh," warned Moran as he studied the place. "They are drunk but we have to make for the boats very quietly."

They tiptoed between the drunken river guards and untied one of the boats. As they pushed the boat into the river, they heard a loud horn going off in the city.

Moran froze.

"What was that noise?" Mashaka whispered.

"They have found out. That is the horn of *Hatari*. It is the horn of danger. They only blow it if attackers have been sighted or if there is an escaped prisoner. Quick! Get into the boat and row with all your might."

"Aren't you coming too?"

"No, you ..." He did not finish the sentence. An arrow whizzed through the air and struck him. He arched back in pain.

"Go, go now!" Moran gasped as more arrows rained on him.

Mashaka rowed like a man possessed with thirteen demons as arrows whooshed past him. Behind him, Moran lunged at the pursuing guards with arrows still lodged deep in his back. He grabbed a machete from the guards and engaged them in a vicious fight. This bought Mashaka some valuable escaping time. But Moran, overmatched by the guards, was soon overwhelmed.

Mashaka reached the other side of the river, jumped off the boat and swam to the riverbank. A volley of arrows missed him narrowly and some even landed on the sand just inches away from him. He ran for his life, heading into the forest that stood not too far away from the riverbank. As more arrows rained all around him, he dashed into the protective confines of the awaiting forest. But just as he leapt into the thickness of the welcoming forest, one arrow lodged deep into a tree, just a fraction of an inch from his head. Mashaka flew through the air and disappeared into the trees.

He had never been happier to see the dark enclosures of a forest.

CHAPTER 9

Land of the Falling Skies

Moran fought the guards with all his might. He swore to himself that if he was to go down he would take with him as many guards as possible. But most important he knew he had to buy Mashaka valuable time to get across the river and into the forest beyond. He slashed deftly at the charging guards, valiantly displaying his fighting skills. But his mortal wounds soon got the better of him and the guards finally brought him down. He lay on the sandy riverbank, gasping for breath, his clothes drenched in a crimson wetness. He slowly turned his head towards the other side of the river just in time to see Mashaka hit the riverbank and run to safety into the forest. He turned his head towards his tormentors who were now staring aghast as the boy escaped right before their eyes.

As if in celebration, Moran smiled weakly at the guards. The last thing he saw was a guard's machete swinging towards him.

The pain was intense but brief. It disappeared as quickly as it appeared. A sense of peace and calm engulfed him. It was as if an ethereal painkiller was running deep inside his veins. He felt light and free from burden. His mind was as clear as the sparkling water from the local springs. His depleted energy stores suddenly filled with renewed vim as a bright cloud descended to envelop him. From it, a familiar voice emerged.

"You have done it great warrior. The boy is now safe."

"Seer is that you?" Moran asked.

"Yes my son, it's me. I have come to congratulate you on your good deeds. You are a great man and you will be remembered for that."

"But am I going to die Seer?"

"My son, a good soul keeps forever. It does not matter where and how, but a good soul keeps forever."

"My mother, my father …"

"You will soon be reunited with your people, great warrior. They will be very proud of you. They will be very, very, proud my son."

"I feel calm and peaceful. I have never felt this way in a long time. I have never felt this way since I was little boy."

"That's because you have recaptured the real essence of life great warrior. You have washed away the ills the world imparted onto your system throughout your life. There is not too much difference between you and a newborn. You are in a perfect state of existence. Great warrior, you are free from all the chains and restraints life clamped on you. You have just drank from the elixir of everlasting existence. You, Moran, are about to head to the land of the free!"

"I can feel it Seer. I can feel the freedom."

"Then it is time you enjoyed your new freedom my son. Where you are about to head, no man shall put his chains on your feet. No man's shackles shall touch your wrists. No man's spear shall be strong enough to penetrate your skin. And most important, no man shall ever trouble your soul again."

"I am going to the land of my ancestors?"

"Yes my son, it's about time you joined the great ones. You have made them so, so, proud, great warrior."

"Oh, how I have longed for freedom. I have thirsted for freedom for a long time. I can't believe that I finally get to taste it."

"You have earned every ounce of your freedom great warrior. Now my son, it is time to taste the fruits of your labor."

"Yes Seer, I'm eager to taste the fruits of my labor."

"Now get up my son. Get up and take your first step in freedom," the Seer cried out.

Moran got up and took a few steps. He felt as light as a feather. It was as if his body was totally weightless. He took another step and this time his feet left the ground.

"I can walk in the air!" he shouted in amazement. "It feels so good Seer, it feels so good!"

"Ha-ha-ha, it must feel so good my son."

He took a few more steps and each time he did that, he went higher off the ground. He threw his arms out and started gliding through the air.

"I can fly! I can fly!" he shouted as he flew higher.

"Fly on great warrior, fly to your freedom, fly to your new home!"

Within no time Moran was flying over the city. He kept going higher and higher until he disappeared into the dark night sky.

❧   ❧   ❧

Back in Gereza, word had reached of Mashaka's escape. It would be an understatement to say the high priest was irate. The man was raving mad. He had finally lost it. The evil pent up inside him for all these years came gushing out in powerful torrents. His ire was about to scorch those around him.

"How could he escape right under you noses?" he hissed at the prison guards, who now knelt as his feet, shackled at the wrists.

"He … he stole my key your holiness," said Askari.

"And how did he manage to do that?"

"I don't now, I was walking then I tripped over something … I cannot remember," the guard answered, shaking under the frightening gaze of the high priest.

"You know prison guards are not supposed to drink on the watch! What kind of guards are you?"

The high priest's hand cut through the air and landed soundly on the guard's face. The man went crashing to the ground. He remained down, whimpering and bleeding as the high priest simmered some more.

"Call the celebration off!" the high priest called out to the temple guards. "I have to prepare for a journey; a very long journey."

The temple guards glanced at each other nervously. Never before had the feast of *Karamu* been cancelled. The magnitude of Mashaka's escape started sinking in.

"Vacate this scum from my presence!" the high priest hissed and spat on the kneeling prison guards.

The temple guards quickly whisked them away. The high priest then turned to the chief temple guard and hissed softly.

"Prepare the best hyena horses you have."

"Yes your holinesses, I will have the best hyena horses ready for you in no time," the guard said as he hastily turned to leave the room.

"Hold it there!" the high priest called, leaning close to the guard's ear. "I want the traitor's body dismembered and burnt to ashes. No trace of him shall remain."

"Yes your holiness," the guard answered, visibly shaken. He was so scared he could not bring himself to look the high priest straight in the eye.

"Look me in the eye!" the high priest hissed, jerking the guard's chin around and forcing him to look straight into his burning eyes.

What the guard saw in those eyes would have sent shivers down the spine of the bravest and most battle tested warrior. The eyes were squinted like those of a large cat. But it was what the guard saw in them that sent his skin crawling. The whites of his eyes had turned into a blazing bright red color. The eyes were practically on fire and tiny flames blazed and burned fiercely inside them. But the strangest thing about the eyes was his pupils. They were dilated and looked icy cold, standing in sharp contrast to the blaze around them. They looked as though they were frozen in a lifeless and monotonous bluish white color. But the more the guard gazed in them, the more he realized that the pupils were not lifeless. They were just rotating at a speed so amazing it made them look deceptively stationary. This was a reflection of the malevolent tempest brewing inside the high priest's heart. The stormy rage that had consumed him from within was now boiling over into his eyes.

"Are you afraid of your duties?" the high priest hissed the question.

"No ... no sir, I ... I am not afraid of my duties."

The high priest smiled wickedly. He was enjoying this. "Then you better do everything I tell you. Otherwise you know the fate that befalls those who disobey the high priest."

"Yes your holiness, I will do everything you say," the guard whispered back, totally devoid of his wits.

The high priest took a long look at the prison guards now kneeling at the temple entrance, still shackled at the wrists.

"The lord will need some appeasement. Collect the blood of those foolish ingrates!"

The temple guard's mouth fell open in disbelief. On seeing this reaction, the high priest approached him and in a matter of fact manner stated, "I know your brother just had a new baby. It is either the baby's soul or their blood. You choose. Ha-ha-ha!"

"I will do what you order, your holiness," the guard whispered in fright.

"Now be gone from my sight!" the high priest finished and shoved the guard straight to the floor.

The frightened guard picked himself up and stumbled out of the temple, leading the prison guards away to their fate. The high priest swung back onto his throne, leaned back and sighed.

"I will get you Seer. I will get you for this you old fool."

He braced his hands on his throne, knuckles straining against the skin, blazing eyes staring in a trance as he turned east and screamed.

"The last passage, nooooh!"

❦   ❦   ❦

In the dark, Mashaka dodged between the trees. He stumbled several times but picked himself up each time. He knew he had to put more and more distance between himself and the river. Occasionally he heard an unfamiliar sound that he mistook for a pursuing river guard. He would turn around nervously only to see nothing but the empty forest all around him. He finally came to rest when he was sure no one was following him. He gasped and collapsed on his knees, hardly able to catch his breath.

He peered at his surroundings through the eerie dark. The forest was extremely quiet. It was almost as quiet as the land of the living statues. He groped around in the foliage, trying to get some bearing of his surroundings. He was sure his adventures were not over. His heart raced in fearful anticipation at the mere thought of what he would encounter next.

It started with the *Damus* out in the pastures back in the village. Next were the speed runners, sent by the council spokesman to retrieve the stave. Just the mere thought of the *Gizas* and the land of total darkness sent chills down his spine. In the land of the living statues, he was almost killed by the guardian imps and soon after almost trampled to a pulp by the fighting brothers. The night runner's frightfully masked face kept flashing before his eyes every time he shut his eyes, not to mention the transformation of the one-eyed ogres. He did not even dare to think what would have become of him had Moran not helped him escape from Gereza.

What could have happened to Moran? Was he still alive? Had they captured him and taken him back to the prison for more torture? Or had he died? *No, he can't be dead!* Mashaka lamented to himself.

Only one person would know the answer.

Without thinking twice, Mashaka quickly took the bracelet off his wrist and held it in his palms. The familiar tingling ran up his arms. It was such a welcome sensation. He called out to the Seer.

"Did you call me my son?" the Seer's voice boomed from within the forest.

"Seer is that you? I am so glad to hear your voice."

"It is me my son. You have done wonderfully."

"Thank you Seer, but what happened to Moran?" Mashaka asked in anticipation.

"He was a great warrior, and he will forever be remembered as a great warrior." The Seer sounded solemn.

"Was a great warrior? What do you mean was? Is he dead?" Mashaka labored to bring these words out.

"He is not dead my son," the Seer corrected.

"So he is alive?" Mashaka said, jumping to his feet.

"I did not say that either."

"Then what is it?"

"Be patience my son, be patience. He is with us, but not in the repressive human form in which you met him. He is now free Mashaka. He has gone to be with his ancestors."

"Oh," Mashaka groaned painfully and fell to his knees.

"Mashaka! Do you weep for a free man? Save your tears for those who suffer under the cruel tyranny that permeates your entire world!" the Seer answered sharply. "Moran's soul rests in peace and it will live forever. My son, I promise you that you will meet him one day."

"How much longer do I have to go before I reach the land of the Rainmakers? I am tired and scared. I don't think I can take it any more."

"You are very close my son, you are very close. Now you need to rest. You have had a long day and you will need fresh legs to get to the land of the Rainmakers."

"Thank you Seer." He knew it was no use arguing with the Seer.

With that, Mashaka scaled a tall tree and soon fell fast asleep among its leafy branches. He did not know how long he had been asleep up the tree but when he woke up the sun was already shining bright. At first he did not know where he was. Then, like an angry bull, the events from the previous day came charging into his mind. A sharp pang of sadness cut through his heart when he remembered Moran. The man sacrificed himself for his sake. He gave himself up so the people of the world could live to see better days. Mashaka's heart rendered itself into shreds of pain as he wondered how Moran's last moments would have been like. The last time he saw Moran was when the man took on the small army of river guards. The voice still rang very clear in Mashaka's mind. He remembered Moran shouting defiantly at the attacking guards, moments before he jumped on them. But just before he dashed into the forest and into safety, Mashaka heard the scream. It sounded much similar to the one he heard earlier from the prison torture chambers. But this time it sounded a little bit different. It had a strange ring of finality to it.

But the Seer said Moran was now free. Mashaka had been told that those who made it to the spirit world lived an eternal life of joy and happiness. Surely, for a man who sacrificed himself for others, Moran must be in the spirit world by now. *In that case he must be able to see me now.* Mashaka looked around anxiously as if expecting to see the man who saved his life to emerge from within the forest. But the forest was empty. He was the only human being there.

Mashaka looked up to the sky, wondering whether Moran's spirit was floating high in the clouds. It might have been his imagination but Mashaka though he caught something up in the sky. A lone cloud came floating over the otherwise blue sky and stood still somewhere high above the tree. Mashaka was very perplexed as he looked at the cloud. Then he remembered the superstition. People dismissed it as an old wives' tale. The superstition told that when an important person died and went into the spirit world, the clouds actually paid homage to him. This was a way through which nature signaled that the person had successfully made the journey over into the spirit world. The mysticism of these clouds was propounded further by the fact that they were visible only to the deceased person's loved ones. They called them the clouds of the last passage. These clouds looked different from any other that ever formed in the sky. Their formation was supposed to be unique and very distinct. They would form unmistakable stripes uncannily similar to a zebra's back. But nestled between these stripes would be the delicate luminescence of an unlikely rainbow. Those who claimed to have seen them said it was a sight to behold.

To Mashaka, this could have remained a superstition had he not been sitting up the tree, staring at a distinct cloud formation, shaped exactly as the tale described. It did not take but a moment of thought for the boy to realize what they meant. Moran had finally made it to the spirit world. A deluge of joy and happiness quickly displaced all the sadness chocking his heart. But that was not all. The clouds remained in their unique formation for just a few moments. Then slowly, they twirled around to form a visage that almost knocked Mashaka down the tall tree. It was Moran's face in the clouds. The features were so distinct Mashaka could have as well been staring at the man face to face. He looked very peaceful as he smiled lightly towards Mashaka. But just as the mysterious clouds formed, so did they quickly dissipate into the vastness of the blue sky.

Mashaka looked on as the clouds vaporized into the clear sky. What the Seer promised him came to fruition. He said he would meet Moran one day. That day arrived sooner than the boy would have ever expected.

Still reeling from the experience, Mashaka peered over the horizon and noticed that the vast forest disappeared into a cloudy fog farther east. Did that mean he had to go through the fog? At first he hesitated then he remembered how the Seer assured him he was getting very close to the land of the Rainmakers. He quickly descended the tree and headed towards the fog.

The fog was thick and Mashaka's visibility was limited to a few feet. He peered into the semi-darkness of the fog, expecting an attack from some strange creature anytime. *What would it be this time? Tall wispy creatures the fog wrought? Maybe an evil mist that sucked the life straight from inside of you as you stood watching? Even worse, probably an evil spirit that ruled this foggy land and destroyed all those who passed through? Probably that is why none of the guards bothered to cross the river to pursue him.*

But the more he walked into the fog, the more it thinned out and soon the sun broke through. It shined bright on a sight that snatched the breath right out of Mashaka's mouth.

He stood in amazement, his jaw practicality dropping to the ground.

The sight before him shone bright and clear. The green vegetation looked darker than any he had ever seen. It was darker than the deep green grass he saw in the burial grounds in the land of the living statues. The ground was soft and fluffy and Mashaka could not stop walking up and down on it. The soil looked and felt different too. It was rich and dark with a fine smooth texture, and despite its moistness it did not stick to his feet. Even in the hot sun the dew still sparkled very bright on the grass. The sun itself seemed to hang much lower than he had ever seen. Even the clouds went floating by just slightly above the trees. In fact if he was to climb up a tall tree he was sure he would be able to touch them. And that is exactly what Mashaka did. He hastily scaled a tall tree and was soon caressing the soft clouds as they passed right by his face. The air was crisp and pure and Mashaka inhaled a lungful. He closed his eyes and felt the soft feathery touch of the clouds gently brushing his face.

With his eyes still closed, he kept reaching farther and farther into the clouds. He was lost in the feeling of celestial bliss that now engulfed his whole being. Then his hand hit something solid. Instinctively, he pulled back. *Probably it was a branch,* he thought to himself. But whatever he hit felt very cold. He reached into the clouds again, and this time he felt something crunch in his hand. Curiously, he reached out and grabbed a handful of the substance.

It felt cold in his hands and it crushed easily in his light grip. As it melted slowly in the warmth of his hand, the substance turned into a bluish liquid. Curious, he dipped a finger in the substance and tasted some with the tip of his tongue. The substance tasted good. He put a whole piece inside his mouth. The substance dissolved quickly in his mouth, sending a strange sweet smooth creamy taste down his palate. It was like nothing he had ever tasted. He ate some more, and the more he ate, the more he liked it. He shoved more of it into his mouth, continuously doing so until his mouth was bursting full. No matter how much of the strange substance he ate he could not get enough. Soon it was dripping down the sides of his mouth, past his chin and sticking fast to his clothes. But Mashaka did not even notice that.

As the sun grew hotter and the wind picked up, the clouds started thinning out. It was at that moment that Mashaka saw exactly what it was he was consuming. His mouth fell open as he looked at his hands in disbelief. He quickly pinched himself to make sure he was not dreaming.

Please let me not wake up if it is a dream, he pleaded to himself. But this was no dream. He looked skyward and the reality hit him. His heart almost stopped short. He had done what probably no human, at least none from where he came from had ever done. He had just partaken in an activity all children from Amani and other far off villages would literally die for. He looked down at his hands one more time and in disbelief, he cried out.

"The sky!"

That was what he had just consumed.

When he learnt of Mashaka's escape, the high priest did not scream out in anguish for nothing. He knew that once

Mashaka crossed the river he would be out of reach of evil. By crossing the river, Mashaka entered the last passage. It was also known as the land of the falling skies—the land that time forgot.

This place represented the lingering vestiges of the bygone era of the great optimal world of Sadikia. It was the ancient world of the Great Trust and this legendary world existed for hundreds of years. It represented a period when, for the first time ever, man and nature formed an unbreakable bond based on pure trust. This was the one and only time man literally become one with nature. In return for their trust, nature provided humans with whatever it was they needed for survival. But they were bound by two conditions; man would not interfere with nature's processes, and man would not waste nature's gratuity.

People lived and prospered under this truce. They did not have to lift a finger to perform any work. Nature provided everything to the humans, from fresh water to the very clean air they breathed. People did not have to farm because from the earth, emerged mature crops ready for harvest. People did not get sick because nature got rid of all pathogens that caused maladies. People did not die because nature held death at bay. Men and women did not age because nature held back its ravages. Whenever the weather got too hot, nature would send in cool breezes from the cold mountains to bring down the temperatures. Inversely, whenever it got too cold, nature would turn on its own heating system.

The great era of Sadikia was the apex of human existence.

But the human spirit is fickle. The human mind is easily corruptible, and human will is fallible. At some point, dark temptations seeped into the minds of some humans. As a bad

tomato does to a good bunch, a few evil minds soon cor-
rupted and poisoned man. Within no time humans wanted to
usurp nature off it powers. The humans grew so bold, so
greedy and so ungrateful they wanted to snatch the very
benevolence nature bestowed upon then.

One such benevolence was the sky. Nature lowered the sky
so low humans could easily climb up the trees and harvest as
much of this delicious substance as they desired. But as greed
spread throughout the land, people harvested more sky than
they could consume. Then they carelessly threw the leftover
sky into the rivers. Soon the rivers turned blue from the abundance of the sky disposed off that way. Legend has it that after
the rivers deposited this substance into the seas and oceans,
they turned blue and remained that way to this day.

After several warnings that no one heeded, nature decided
to strike back at humanity. The first thing nature took away
was the sky. It pushed this delicacy deep into the atmosphere,
way out of reach of any human. The humans reacted violently.
They went on a rampage, bringing down anything that represented nature. They cut down trees, they burned forests, and
they deposited dirt and waste into the waterways. All the
while they cursed nature with such vitriolic language that had
never been uttered before. In fact, it is widely believed that
most expletives and curse words used to this day were coined
during that time.

The era of Sadikia came crashing with a bang as nature
counteracted with vengeance. It held back the rain for years. It
sent balls of fire raining down from the sun to the earth. It
sent thick torrents of rain that fell for days. For weeks on end,
nature denied the humans any light and the earth was covered

in total darkness. Remnants of this darkness now remain in the mysterious rocks Mashaka was once trapped in.

When the humans did not repent, nature meted out more punishment for their ungratefulness. It sent all kinds of sicknesses down on earth. It even put pathogens inside some insects and sent out armies of them to attack humans. One such insect was the mosquito. A bite from this formerly benign insect now transmitted to humans, a deadly fever that turned fatal in a matter of days. Insects and bugs whose bite had been harmless so far turned lethal. Ticks spread all kinds of diseases to livestock, fleas jumped from rats with deadly germs, and some insects spread a variety of blight that killed off all plants and crops.

Finally defeated, the humans fell to their knees and begged nature for forgiveness. Some people however, remained defiant. In a last stand with nature, a small band of rebels led by an eccentric man embarked on a last ditch effort to overthrow nature. They were quickly defeated and banished into the fiery bowels of Mount Elgon. This eccentric man would later be known as Lord Kifo, or simply, the evil lord, or, the lord of death—his quest to control nature has never ended.

A small band of people remained loyal to nature and they soon gained its forgiveness. Nature then bestowed upon these people different powers. One group received nature's mightiest gift—the power to make rain. It is to the land of these people that Mashaka was headed.

It was on the second day that Mashaka finished traversing the land of the falling skies. Not sure how much longer he had to go on, he kept on pushing east through the forest of Sadikia. Little did he know that his journey was soon to come to a tantalizing end. On the morning of the third day through the land of the falling skies, he woke up to a sight mere words fail to describe.

For what seemed like eons, Mashaka stood transfixed on one spot. His eyes were glued to the sight for what seemed like an eternity. His legs liquefied in awe and he fell to his knees. His mouth agape, his eyes starry, he beheld the scene unraveling before him.

This was the price he left his beloved mother for. This was what he left his home village for. This was what he went through all the hair-raising adventures for. This was what Moran died for. It was now sitting right before him. It was so close he could almost touch it.

Mashaka's eyes marveled at the indescribable sight—the land of the Rainmakers.

PART II

LAND OF THE RAINMAKERS

CHAPTER 10

Land of the Rainmakers

Mashaka, still on his knees, stared in bewilderment at the magnificent sight before him. This was the culmination of his long and arduous journey. This was what he risked his life for, time and again. This is the place that held his answers. Somewhere in there lay the key that would unlock the mysteries of his life. Here, his world would unravel anew. This was also the place that was about to open a conduit through which he would rid the world off an unimaginable evil. In return, he would earn a one way ticket to reenter his home village and reunite with his family. What the Seer said was true. His long journey had come to an end.

Right before his eyes was the land of the Rainmakers.

Even from a distance, the land of the Rainmakers still exuded its majestic and mystic presence. Its significance rang deep in the minds of all who may have had the rare chance to visit and see its secrets. This was where people skilled in the art of creating rain resided. They were the sole keepers of nature's most powerful element—water. The substance that gave life to all living organisms in the world was forever in their custody. Without water, not a single organism could survive on this earth. Water comes from rain, meaning these people literally held all life on earth in their hands.

They had the power to grant and withhold this vital lifeline so many depended on. But how did they do that? How did they make rain? From what substances did they obtain all the moisture to make the clouds and the rain? How did they distribute rain to all the lands that covered this earth? These are answers Mashaka was about to find out.

He rose to his feet and took his first step into the magical land.

The land of the Rainmakers itself was a mystery; a mystery no one on the outside knew of its origins. Legend had it that the Rainmakers were the descendants of the ancient people who dissented from the rebellious majority to make peace with nature. In return, nature awarded them the power to create and control the rain forever. Of course, those who held on to the rebellion against nature were banished into the fiery bowels of Mount Elgon, to burn in the intense fires eternally.

But right now Mashaka was not concerned with legend. He was in the land of the Rainmakers and he was about to get the answers himself, first hand.

The land of the Rainmakers was in fact a large island that stood in the middle of the Great Lake Sango. The treacherous waters of the lake boiled continuously to form huge and intimidating waves. The violent and relentless currents churning deep inside the lake did not allow for boat travel. Swimming was definitely out of the question. So Mashaka stood by the lakeshore alone, wondering what his next move would be. As far as his eyes could see over the vast lakeshore, there wasn't a single soul from whom he could ask directions.

He glanced up and there stood his prize—so close and yet so far. The city that stood on the island was absolutely breathtaking even at a distance. Mashaka, still feeling stranded and lost on the lakeshore, took in the magnificence.

The bigger part of the city was situated right on the highest point of the island. Even from afar, Mashaka could see its buildings sparkling in the sun. He wondered what material it was that made the city sparkle like so. *Is it made of pure jewels?* Even the city walls sparkled brightly at a distance. But it was the architecture of the buildings that mesmerized him the most. All the buildings were extremely tall and reached very high in the air. They were all shaped differently and in fantastic patterns too. There was a spiraling tower that ended up in a long sharp spire. All around the structure, huge bands of blue worked their way up to the spire, on top of which stood a large rotating ball of light. The light from the ball was powerful even in broad daylight. Mashaka had to cover his eyes momentarily until they adjusted to the intensity of the light.

Another spectacle was a set of three buildings shaped like long cylinders. They stood right behind the spiral tower but reached much higher into the air. But Mashaka also noticed that the buildings did not just stand still. They kept moving up and down in sequence. He watched in amazement as the three structures pistoned up and down. Each time one of the buildings emerged in the air it would monetarily change color from a glassy blue hue to clear water-like transparency.

Another breathtaking structure looked like two gigantic bull's horns facing each other to form an arch. The tips of the two horns were a small distance apart and were joined by a constant bolt of lightning burning in a bright blue electric color. But what caught Mashaka's interest was the huge set of

Ferris wheels rotating in a fantastic formation inside the arch. One upright wheel rotated clockwise. Inside it, another one rotated vertically on its axis, while yet the third rotated diagonally inside the second wheel. Even more amazing was the fourth wheel hanging below the three. This one just rotated on a fixed horizontal axis. Strangely enough these wheels where not attached to the two gigantic bull's horns. It looked as though they were suspended midair.

Not too far from the arch was a set of three mesmerizing gigantic pyramids. These did not stand side by side like any ordinary pyramids. These crystal architectural wonders stood one on top of the other. Just like the pistoning cylinders, the three pyramids were not stationary. They rotated in reverse motion of each other. Mashaka could not help but wonder what magic the Rainmakers used to prevent the pyramids from crumbling under the pressure of the rotation

But it was two other buildings that had Mashaka's mouth literally open and involuntarily drooling. The two rectangular buildings stood side by side and ran probably a couple of miles in width. They did not have much fanfare to them expect for one thing. They were the tallest buildings in the whole city. No matter how far Mashaka craned his neck he could not see the top of the buildings. But how could he? The buildings were so tall they disappeared right into the sky. However, it was not just their height that made them stand out. It was their color too. They were a solid and unceremonial deep blue color, different from all the sparkling structures around them. Instinctively, Mashaka knew these two buildings held special significance to the Rainmakers.

He would soon find out.

Outside the city walls he could also see the dark green forest that covered the island. At a distance, the scenery looked picture perfect and Mashaka longed for the means to get to the island.

He would not have to wait too long.

At first it looked like a tiny white speck but as it approached the lakeshore, Mashaka could see it was indeed some type of large bird. Instinctively, he started backing up. He was not in the mood for any more adventures with fantastic out-of-this-world creatures. The bird drew closer and the more it neared him the larger it became. Soon it was floating right above him, its giant wings flapping and sending powerful wind currents all around him. Now he could tell that it was a giant kite. The giant bird landed gently in front Mashaka and before he could think of any defensive moves it opened its beak and spoke to him.

"Mashaka, welcome to the land of the Rainmakers," it said in a soft female voice.

He was speechless.

"Don't be afraid, Mashaka. I have been sent by The Rainmaker to come and fetch you."

"You … you … talk …" Mashaka stammered. He was pointing at the bird with the innocence of a toothless toddler.

"Of course I do talk. Remember, I am from the land of the Rainmakers. Where I come from, all the birds talk."

"That is just so amazing that a bird can talk," he gasped. "So you are not going to hurt me, are you?" Mashaka asked with a sense of relief.

"Not unless you give me reason to … okay, that was just a joke. I would never touch an innocent young soul like you."

The gigantic bird seemed to tower over Mashaka. Its feathers were as white as chalk, forming a perfect contrast to its jet black wings. Its huge claws sank into the soft sand as it impatiently swung its large black tail in the light wind. On its neck were two leather straps that had some kind of handles on them. Mashaka, who had never seen reins in his life, could not make sense of them.

"What are those things on your neck?"

"Those are my reins. We will be doing a lot of flying together. That means you will need something to hold on to."

"I have always wanted to fly like a bird, far above the ground," Mashaka gasped some more.

"And now you will, Mashaka."

"But how did you learn how to talk? The birds in my village only know how to sing and chirp. They cannot talk," Mashaka asked, now brave enough to reach out and touch the kite. Its feathers were soft and silky.

"That is a long story Mashaka. But hey, you have come to the right place to get all your answers."

"How do you know my name? And how do you know about the answers I seek?"

"We know a lot about you and we know why you travel to our land. Now we must leave before it gets too hot. I don't like flying in the hot sun. Now jump on my back," she cried out.

Mashaka jumped on the bird's back and grabbed the reins. Soon both bird and boy were airborne, headed to the magnificent land of the Rainmakers. Below them, the dark waters of Lake Sango churned and boiled furiously. Mashaka watched the sight in sheer amazement.

❦　　　❦　　　❦

What Mashaka saw from afar was nothing compared to what awaited him from inside the city walls. Everything looked like it was made out of crystal. That was the material that sparkled so bright from afar. The substance shone so bright in the sun it took his eyes a few minutes to adjust to the intensity of its reflection. The kite landed on a large courtyard just outside a huge crystal building. The building was so tall Mashaka had to crane his neck backwards to see the top. Everything looked so big and intimidating, but at the same time so beautiful and breathtaking.

"Step inside Mashaka. The Rainmaker waits for you," the kite said to him.

"Thanks for the ride," he said as he climbed the crystal stairs into the building.

The huge crystal doors swung open as soon as he approached them. Two maids dressed in blue waited inside and they kindly waved him through.

"Wait here while I inform The Rainmaker that you have arrived," said one maid.

As he waited, Mashaka studied his surroundings. He felt as though he was in a dream. In fact, he pinched himself several times to make sure he was not asleep. The walls inside the building were all crystal. Everything was crystal and even inside, everything glistened brightly. All kinds of crystal statues and figurines donned the walls. Huge crystal torches burned in a powerful bluish white flame that did not produce any smoke. Massive and elaborately designed crystal chandeliers hung on the arched roof above. Mashaka wondered what the powerful flame was. On closer examination, all he could conclude was that it looked like miniature lightning bolts. Everything seemed to baffle his young mind. Even the roof took him by surprise. It looked exactly like the sky. His admiration for the Rainmakers was growing by the minute.

"Come this way, The Rainmaker is ready for you." The maid had returned, unbeknownst to Mashaka, who was still transfixed by this crystal heaven.

He followed her through a huge set of crystal double doors that automatically swung open to reveal a large room, still made out of crystal. It was adorned with all kinds of crystal decorations but the most amazing presence in the room was The Rainmaker, who sat on a crystal throne facing away from Mashaka. The throne was suspended midair on a small silver cloud. The cloud rotated slowly and Mashaka came face to face with The Rainmaker.

"Mashaka, welcome to our city." The voice was rough, aged, but steady.

"Thank you," Mashaka said, studying The Rainmaker intently.

The woman sat on her throne majestically, garbed in a simple but elegant blue robe that flowed to her feet. On her head she wore a blue hood from whose edges her dreadlocked hair hung. Her face, though wrinkled, was strong and confident, and her gaze, steady and piercing. But that is not what caught Mashaka's attention. He stared in shock at her hands. Her fingernails must have been inches long and they had intricate blue patterns painted on them. Yet still that is not what Mashaka was staring at. In her right hand she held a stave exactly as the one the Seer gave him.

Mashaka looked down at his stave then at The Rain-maker's.

"Yes I know. You hold a stave just like mine," she said.

"Did the Seer give that to you?"

"Now, now, my boy, we have plenty of time for questions. But right now I can tell you are famished. You know we have prepared a feast for you. Follow me now."

She tapped the throne twice and the cloud descended to the ground. It bounced softly several times before it came to a halt, engulfing both The Rainmaker and her crystal throne. She emerged from the cloud in all her elegance. Although she was well advanced in years, she walked with a majestic and upright posture. She held her head high and proud, her flow-ing robe sweeping the spot free crystal floors. She led Mashaka into an adjoining room in which stood a huge din-ing table filed with all kinds of delicacies.

"Make yourself at home Mashaka. You have traveled far and you need the nourishment. Do not be afraid to dig in."

And that is exactly what Mashaka did. After he was fin-ished, The Rainmaker had him shown to his quarters where he soon fell sound asleep. It was long since he laid his head on a comfortable bed. But this was not an ordinary bed. This was the land of the Rainmakers and it was evident to Mashaka that these people did not practice the word ordinary. The bed they offered him was made out of clouds and crystal.

It was made from the crystal material that seemed to be very popular with the Rainmakers. But the mattress had a fluffy filling that sent Mashaka guessing. Well, he would not wonder for long, for when he finally jumped into the bed he discovered that the white covers were not made from white sheep skin. They were actually made from thin clouds. He snuggled inside the warm cloud covers, totally engulfed in an ethereal feeling he had never experienced.

But suddenly the bed moved with a slight creak and Mashaka felt blood rushing from his brain. He felt as if he was floating in the air.

It's probably just the fatigue.

But when the bed seemed to rise in the air some more, he decided to investigate. He leaned over the edge and almost toppled over. From the reflection on the crystal walls Mashaka saw what was happening. The bed was way off the ground. His crystal bed was actually floating on a small silver cloud just like The Rainmaker's throne. His jaw dropped in amazement. *How will I ever explain this to anybody?* Mashaka agonized joyfully to himself. He was lying in a crystal bed, on a mattress made out of cloud filling, covered in cloud sheets, and all the while suspended midair on a silver cloud? He did not have to wonder about that for long as the exhaustion of his long journey overwhelmed him.

He slumbered like a newborn.

❦   ❦   ❦

The village looked just like he left it.

He walked slowly, not sure what he would find. He could see his mother's house from a distance. The sight spurred him on. He walked faster and as he drew nearer he saw his mother outside. She was feeding the chicken, which jostled around her, each trying to be the first to get the grain falling from her hands. Just then a sudden gust of wind picked up and started blowing strongly against him.

Mashaka was now very close to the house and he walked faster, now taking bigger steps towards his mother. But he just kept marching on the spot, unable to move any farther. The powerful wind was blowing against him so hard it kept pushing him backwards. He tried to push against it with all his might but the effort was futile. Finally he gave up and stood helplessly watching as his mother went back inside the house.

He tried calling out to her but the wind blowing against his face snatched his words and carried them away from his mother's direction. But then his mother reappeared with more grain for the chicken. Again, the birds rushed to her feet for more food. He called out again but the wind grabbed away his words. Mashaka was growing desperate.

Then something caught his eye.

One rooster strayed from the feeding flock and went around the corner, out of sight of his mother. Mashaka watched as the bird stood in a trance momentarily. Something was not right. The rooster then shook its feathers vigorously and they flew off its body. The feathers hovered midair for a while, engulfing the de-feathered rooster before they amazingly transformed into a blood sucking monster—a *Damu*. The monster emerged from the corner and approached Mashaka's mother from behind. He shouted at her with all his might but again nothing happened. The wind was blowing against him even harder. But he kept shouting regardless, trying to warn his mother of the danger right behind her. Just when the monster was about to leap on her, a hand reached out through the strong wind and grabbed him from behind. With a stifled scream, he turned around—it was The Rainmaker.

"Mashaka, you are having a bad dream."

"It's my mother. The *Damus* are attacking her!"

"You were just having a nightmare. That happens when one is very tired you know."

"But my mother."

"Don't worry, she will be okay. You need to get up from bed now. There is a lot that you have to see today. And I have to show you our city."

*   *   *

What Mashaka had seen so far did no justice to what the rest of the city looked like. Of course the whole city was made out of crystal; even the fruits hanging on the green trees lining the city streets.

"Those are ice guavas," The Rainmaker informed him.

But then everybody was dressed in blue. Mashaka wondered about this and inquired about the blue attire.

"You see we control the skies too, and that is our color. We all wear blue to symbolize our relationship with the skies."

"What about the crystal … and … the clouds?"

"What you see is not real crystal. It is actually ice rain that looks exactly like crystal."

"Ice? But how come it is not cold? How come it doesn't melt?" Mashaka sounded confused.

"Well, the ice in your village melts. All ice everywhere melts but here. We have powers to control how it melts. Over here, it melts when we say so. And ice is the cleanest building material you can ever find. It's just another form of clean water. Clean water never brought harm to anyone, did it?"

"No."

"Water is the purest element in the whole world. Water cleans your clothes, it cleans you body, it cleanses the earth, and it cleans everything. We also use the purest and most natural water here."

"Where is the kite that brought me here?" Mashaka asked, remembering the fantastic ride the kite gave him.

"She is around. If you want to, she can take you flying sometime this afternoon."

Mashaka and The Rainmaker chatted as they walked down the city streets. They passed the huge and elaborate ice crystal buildings that stood on both sides of the street. Even the streets were paved in ice. Each building had its own unique architecture. One building looked exactly like a gigantic rain drop. From outside, he could see people going about their business. Another building was made in the form of a gigantic statue standing hundreds of feet above ground. Mashaka wondered who the statue depicted.

"That is our founder. He lived a long time ago but his spirit still remains with us."

Mashaka was awed. "This is all amazing."

"That is what all visitors say. But I am sure you have other things on your mind that you need answers to."

"Yes, the Seer said I will find my answers here."

"He was right. You will find all the answers here. But now I have to show you the most important part of our city. I am about to show you the place in which we make the rain. Come this way," The Rainmaker said and led Mashaka into an open field where a group of clouds stood suspended in midair. She pointed her stave at one cloud and it slowly approached them, landing softly on the ground before them.

"This is our ride. My old legs can only take so much walking. Now get in," she called out.

Mashaka approached the bobbing cloud hesitantly.

"Come on Mashaka, it is just a cloud. Get on it."

He approached the cloud nervously. It had a few ice crystal steps that led to a couple of chairs, all made of ice. He climbed in and sat on one.

"It feels nice and comfortable here," Mashaka said, finally getting over his fears.

"I told you."

She tapped the cloud three times and it slowly lifted off the ground and soon both passengers were airborne. The cloud floated way above the city streets and from this angle, the whole city looked like one shiny crystal forest. Other passengers floated on clouds not too far from them.

"Is this how you get around here?"

"Yes, but just within the city. If you have to across the lake then you use the kites."

"Kites? You mean to tell me there is more than one kite?"

"Well of course there is more than one kite. We have a whole army of them. There is so much you will have to learn about our city."

They flew higher and higher, but even at this altitude, Mashaka could not see the top of some of the buildings. That is how tall they were.

"I guess you miss your mother deeply."

"Yes I do. I miss the Seer too. You know he died the night I left, right?"

"Well, he did not exactly die. He is still with us. You want me to summon him for you?"

"I can do that. See here, he gave me his magic bracelet," Mashaka said proudly, pointing his wrist at The Rainmaker.

"Just like this one right?" she said, showing him her wrist, on which was a bracelet just like the one the Seer gave him.

"Yes, that's just like mine. Does it work the same?"

"No, it works a little bit different."

"It does? How?" Mashaka peered at The Rainmaker's bracelet.

"For example, right now mine works and your's doesn't. Try and see what happens."

Mashaka reached for his wrist and held the bracelet in his palms. Just like he had done several times earlier, he concentrated hard and called out to the Seer. But this time the familiar tingling sensation was not there. Neither was the Seer's voice.

"Try rubbing your stave."

He rubbed the stave gently but nothing happened. It failed to purr and produce its golden glow.

"What just happened? Did the magic powers die off just like that?"

"Ha-ha-ha," The Rainmaker laughed softly. "No, the magic powers are still there. You just can't use them in our city. You see, we took extra precautions after the terrible breach into our guardian system."

"Who did that?"

"The evil lord did. He sent his sentinels and they broke into the rainmaking plant. That is where we are headed you know. It happened a few weeks ago. That should be about the same time he sent the *Damus* to your village."

Just like The Rainmaker said, the attack coincided with the *Damu* attack on Amani. To the land of the Rainmakers the evil lord sent, not the ferocious four-legged blood suckers, but his sentinel kites. But these kites differed from the ones in the land of the Rainmakers in two fundamental ways; in their smell and in their appearance. Since they lived in the depths of the fiery Mount Elgon, they were exposed to the volcanic smoke constantly. They simply could not shake off the accompanying smell no matter what they did. Their smoky stench preceded their arrival by several minutes. It lingered for days after their departure. Their feathers looked different too. Unlike the fine silky plumage the kites from the land of the Rainmakers wore, these evil birds were swathed with a bristly and offensive coat of charred down. It must have been harvested from some type of abominable material only found in the fiery and distasteful furnace they called home. But for what they lacked in aesthetics, they made up for in speed and vice, tenfold.

It was the same speed and viciousness with which they attacked the rainmaking plant.

Things had been peaceful in the city for years. Although the residents knew that the evil lord would try his hand at usurping nature one more time, no one knew when or where that would happen. Over the years, people became desensitized to the danger and the guardian system quickly fell victim to this complacency and hence it became extremely vulnerable to attack. This was exactly what the evil lord had been patiently waiting for.

His kites came to the city under the cover of darkness. No one really knew how that happened. At the very least, the magical blanket of the invisible guardianship that covered the island should have warned the residents of an intruder. But the guardian blanket did not stop the sentinels from coming through, thanks to the shrewdness of their evil master. It was only after the kites were well into the city's airspace and fast approaching the rainmaking plant that people realized something was wrong. They hardly ever used kites for errands within the city. More so, kites were not supposed to fly near the rainmaking plant unless the rider had express permission from The Rainmaker herself.

But it was too late.

The kites swooped down on the plant and breached through its crystal walls. They attacked and killed anyone they could find. In the process, they also destroyed as much of the rainmaking equipment as they could. They even tried to snatch the chief rainsmith and carry him off to Mount Elgon. But the city guard put up a dramatic rescue effort and freed him before it was too late. The sentinel kites however got away and returned to their evil master.

Since that day, the security blanket was reinforced and only certain people were allowed to carry objects that had magical power. That is why Mashaka's stave and bracelet were useless within the city limits.

"But now we are much, much, safer, not to say much, much, wiser too," The Rainmaker said. She proceeded to hold her bracelet in her palms, concentrated hard, and then called out to the Seer.

"Seer, Seer, can you hear me?"

"Yes I can hear you very well my friend," the Seer said.

"I have Mashaka with me right here."

"I guessed so. I am so happy he has finally reached your city. I was getting worried about him."

"Do not worry about the boy Seer. He is very safe in my hands."

"I know he is. Mashaka, are you all rested?"

"Yes Seer, I feel fresh as the morning sun."

"That is good to hear my son. How do you like the land of the Rainmakers?"

"It is wonderful. I have never seen anything like this Seer." Mashaka was as excited as a little birthday child.

"I know that my son. We don't have kites that talk in Amani, do we?"

"No, and I also slept in an ice crystal bed that had cloud sheets."

"And it was not freezing cold?" the Seer asked jokingly.

"Not at all Seer," Mashaka replied innocently. "The Rainmaker says they have special powers to control the clouds and the ice. That way, the ice does not melt and the clouds can even keep you warm. Isn't that so amazing?"

"I know that Mashaka. I was just trying to see if you paid attention to The Rainmaker's words," the Seer laughed in reply.

"I am taking him to the rainmaking plant," The Rainmaker said.

"Oh, that is wonderful. Mashaka, you will be amazed at what you will see. I promise you it is something out of this world."

"But when am I going to see you Seer?" Mashaka asked, a tinge of sadness in his voice.

"One day we will meet my son, and we will sit down and you'll tell me all about your adventures," the Seer replied solemnly.

"Yes Seer, I would like to share my adventures with you."

"Alright now Seer, we have arrived at the rainmaking plant. Let me show the boy his surprise," The Rainmaker called out.

"Thank you so much Rainmaker. May peace be with you and your people."

"Thank you so much Seer, goodbye."

"Goodbye Seer," Mashaka called out as The Rainmaker put the bracelet back on her wrist.

"Mashaka, we have arrived."

Mashaka looked up and almost fell off the cloud. He was staring right at the rainmaking plant. It was like nothing he would have ever expected.

❀   ❀   ❀

The rainmaking plant was in fact the same pair of tall rectangular buildings he saw so clearly from the lakeshore. The massive buildings stood stoically side by side before him, reaching all the way into the sky. These twin towers looked different from the other buildings in that they were all blue, the same color all city residents wore. Although they were made from ice crystal like all other buildings in the city, they had a constant sheet of clear water flowing down on all sides. Through the water, the ice crystal wall glistened in a cool blue hue.

The cloud they were riding finally landed gently on the ground. Mashaka and The Rainmaker emerged from it and made straight for the building.

"Let us step inside," The Rainmaker said.

"What about the water?"

"Are you afraid of water? If that is the case, then you might just as well be afraid of life itself."

"I guess I can handle a little bit of water."

"We all can. But you guessed right. No one wants to be all soaked and wet."

"I can't see a door," Mashaka said, looking at the solid ice crystal walls.

"Mashaka, there is always a door. You just have to look hard enough."

As they approached the building, a section of the water curtain started churning outwards in a semi-circle, forming an arch that exposed part of the blue wall. The Rainmaker then raised her stave towards the arch on the wall which then split in two and slid apart just like two massive sliding doors. Behind the arch was a real door made of blue ice crystal.

"Let's get in," The Rainmaker said, ushering Mashaka.

"Uhm, but the door is still closed."

"No its not, look." She approached the crystal door and marched right through it. The ice closed in behind her.

In shock and awe, Mashaka cautiously approached the door. He extended his hand slowly and indeed it went through the ice. But he quickly pulled back when the crystals started closing in around his fingers. Deep inside he knew he would have to go through the door eventually and that he was postponing the inevitable. He shut his eyes and took a timid step into the crystals. He felt them crunch gently around his leg. He took another step forward, this time with a little bit more dexterity and he felt the ice crystals crunch all around him as he stepped inside the plant.

"You can now open your eyes," The Rainmaker said, a soft smile on her face.

Mashaka did, and almost doubled over. The whole place was bustling with activity as people hurried back and forth, going about their duties. But as he looked around, it was the endless network of rainmaking equipment that astounded him the most. But also, high above ground in the air flew small birds of all colors. As they flew around merrily, they chirped and sung, ducking between man and machinery.

"How do you like it?" The Rainmaker asked.

"It's amazing."

"I know. Now let me give you a tour," she said, leading him through the plant.

"These are the rain workers." She was pointing at the bustling crowds of people, all dressed in white gowns and blue turbans. "Let me first show you the fountain of the living water."

The gigantic fountain stood isolated in a large corner area. It looked like any other expect for one aspect. The water spouting from this fountain had the capacity to give life to anyone who tasted it. But not just anyone was allowed to drink from it. The water was reserved for special groups of people. Only very sick children and those born with rare conditions where allowed to drink the potent water. Pregnant mothers were also allowed to drink the life giving water in order to nourish the developing fetuses inside them. The only other people who could drink from the fountain were young married couples. It was believed that the water ensured they would have healthy offspring. This explains why the infant mortality rate in the land of the Rainmakers was almost zero.

"We also use some of this water when we send out the rain to different places," The Rainmaker explained.

This was true. Without the life giving capacity of the living water, the rain they sent out would be barren. This type of impotent rain would doom all those who consumed it. It would be poisonous, not just to man but also to plants and animals.

Mashaka watched as the living water gushed out in small jets from the fountain. Occasionally the water would collect in small puddles that quickly transformed into the shape of a bird. Right before his eyes the puddle would come to life in the form of a colorful bird that flew up in the air.

"Is this where all those birds came from?" he asked.

"Yes," The Rainmaker replied. "These are the harbinger birds. They herald the coming of the rain. We send them to guide the rain to the right place."

Mashaka then remembered. Every time before it rained in his village, there would be flocks of birds flying overhead. People said that probably the birds were afraid of getting wet and that is why they flew ahead of the rain. But that was all wrong. The answer was right before his eyes. The birds where not running away from the rain. These birds were in fact ushering the rain.

"Of course, once in while some evil people have captured these birds and sent the rain the wrong way, causing drought in some areas."

"What are those things?" Mashaka asked, pointing to the huge ice crystal pipes crisscrossing overhead.

"Those are the rain mixers. We have different types of rain and we have to mix them very carefully in order to get a good balance. We have storm rain, we have drizzle rain, we have hailstorm rain, and we have night rain."

Mashaka looked up at the churning water in the crystal pipes. Some of the water seemed darker than others, and indeed, some pipes carried water that had small white particles. *That must be the hailstorm rain.*

"Here, let me introduce you to the chief rainsmith."

The chief rainsmith was a tall gaunt man with a long gray beard.

"It is so nice to see you here Mashaka. It must have been a harrowing journey for you to reach our land," he said in a deep steady voice.

"It was, but now I am happy to have finally arrived here."

"I was just explaining the rain mixers to him," The Rainmaker said.

"Oh, those, I'll explain. You see we have different types of rain. We have to mix the right type of rain before we send it out. For example, you cannot send night rain in the daytime. It is very dark and it has the power to make people sleepy. That is not good for hardworking people in the village, right?"

Mashaka shook his head.

"At the same time, you cannot send drizzle rain in the afternoon during planting season. You need lots of water for the seeds to sprout. That type of rain is good for the dry season, when harvest has already taken place and the earth is dry and hot. That way, it gets to cool the ground on which your people walk."

"So that means when we have drought, you people decide not to send us rain?" Mashaka challenged.

"No, no. It does not work that way. You see, nature gave us the power to make rain. But nature can override our work any time and divert any rain we send out. We only make the rain my boy, nature still decides who gets it."

"Come this way, let me show you how we really make the rain," he said, leading them into an underground chamber.

The place was dimly lit but Mashaka did not need any light to see his surroundings. Small blue cubes of about a foot square floated in the air alongside clear bubbles of about the same size. The cubes and bubbles shined luminously in mid-air as they gently bobbed and bumped against each other. The low roof was nothing but a mesmerizing mass of boiling silver clouds.

"This is the rain?" Mashaka asked, confused.

"No, that is not the rain. Come this way," the chief rainsmith said.

He led them to a small room which had a huge clay cauldron sitting on simple traditional fireplace. The huge cauldron sat on three firestones. Underneath it were pieces of firewood burning with a fierce bluish white fire. Instead of sending sparks in the air, the fire sent long thin miniature lighting bolts that slithered over the cauldron and disappeared inside it.

"What is that?" Mashaka asked, backing up a few steps.

"Relax my boy. We are in the sphere of the first elements. That is the fire that creates the rain. This is what nature gave to us when we agreed to the peace. These are among the very first elements of nature to exist."

The fire was not burning on regular firewood. This was special wood nature gave the Rainmakers together with the cauldron. The wood was harvested from the very first tree to grow in the whole world. The wood was so potent it burned, not to produce fire, but lighting bolts. Inside the cauldron was the first rainwater to fall from the sky to the earth. It was the earliest water known to this world. The only other water rivaling it in age was the one flowing from the fountain of the living water. That was but a little bit older and more potent. The cauldron was made from the first soil to form on the earth's surface.

A few feet above the cauldron was a small cloud and Mashaka quickly inquired about it.

"That cloud produced the very first rain to fall on earth. That is the very first cloud nature created. It has been preserved to this day. From the fire, the water in the cauldron, and the cloud, comes all the rain that falls on the whole world."

By this time Mashaka's mouth was practically open. "So how do you get rain from the cauldron?"

"You see that crystal thing standing above the cloud?" the chief rainsmith said, pointing to a wide funnel-like structure hanging upside down above the cloud. "That is the rain grabber. It collects the moisture from the cauldron and leads it to the rain towers."

"The rain towers?" Mashaka asked, totally bamboozled by the terms he was hearing.

"Yes, the rain towers. That is where we store all types of rain. I will take you there right now."

They walked out of the underground chamber and headed farther into the plant. Soon they were standing facing a huge wall of gushing water. Mashaka could not see the source of the water wall no matter how much he leaned back. The water curtain fell silently, disappearing into the ice crystal floor without letting a single drop loose.

"This must be the rain tower," Mashaka announced excitedly.

"No my friend. It's just a simple water curtain," the rainsmith corrected. "But watch this."

He stretched his arms towards the water curtain and then swung them in a parting motion, as if to open a massive door. In response, the water curtain split in the middle and the two halves slowly slid away form each other to reveal the rain towers. Just as he did when he first saw the land of the Rainmakers, Mashaka went limp at the knees. His legs turned to jelly and he remained on his knees as he stared at the rain towers.

The cylindrical towers were located a few hundred yards from where they were standing. They must have been at least fifty meters in diameter and they stood about half a mile apart from each other. But they were all so tall they reached right up to the sky. This is why the rainmaking plant was so wide and so tall. It was the storage for the rain towers and it had to be that big to contain these huge columns. The towers stood on a round crystal platform that rotated clockwise.

Each tower contained a different type of rain. Right now the storm rain tower was passing by. The furious water churned in a violent spiral that disappeared into a boiling cloud storm high above them. Huge lightning bolts worked their way up and down the column as it rotated from view. The night rain tower came in next. The dark waters also churned violently skywards, also ending up in a dark cloud storm. But this storm looked different. The clouds standing at the top of this column were pitch black and looked like thick black smoke as they boiled angrily in the sky.

The hail storm rain tower was next and it was a wonder to behold. The hail stones looked like miniature juggling balls as they worked their way to the sky, finally falling back to earth through the inside of the tower in what seemed like a streak of long white lines. Next to it was the shower rain tower. The rain in it fell gently in long thin strands that returned skywards in an elaborate spiraling manner.

However, Mashaka noticed that the rotating platform had a strange hole in the middle. He asked the rainsmith abut it.

"The cauldron you just saw in the sphere of the first elements lies exactly beneath that hole. The moisture from the cauldron collects to form these rain towers.

"You mean to tell me that all these came from the cauldron downstairs?"

"Yes."

"But it looked so small."

"It does, to the human eye. In reality, it is much bigger. In fact, it is so big you can fit all these rain towers inside it with room to spare."

"But what keeps the rain towers from falling? There is nothing holding the water columns together. They do not even spill," the ever so inquisitive Mashaka asked.

"That is the power of nature. Inside this building we have the perfect balance of elements. If the balance goes out of place just a little bit, everything goes awry."

"So what happened the night the evils lord's kites came here?"

"Some things went out of place but luckily they never reached the cauldron. If they had reached it, they could have definitely carried it off to the evil lord and who knows what might have happened then. Most probably the rain towers would have collapsed and inundated the whole island." Fear flashed across the rainsmith's eyes as he contemplated the possibilities.

"So if you are the only people who can make rain, how did the evil lord send the *Vuas* the evening I was born?"

"I will answer that," The Rainmaker stepped in. "He is a very powerful man and that is a fact no one denies. He has the power to divert the harbinger birds and put evil in the rain they guide. He has been doing more of that lately and that is one of the reasons he has to be stopped."

As they turned away from the rain towers, Mashaka could not help but keep glancing back as the water curtain slowly closed in on the rotating columns.

"Come on Mashaka, we will be late for the council meeting," The Rainmaker said.

"What council meeting?" Mashaka asked absentmindedly, still glancing back at the rain towers.

"The council of the Rainmakers. It's time you met them."

❦   ❦   ❦

The council of the Rainmakers met in their official chambers which were similar to any other room in the city save for one difference. The floor was not made of ice crystal. It was nothing but a deep pool of clear blue water. Mashaka hesitated at the chamber's entrance, despite of The Rainmaker's repeated assurances.

"Don't worry Mashaka, you will not drown. In this chamber you can actually walk on water. Watch me."

She gently stepped on the water and walked to her position at the head of a long table. On each side of the table sat all the council members. All eyes now turned towards Mashaka. Some council members even had knowing smiles on their faces. Mashaka did just as he did earlier when entering the rainmaking plant. He timidly put one foot forward and touched the water with his big toe. He saw a slight ripple and quickly stepped back.

"Mashaka, just step forward. You will not fall into the water. Trust me."

He shut his eyes and put his foot on the water, expecting the worst. He felt as if he had stepped on a soft smooth surface that had a little bounce to it. He opened his eyes and put his other foot forward. He was now standing on the water. Filled with excitement and new courage, he took his first steps on water.

"You see, you did not drown. You are now walking on water," The Rainmaker said as the whole council burst out into laughter and applause.

Mashaka looked down at his feet as he carefully treaded the water to the chair the council had reserved for him.

"Council members, I would like to introduce to you our visitor, Mashaka from Amani," The Rainmaker announced to an applauding council.

Mashaka went around the table greeting each council member and then sat in his designated chair.

"We all know we are living in very dangerous times people. Danger and evil have permeated the earth one more time," The Rainmaker announced.

The council murmured its agreement.

"Many have suffered. Our visitor from the far off village of Amani is living testimony to this. His people have suffered the pain the evil lord brought upon their village. Now they stand to suffer even more from his wrath. The evil one has risen again. From the fiery bowels of Mount Elgon, he has built his vile empire and soon he will try to conquer the whole world and spread his evil domain."

The council agreed in unison.

"Long has been the time since nature cast him away into his fiery hell. But his evil spirit did not die, neither did it repent. He consumed the fire and used the resulting pain to light and nurture the evil inside him."

She stopped briefly and looked at Mashaka.

"But right before us sits the chosen one. He is the only person on this good earth who can stop the evil lord from defeating the whole world."

Everyone turned towards Mashaka, deep concern in their eyes.

"He has come a long way to seek us. He has come to seek us, the people who are still one with nature. He has traversed dangerous lands and he has met a lot of peril in his journey. For forty days and forty nights, he has traveled in the wilderness to reach the land of the Rainmakers."

It had been that long? Mashaka knew he had long lost count of the days but forty days? That sounded like a lifetime to his young mind.

"But he comes here with a heavy heart," The Rainmaker continued. "He comes here, not with joy, but with sorrow and longing. He comes here to seek answers to questions that plague his young mind, answers the Seer instructed him to seek in our land. He has fulfilled the first part of his quest. But there lies the problem." She paused and turned to Mashaka.

"Mashaka, I know your heart is filled with sorrow, and your young mind is parched for answers. But you have come to the right place, for here, in the land of the Rainmakers, you will find all the answers to your questions."

The council burst out into more applause.

"But Mashaka, are you ready for the answers?" She paused to let the boy ponder the question for himself. "Only you can tell if you really are prepared," she continued softly, still looking at him.

He kept quiet. He knew he longed for the answers. But right now when they lay just within reach, his mind quickly filled with doubt. Was he even ready to hear the truth about himself? The truth about who his father was? The truth about why he was the chosen one?

"Mashaka, we cannot force the truth upon you. You will have to either reject the truth or accept it. But the answer has to come from your heart. Listen to your heart Mashaka, listen to your heart!" The Rainmaker cried out.

He glanced nervously at the men and women of the council then hung his head. He was not sure if he was ready to take the next step. Deep in his mind he knew the truth would be shocking at the very least. But he wasn't sure if he would be able to handle it. What if the answers were too brutal for his young mind? What if the answers complicated his life further? He had a choice. He could simply say no and return home.

Somehow, he thought he could devise a scheme to have the village take him back. Probably he would dazzle them with stories from his travels. Yes, probably he could ask the Seer to intervene from the netherworld on his behalf. That would convince the elders back in Amani. But wait, all that would not stop the evil lord from meting out more punishment on the village. If he was to go back and as a result more evil befell the village, the elders, and especially the spokesman would … *Oh no! The speed runners!* He would send the speed runners to finish him off. The glint of their murderous machetes flashed through his memory. He knew he would not last a day back in the village.

He raised his head slowly, looked at The Rainmaker straight in the eye and proclaimed, "I am ready for the truth, Rainmaker."

"And the truth is what you shall receive."

The council members heaved a collective sigh of relief.

CHAPTER 11

The Truth

"Mashaka, we are sending you back in time. You are going back into the era of the old ancient," The Rainmaker announced. "That is where the truth lies. It's in the past that you will travel to find the answers to the questions that have burned in your soul all these years. Now let me warn you Mashaka, what you are about to experience will be very strange to you. But I want you to relax, do not panic. Nothing will cause you any harm."

Mashaka nodded speechlessly. He did not know what to expect.

"Now, council members, we will join our hands and send the boy over."

But Mashaka quickly jumped in, "What do you mean send the boy over?"

"Only nature can give you the answers, Mashaka. You are going to meet nature. You are about to enter the ultimate realm of nature. Now let us join hands."

Everyone joined hands. The council members then started chanting in a strange language Mashaka had never heard before. This was the language of nature, an ancient tongue now long forgotten. In fact, it is so old it was the first real language spoken by human beings. This language could not be learned like other human languages. It was only transmitted subliminally to an individual who had reached a high level of purity as the council members had done. The joining of the hands was simply a way to transmit the language to Mashaka so he could understand what nature was about to tell him.

Initially, Mashaka did not feel anything. But then it came—a small tingling sensation in the center of his palms. It soon grew to engulf his whole hand, then his arm, and soon his whole body was shaking in powerful spasms as the energy from the council members filled up inside him. It felt like a force was running amok inside him, churning his insides into a quick mash. The water beneath him started flapping and within no time he perceived a sinking sensation.

He opened his eyes quickly and noticed that he and the council members were going underwater. But strangely enough none of them seemed to be bothered about rescuing themselves. He knew he had to do something or he was bound to drown. The significance of the answers vanished from his mind that instant and his survival instincts took over. But try as hard as he could, he could not move a limb. Some kind of force was holding him in place as he felt the water rise higher. First it rose to his ankles, then to his knees, and soon he was waist deep in the water. He watched helplessly as the water finally reached his neck, crawled upwards to cover his mouth, his nose, his eyes, and finally he was completely submerged under water.

That is when the spasms stopped.

He had crossed over.

Mashaka opened his eyes slowly, expecting to see the worst. They were no longer underwater. Matter of fact all the water was gone, but so was everyone else. He was alone, standing on dry land. He looked around for the council members but he could not see any of them. Then someone tapped him on the shoulder. He jumped around in shock.

"It's me," said The Rainmaker.

"Where is everybody else?"

"They are in the city. We needed a lot of energy to make the crossing. They will remain as our link to the human world."

"Where are we now?"

"We are in the absolute realm of nature."

Mashaka looked around. The place looked no different from his world. The trees looked the same, the sky looked the same, and the wind blew just like it did elsewhere. But then, when he concentrated harder on his surroundings, he noticed one difference. The place was completely quiet. But this was a peaceful kind of quiet, not the eerie quiet he experienced in the land of the living statues. And it definitely was not the type of silence that existed in the land of total darkness. This was a silence he welcomed. He felt peaceful in the realm of nature.

"So where is nature?" He sounded impatient.

"Patience Mashaka, nature will be here soon. That is why we came here; for you to meet nature."

They stood still for a moment while Mashaka fidgeted with his fingers both in angst and anxiety.

"Remember, whatever you do, don't move, and especially, do not run. Nature will not harm you no matter what manifestation you see," The Rainmaker cautioned.

They did not wait too long.

From the clear and cloudless sky came a loud clap of thunder followed by a bright lighting bolt that hit the ground right in front of them. The thick pillar of lighting remained frozen in place just a few feet from where they stood. The spot on which the lightning hit burst into huge ferocious flames that burned brightly, rapidly growing in size and soon turning into a towering inferno. The tower of fire kept growing bigger and burning higher until it reached well into the sky.

Mashaka looked on in amazement. *Is nature this violent?* He was expecting something more passive, something more benign.

But that was not about to happen. Dark clouds suddenly formed in the sky at the tip of the fire tower. They churned and boiled angrily before they spewed out a humongous twister that spiraled rapidly towards the ground. As it descended, the twister quickly extinguished the fire. Within a short period of time the twister was spinning violently in front of the two, hanging just a few feet off the ground.

The terrified boy was spellbound.

"Who is the young boy you bring to me, Rainmaker?" a voice thundered from the twister in front of them. The mysterious voice spoke the ancient language but this time Mashaka understood each and every word.

The voice, though very powerful, sounded strange. Mashaka could not place the voice since it seemed like it was actually made up of several voices. There was a man's deep voice, but that was accompanied by a woman's voice. He could hear a child's voice but then he could also hear a young boy's voice, just the same way he could hear a young girl's voice. But then there was the voice of an old woman that sounded distinct from the labored voice of an old man, well advanced in age. But one thing Mashaka knew was these voices blended to form a perfect tone.

This was the voice of nature; a voice representing all of mankind's diversity.

"I bring Mashaka, a boy from the village of Amani," The Rainmaker shouted back.

"I see," thundered nature. "Step forward Mashaka!"

Mashaka hesitated.

"Do you fear me Mashaka?" nature asked.

Mashaka hung his head and did not answer.

"Do not have fear Mashaka. You cannot have fear in your heart. You are the chosen one, and the chosen one shall fear no man, no animal, or no spirit. You shall not fear even nature itself."

Mashaka looked up at nature, now a little bit more confident. His confidence faltered slightly however when nature transformed the twister into a raging sand storm that spun sand in a violent column reaching all the way into the sky. But Mashaka's confidence had been building up slowly since he crossed over into the realm of nature.

"I do not fear!" he shouted, standing his ground before the gigantic column of sand.

"That is better Mashaka," nature boomed. "I know you come to me for answers. I know you have plenty of questions. Well today you will get all your answers," nature said as the sand storm, without warning, quickly engulfed Mashaka and The Rainmaker. It picked them up in air, tossed them around and finally deposited then in a strange land.

There where people all around and they too spoke the very strange and ancient tongue Mashaka had just heard nature address him with. He looked around and a force turned his head to face a couple standing at a distance. He peered at the couple, trying to figure out what it was they were saying. That is when something out of the ordinary happened. As he strained to hear what the couple was saying, the ground shifted suddenly and zoomed in the scene right in front of him. It was as if the ground was moving on well oiled giant rollers.

The couple was engaged in some kind of argument. He could see the man's face clearly but the woman had her back turned to him.

"We have everything we need. Why should we want more?" the woman was asking.

"I have dreamt of this moment since the day I was born," the man said. "And no one, and I repeat, no one even you will stop me."

"But it has been good to us. It has given us everything we need," the woman pleaded. "Your greed is going to destroy us all."

"But not before I destroy it first," the man replied sharply.

"And how do you think you are going to destroy it?"

"I have the will. All you have to do is believe you are greater than what you have been told. It is all in the mind," the man emphasized, pointing his finger to his head.

"I will not take part in any such activity."

But the man was insistent. "You have to open your mind. We have been blinded all these years. This is an illusion you see. Look around you. Open your eyes and look around you. We have to tear through this sheer curtain of false reality and get to the real thing. It is time you liberated your mind, my dear."

The woman stood her ground. "I don't believe you. It's probably you who needs to look around. People are happy, can't you see that?"

"That is a blind happiness they think they enjoy. They have to go out and find the real thing. We live in a prison. Look at the people. Everybody follows the rules blindly. Did anyone ask themselves why things are the way they are? No! And that exactly, is the problem. These people have been conditioned not to think. When you think, you break down the gates of your mental prison. It's all in the mind, all in the mind."

The woman shook her head tearfully. "I would rather live in this happy prison than forsake it for the unknown. We have an agreement, a truce. It is all based on trust!"

"That is the same truce that was used to pry the power to rule this world from your very own hands. That is the same trust that blinds your eyes from the truth. This world belongs to us. This world is our legacy, and we can do to it whatever it is we want to!"

"I … I … can't, I can't," the woman whispered quietly as she sobbed.

"Then I shall go on without you," the man retorted. "And when I succeed, you shall come begging on your knees for my mercy."

"But what about us?" the woman begged, tears streaming down her cheeks.

"You were supposed to stand by my side through thick and thin but you let me down. There is no 'us' anymore. We are going to carry out the rebellion whether you join us or not!"

"Please don't … please …" the woman wailed as she reached out to grab the man's arm.

"Let go of my arm, slave of nature! You are not worthy of my affection!" he shouted as he walked away.

The woman collapsed on her knees and wept her heart out. Mashaka looked at the crying woman in pity. She then turned her head slightly towards his direction momentarily, just in time before the ground zoomed out the scene.

Mashaka turned sharply to The Rainmaker and blurted out. "You were married to him once?"

"Not married. But we were engaged," she said as her eyes glazed over with emotion. "But that's a long time ago."

From a distance, they could hear screaming and wailing that was accompanied by shouting and cheering. Mashaka looked at The Rainmaker askance. She looked back at him and gently put her hand on his shoulder, squeezing it as if to give him assurance. Again, the ground shifted, zooming in a new scene before them.

People were running around screaming and wailing. Mashaka wondered what it was they were running away from. Hot at their heels were other people, all dressed in red. Each held a long machete in one hand and a burning torch in the other. Mashaka quickly recognized the man leading the charge. He was the same man who had been arguing with The Rainmaker in the previous scene.

"Come, my people. It is time we started the rebellion!" he shouted as his people cheered wildly at his words. "We have been fooled for a long time but now our minds are enlightened. The blindfolds that once covered our eyes have been lifted. We have drank from the cup of truth. It is time to take what is ours. I command you to destroy nature and all those who stand in its name. Destroy it and destroy it completely!"

The crowd cheered loudly and charged forth, cutting down anything that was in the vicinity. They cut down crops and uprooted the grass. Their sharp machetes slashed at innocent animals and at anyone who was not dressed in red. They even used their blazing torches to set the large trees on fire. There was pandemonium everywhere. While some continued to set everything ablaze, others collected dirt and threw it into the river. All the while they cursed at nature. The language they used was so caustic to the ears The Rainmaker quickly covered Mashaka's ears with her hands.

"May your powers be defeated today," cursed one man.

"I spit on you nature! I spit on you!" shouted a woman as she spat in the air.

"Yes, may this be your last day on this good earth. Man shall finally rule this world, ha-ha-ha," laughed a young man as he deposited more dirt into the river.

Soon the whole crowd was chanting in unison, "Bring nature down. Bring nature down. Bring nature down."

The rampage went on for what seemed to be hours. When the picture finally zoomed out, Mashaka turned his head slowly towards The Rainmaker.

"So that's how they rose against nature?"

She nodded.

"But nature struck back at them, didn't it?"

"Oh yes it did," she replied as another scene zoomed in.

There was more screaming and wailing but this time it was coming from the people in red. They wailed in pain and anguish as the apocalyptic scene unfolded before Mashaka's eyes. From the sky, huge balls of fire descended with such magnitude and ferocity they lit the whole sky in a bright red glow. The ground simmered and seethed as the people in red burned to their demise. Some were so badly burnt they lay helplessly on the red hot ground. The ground they lay on was so hot the soil boiled and bubbled like a thick sticky liquid on a hot fire. Slowly, they all sunk deep into the seething ground until no one in red remained to be seen.

The ground soon shifted to present another scene. This time the people in red were facing nature's torment through rain and wind. Mashaka watched as large amounts of hail fell from the sky. The hail fell so quickly and in such abundance that most people, if not killed by the huge stones, were soon buried under whole piles of them. The wind blew ferociously, sweeping people high above ground and depositing them over the rugged mountain tops. Here, they crashed with loud breaking noises. But that was not all. Nature proceeded to send forth its cleansing agents. These were supposed to sanitize the earth off the evil carnage consisting of the remains of the rebellious people. Mashaka watched in disbelief as the torques of nature descended. The torques of nature were ultra violent twisters that descended from the stormy skies in hundreds, but touched down in sets of three. The dark waters inside the twisters churned and spiraled with such velocity that within no time not a single person in red was to be seen. The torques had washed them away and deposited them into the deep seas.

The next scene nature revealed to Mashaka depicted a coastal settlement. The people in red ran around wild and confused. They were trying to get leverage against a forceful gale that easily picked them up from the ground and tossed them yards away. Whole houses were uprooted with ease and flung high into the air. They would come crashing down, sometimes on some hapless rebels. The wind was so strong, tall mature trees easily bent over double. Matter of fact most trees did not have any foliage left on them anymore. The wind had stripped them clear off leaves and small braches. They now looked like ghostly fingers scratching an invisible skin in the wind. The wind then picked up over the sea, while simultaneously the sea bed shook in a series of powerful earthquakes, causing a monstrous tidal wave to form. The wave grew bigger and bigger until it stood so tall its peak was almost caressing the clouds in the sky. It rushed to the coast with the speed of an evil sentinel kite. People frantically fought the wind, trying to get as far away from the coastline as possible. But no one made it. The gigantic wave crashed the coast with the explosion of ten angry volcanoes. It was so big it inundated the adjoining area hundreds of miles inland then washed everything standing in its way back into the sea. Mashaka stared in horror as the people in red drowned in the boiling waters of the angry dark sea.

What nature revealed next was probably the most astounding scene. This scene was shocking beyond description. It was so horrific it sent pangs of pity cutting through the boy's heart. For once, he felt sorry for the people in red. This scene depicted the four afflictions of nature. It was set in an extensive settlement on the edge of a large dark forest. The victims' screams were the likes of which the boy had never heard before. They made Moran's screams from the torture chambers in Gereza sound like an infant whimpering for its mother's breast.

A female rebel sat on the ground, leaning on a tree and shaking violently. Her mouth was open in a perpetual scream from the severe pain and suffering she was undergoing. It was one long scream that seemed to go on forever and Mashaka saw why. It was her limbs. As she sat shaking in powerful spasms, her limbs were self-dismembering piece by piece. First it was her finger tips. They just fell off her trembling hands. Then the rest of her fingers fell off, followed closely by her hands. The body parts now lay next to her, very much alive as they twitched and twisted in severe pain on the ground. Desperate to regain the possession of her lost appendages, the woman tried to reach out to the ground with the stumps that were now her arms. Her arms just popped at the elbows and both her forearms fell off. Just like the fingers were doing, these too remained twitching and twisting on the grass. Soon, all her arms were lying on the ground next to her. Her legs came off next. They simply fell off at the toes, at the ankles, at the knees, and then at the hip. But the affliction did not stop there. Her torso trembled and heaved once, forcing her head out of her neck. The head popped out of the neck and landed on top of the pile of twitching body parts.

But the head kept on screaming, eternally.

This was the worst affliction nature could unleash on the human body. It was the deadly affliction of *ukoma*. It is very similar to modern day leprosy except for two things: Once infected, it took but a few seconds for the disease to spread throughout the whole body. Second, unlike leprosy, it caused the body to self-dismember in a matter of minutes.

Just a few yards from the pile that was the dismembered woman, a man stumbled by. The low gurgling moans escaping from the hole in his throat sent chills of fear down Mashaka's spine. He was infected by the affliction of *raruka*. In terms of pain and suffering, this was second only to the affliction of *ukoma*. *Raruka* was characterized by the violent tearing of the flesh. On their own volition, chunks of flesh simply tore away and leapt off one's body. A huge piece of flesh had just torn itself off the man's throat. As he stumbled along, he desperately held on to different pulsating parts of his body. The pulsation signaled to him where the next chunk of flesh was about to tear away. Right now he was holding fast to his chest.

But alas, nature was yet to receive the man's repentance. Huge chunks of flesh ripped off his chest and flung themselves to the ground just a few yards from where he stood. He fell down on all fours, staring at his own twitching flesh. That is when long thick strips of flesh started pulsating down his back. They proceeded to tear and leap off, landing way behind him. Ironically, the pain seemed to energize the man because he jumped to his feet and started running wild. The pain had actually sent him raving mad. He ran around a corner, screaming in the guttural sounds escaping through the hole in his throat. As he disappeared around the corner, more chunks of flesh kept flying off in his wake. It was not long before he reappeared around the opposite side.

Or was that really he?

The man's body was totally devoid of flesh. He was not even screaming any more. His bony jaw just clanged against his teeth as the skeleton that was now him pranced around. But to demonstrate how severe his affliction was, his bones started breaking in sequence, accompanied by loud popping sounds. First to break were the radius and ulna of his forearms. Next were the humerus bones in his upper arms. They just snapped with a clap like a breaking twig. They were followed by a series of shattering noises as his ribs imploded within themselves. The bones of his lower extremities weren't spared either. One by one they shattered and soon he was nothing but a pile of raw skeletal bones. But these bones remained alive. Just like the twitching body parts of the dismembered woman, his bones kept on prancing on the ground in mortal pain.

Not too far from where the two piles of human parts juggled in an unlikely death dance, nature was venting its anger on yet another victim. This time it was a young girl. Mashaka quickly recognized the girl. He had seen her in another scene during the rebellion. She had spit in the air and vehemently cursed nature. The girl had also attacked an innocent young child who was not part of the rebellion. It looked like she was reaping the fruits of her unwise and evil doing. Her affliction was different. It was a painless affliction that caused as much suffering and misery as any other. She had been hit with the affliction of *jasho-kuu,* or simply, the ultra chronic sweat.

Usually, one's skin pores are very small and it takes a very close look to see them. But the girl's skin pores had enlarged so much that even at a distance, Mashaka and The Rainmaker could see the sweat gushing out. This affliction is characterized by an abnormal enlargement of the skin pores followed by a severe bout of sweating. The girl now sat in a large pool of her own sweat which grew bigger as each drop of her body fluids was forced out through her distended pores. It was not long before she was completely mummified. But even in this new state of involuntary preservation, she remained very much alive. The weak cries she produced were accompanied by no tears. There simply were no more body fluids for that. When she chocked and coughed in her sorrow, nothing but a dry dust puffed out of her mouth. This dust was what once used to be her internal organs.

One would think that the pain of a fatal disease ends with one's death. This might be true today but it did not apply to nature's wrath that time. As the woman lay twitching in a pile of her own body parts, as the de-fleshed man pranced around in the form of a dismantled skeleton, both still felt the full effect of the searing pain from their respective afflictions.

These were the afflictions that caused the pain of the ages. This pain took decades to subside. The rebellious young girl would suffer an equally long period of severe thirst and dehydration.

Just before the scene zoomed out, Mashaka heard a loud buzzing sound emanating from the direction of the dark forest. But the forest looked very different now. The greenery was all gone, leaving nothing but an expanse of dry leafless trees. At first he thought that somehow nature had stripped the once green forest off its leaves. But then he realized these had not been leaves in the first place. It was an army of biting insects, laden with virulent pathogens that would finally bring down the rebellious people once and for all. The insects swarmed in the sky so thick they covered the sun, turning broad daylight into an instant dusk.

Nature had meted out all its punishment.

The horrific scenes vanished and in their place stood a gigantic talking tree. From it, nature spoke.

"Mashaka, you have seen nature's wrath. But you have not seen everything. Prepare your eyes to see your nemesis, the evil lord. His name is Lord Kifo; the lord of death!"

With that, the tree shook violently, shedding all of its leaves into the air. The leaves collected to form a slithering snake-like formation that came straight for Mashaka and The Rainmaker. Before they could run for safety, the snaky leaves hit them with such an impact they went sprawling to the ground. They lay motionless for a moment. When they finally collected themselves and got to their feet, they were in a totally different place. They looked around, lost and nervous. All they could see was the rocky surface on which they stood. A dark foggy smoke hovered everywhere, reducing visibility to just a few feet. They got up slowly, huddling together, not exactly sure where they were. They slowly turned their heads around and behold, right before them was the peak of Mount Elgon—home of the evil lord.

But they quickly turned around when they heard someone coughing and choking in the hazy smoke. From a distance, they saw a group of men and women struggling up the mountain. As the group drew closer through the foggy smoke, Mashaka and The Rainmaker noticed they were all dressed in red. Their red clothes were tattered and the group seemed to have walked a long way. They struggled up the slope, holding on to each other as their leader, the same man Mashaka saw arguing with The Rainmaker earlier, urged them up the mountain.

"Walk, my people, walk!" he shouted. "We have almost reached our new home."

"I can't," gasped one man, falling to his knees. "The ground is hot and the air poisons my lungs. I don't think I can make it."

"You have to have faith in me. Yes, nature has cast us away from our land but we have to finish our journey and regain our strength. We will rebuild our broken bodies. We will build a new empire and one day we will be strong enough to defeat nature for good!"

Full of encouragement and renewed determination, the team of castaways trudged up the mountain, past Mashaka and The Rainmaker, and steadily climbed towards the peak. Silently, Mashaka and The Rainmaker followed the party up the mountain. Towards the peak, Mashaka could tell that the temperatures were getting hotter. Although he and The Rainmaker could not physically feel the heat, they saw the sweat coming down the castaways' backs in thick rivulets. They were also treading the ground gingerly, the way one does when walking over hot coals.

A bit farther up the mountain the air seemed to get hotter and sparks started flying all about. It was not very long before small amounts of hot molten lava started flowing past their feet. They were almost at the top of the mountain. Farther up, the molten lava started flowing in thick streams but the castaways, drawing from some sort of mysterious power, just walked through the thick hot liquid towards the peak. Occasionally they would stop to help a struggling colleague but otherwise the party made its way up mountain slowly but steadily.

By the time they were a few hundred feet from the peak, the size of the lava flows had increased considerably such that the men and women were practically plodding waist deep through the thick red liquid. Mashaka and The Rainmaker, who were now floating over the rivers of molten rock looked at the scene in sheer amazement.

"My people, I know the heat burns your skin. But I want you to feed off the pain and build strength. Let it burn, but let it strengthen you too," the leader called out as the party cheered in response. They seemed to have gained immunity to the heat because the more lava they walked through, the more their strength increased. Soon they were running through the thick lava up the mountain.

They finally reached the mountaintop where a huge boiling crater continually spewed out the molten rock. The leader then teetered on the precipitous edge and made his victory speech.

"We have made it my people," he shouted as the party broke out into shouts of joy. "We have reached the peak of the mountain at last. Here, we shall make our new home. We have not perished like nature wanted as to. Instead, we have escaped its wrath and in the process we have tamed fire. Fire can no longer burn us my people. Look!" he shouted, bent down, scooped a handful of the hot lava and raised it to his mouth. He gulped it like it was cold water from the spring.

In reflex action, Mashaka and The Rainmaker quickly reached out and covered their mouths as if they where about to feel the lava burn their tongues in the man's stead.

"It burns my tongue," he shouted in triumph. "But it burns in a delicious way. It burns my insides, but all I feel is warmth. I feel it give me new strength. People, we have come to the end of a long journey and now we need some refreshment. Drink to your fill!" he shouted at his followers, who clamored to partake in the lava drinking. The more they drank, the more they seemed to thirst so they took more and more of the hot liquid.

Before Mashaka or The Rainmaker could utter a word, a huge spring of lava gushed from the crater, shot straight in the air and came crashing down on them. It landed right on top of the two and for a moment they were buried inside the red liquid. They held hands as the lava swirled around them for a while then splattered on the ground, ending up in small red balls of liquid fire that bounced down slope.

Suddenly the mountain looked different. The air seemed cooler and not too far from the peak they could see some vegetation. Nature had taken them back to the future. This is how the mountain looked presently, ages after the castaways made it their home. All around, Mashaka could see activity. Huge dark lava monsters labored under the harsh watch of supervisors who were all dressed in red

The monsters were a sight to behold.

They were made of the hot lava that was abundant in the mountain. They looked somehow human since they had legs, arms, and heads. They even had eyes and ears, but no other facial features. Their eyes and ears were just bright spots in their heads that burned in a fierce red color. They did not have noses or mouths. Through the dark brittle burnt crust that was their skin, Mashaka could see their insides which were nothing but a brew of hot lava. The lava would occasionally bleed from the cracks in their skin and stream down in thick bright orange lines.

They heaved and huffed through their mouthless faces under the heavy machinery they operated. Whenever they heaved or coughed, their faces would bloat and red hot sparks would fly through their eyes and ears.

The supervisors were ruthless as they barked harsh unforgiving commands at the lava monsters. They carried long blazing whips made from the molten rock. The long supple whips were thin and they burned in a bright orange color. They would frequently bring these fire whips down on a slow monster. The whips' impact on the monsters was so hard drops of hot lava splattered from their crusted skin. Mashaka wondered what all the activity was for. Then it hit him. It was a huge weapon building operation. The evil lord, having regained his power and created his evil empire, was finally preparing to make war on nature.

"Move faster!" one supervisor called out as he brought his whip down hard on one lava monster. "We don't have time to waste."

The monster wobbled under the strike, almost losing its step as the rocky yoke on its shoulders twisted violently.

"Take him out of the line!" the supervisor called out. Other monsters rushed in and freed their kin from the yoke.

The wounded monster fell to its knees.

"Douse him!" the supervisor ordered.

The other monsters brought in a huge pail of water which they proceeded to pour over the struggling beast. As the water sizzled and entered the monster through its thin crusted skin, it fell to the ground, screaming in pain through its eyes and ears as it convulsed violently. Soon after, the water quickly extinguished its hot insides. The thing now lay spread-eagled on the rocky ground, a useless and lifeless pile of charcoal. The supervisor walked over and kicked the remains out of the way. The monster disintegrated into hundreds of charred crumbs that tumbled down the mountain. Some of the pieces tumbled right by Mashaka's feet as he stood watching.

It was evident the monsters could not stand water.

As Mashaka and The Rainmaker stood speechless at the site, the foggy smoke started blowing towards them with such force that it easily picked them up, tossed them into the air, taking them far away from the mountain. They flew through the air, over the barren slopes of the mountain, over extensive forests, over wide lakes and rivers, and finally they landed on a grassy expanse that cushioned their fall.

The knee-length grass was thick but very soft and it caressed their legs lightly. It seemed to contrast deeply with the barren dryness of the mountain slopes. No sooner had they got on their feet than the grass started pulsating rapidly all around them. Mashaka looked around him as the whole grassy expanse rose and fell as if giant pistons were pumping it from underneath. The pulsating increased in frequency, quickly reaching fever pitch at which time nature's voice boomed from below.

"You have witnessed the evil with your own eyes, Mashaka," nature called out powerfully.

Mashaka nodded in agreement. The Rainmaker looked down at him, her hand resting protectively on his shoulder.

"Evil has rebuilt and it is ready to strike again," nature continued. "Only this time, its might has increased a thousand fold. The evil lord has gained so much power, the only way to bring him down is through war."

"We have seen the rebellion. We have seen the evil lord rebuild his empire. But all that does not answer my questions!" Mashaka shouted in a matter of fact way. His confidence and boldness were growing by the minute.

"Mashaka, all your questions will be answered today." As soon as nature finished the sentence the pulsating grass stopped abruptly and a deafening silence descended upon the field. Mashaka tried to open his mouth to say something to The Rainmaker but nothing came out. The silence was so powerful it swallowed his words the moment they left his mouth. At the same time, The Rainmaker was trying to say something to him but he could not hear her words, despite the fact that she was standing right next to him.

They did not have to ponder their silent situation much longer. Without warning, the grass wilted and withered rapidly, turning the lush green field into a monotonous brown landscape. Then a strong wind picked up and started uprooting the grass and blowing it away as easy as it would do chaff after a thorough threshing. But even as the wind blew massive bales of grass away, Mashaka and The Rainmaker could not hear a sound. Soon the wind swept away all the grass, leaving tracts of arid land that ran for miles on all sides. There was not a single leaf of vegetation to be seen.

It was the distant voices that signaled to Mashaka and The Rainmaker that the silence had passed. They turned around and saw a group of men walking away from them at a distance. Mashaka concentrated on the group and as it happened earlier, the ground shifted and zoomed in the people. The men wore flowing white robes that shined brightly in the hot sun. Their red, green, and black turbans covered their tortured heads from the blazing sun as they wearily trudged in the desert. They were now very close and Mashaka could hear their conversation.

"I still don't think it's a good idea to head that way," said one man.

"I think I have this right. If we keep in this direction, we will hit the great Lake Sango very soon," said another.

The third sounded desperate. "Just say it. We are lost and we don't know where we are going."

"I am thirsty and my legs are weak. We have been walking in this heat for five days and my legs are exhausted. I am an old man and I don't think I can carry on like this much longer," another man complained.

"Why don't you say something," said yet another man, grabbing one of his travel companions by the elbow.

The man turned, took a long hard look at the man hanging at his elbow and continued walking.

But the complainant was relentless. "You cannot ignore me like that. You heard what I said. I know you did."

The first man came to the defense. "Leave him alone. It's not him who got us into this mess."

"All I want is some water and a cool place to rest my head," the man complained once more, paused, put his hands behind his neck and sighed, "What in the name of nature are we doing here?"

These were the seven priests of the ancient *Dini* faith. Word quickly reached their village about the rebellion against nature and they knew exactly what would follow—nature's retribution upon mankind. They feared that although their village did not take part in the rebellion, nature would indiscriminately mete out its vengeance on all of mankind. After days of arguing, they decided to make the treacherous journey to the land of the rebellion. Their mission was to send a message of peace to nature and in return they hoped it would be kind to them and their people.

But they set off shortly after the rebellion and during nature's initial phases of retribution. By that time nature had already held back the rain for weeks and simultaneously sent down streams of hot air on earth. As a result, all vegetation withered and the parched ground turned arid. All streams dried up and there was hardly any source of water. That is how the seven men found themselves in this predicament.

Weak, thirsty, and lost in the wilderness, they were already giving up on the mission—except for one. He possessed the will of steel. He knew that one way or another he would have to reach the land of the rebellion and give the message of peace to nature. But what the men did not know was that the dry conditions and the life sapping heat were not their worst enemies. They were about to encounter evil that surpassed their worst nightmares.

Mashaka and The Rainmaker followed the men closely as they trudged along in the heat. They had to stop once in a while as one priest was going into delirium. It was during one of these impromptu rest periods that they saw what they thought was a would-be rescue party. The men called out to the group of would-be rescuers at the top of their lungs, mustering all the energy they could spare. It was not long before the other party was running to their rescue.

On spotting who was approaching them, the resolute priest held out his hand as if to quiet the rest while he studied the approaching group some more.

"Shh," he hushed them. "Do not move."

"What do you mean do not move. Those men are coming to rescue us," one priest complained.

"I am not sure about that," the resolute priest said, still studying the approaching group.

"You think you are the smartest? You always think you are the smartest one," another priest berated him. "Now tell me, how are you going to outsmart these conditions without rescue?"

"It is not about that. Furthermore, this is not the time to fuss and fight against each other," the resolute priest said in a cool and calm manner.

He took one more look at the approaching party, turned to the others and cried out, "Run for your lives!"

He took off running.

His companions looked at him in confusion.

"That old fool thinks he knows everything. Look at him run away from the rescuers. The desert will consume him in no time," laughed one priest.

"Yes, run you old fool, run even faster!" another priest shouted at him mockingly.

They all laughed heartily as they watched the rescue party approach.

"Hurry, hurry," they all called out to the approaching rescuers who were now running very fast towards them.

"I wonder why they are all dressed in red though?" asked one priest.

Mashaka and The Rainmaker watched in sheer horror as the castaways approached the unknowing priests. It was not long before the six remaining priests lay lifeless on the dry ground.

"We have found the holy men!" their leader triumphed. "Shed their blood and from it we shall draw the power of their faith. From their faith, we shall be invincible and we shall rebuild our spirits and rule forever!"

The castaways cheered as they poured the priests' blood on the ground. The crimson liquid slowly seeped into the thirsty soil which consumed each and every drop it was fed.

"My people, we have done it! We have shed the blood of the holy ones. From their ashes we shall build our new home and we shall be strong once more."

The castaways burst out into cheering, hanging on to their leader's every word.

"Now set their remains on fire so their ashes can mingle with their blood!"

Within no time the castaways had piled up the bodies of the priests in a makeshift crematorium. The fire burned hot and furious, producing a thick green smoke that seemed to rise straight to the sky. It was so hot that within minutes it cremated the six bodies into a small pile of ash. The leader then proceeded to scoop a handful of the ashes into his hands. He walked around and made each member of his party dip his or her finger into the ashes and place it on the tongue.

"Like I said before, from these ashes there will rise our new home. Do you all have faith in me?" he asked, looking around at his followers.

They cheered their agreement.

"If anyone does not want to partake in our new destiny, may he or she leave right now!"

No one moved.

"Then so be it," he said, and dropped the ashes to the ground.

The small handful of ashes hit the ground with the impact of an atomic explosion, jarring the earth and sending the castaways flying through the air and flat to the ground—except the leader, who stood firmly on his two feet, laughing at the spectacle. This time the impact with which the ashes hit the ground was so strong it traversed through time to the present. It tore through decades and centuries of lapsed time to send Mashaka and The Rainmaker flat on their backs too. This exemplified the significance of the lost faith of the six priests of *Dini*. It was a void the world would never again fill. As the castaways struggled to get up, the ground started shaking violently. Huge cracks and crevices developed as the ground split into several pieces. The fissures grew deeper and wider as tremors developed and progressed into a full-scale earthquake. Even then, the ground just split farther apart.

Then it came.

The hot molten lava shot from the bowels of the earth with such velocity that it formed huge red geysers that reached all the way into the clouds. Mashaka and The Rainmaker watched in utter disbelief as the ground creased and rose high, finally forming a new mountain where none existed just a few minutes before.

The soon to be evil lord had just created his new home from the blood and ashes of the six priests of the *Dini* faith. Such was the power of their faith, now lost forever in the tumultuous era that was their world.

Mashaka and The Rainmaker were now standing at the foot of the newly formed mountain. But they were not alone. There was a man standing by their side. He was the resolute priest who narrowly escaped the castaways. The priest turned around and made his way to the land of the rebellion. He knew he had to reach there and spread the bad news. Mashaka turned around just in time to get a glimpse of the priest's face before he turned away.

"Seer!"

But it was no good. They were in different time periods. The Seer was no longer there and Mashaka watched with sadness as the man disappeared over the horizon.

Driven involuntarily by a strange force, Mashaka and The Rainmakers followed the Seer towards the horizon. But they did that in a very strange manner. Instead of walking towards him, days and events just flashed in front of them at lighting speed and when it all ceased they were back in the land of the rebellion. Behind them, the castaways were slowly climbing up the newly formed mountain.

It seemed that the survivors of the rebellion were having some kind of meeting. They also had an unusual seating arrangement. They were divided into five groups, each representing the five clans from the land of the rebellion. This was the meeting of the appeasement. The survivors of the rebellion had come together to make peace with nature. They longed for nature to restore their land to its former glory and the five clans now sat waiting for nature to show up.

As expected, nature showed up in its glorious mightiness. The ground shook as a huge explosion sent huge boulders of the rocky ground into the air, revealing a deep abyss not far from where everybody sat. But amazingly, the huge rocks did not come crashing back to the ground. They defied gravity and remained dangling in the air, floating easily like bits of bird feather. From the abyss, a huge figure slowly emerged—it was nature, fashioned as a gigantic raised fist made of solid black granite rock. As the people watched in awe and amazement, the huge dangling boulders started orbiting the raised fist.

This was nature in its most astonishing manifestation.

"Sons and daughters, mothers and fathers, husbands and wives, I see you have gathered before me today," nature boomed in its unique voice for all to hear.

No one moved. People just huddled in fear amongst their clansmen.

"I see fear in your eyes," nature said. "I hear fear seeping through your ears. I can taste it on your tongues, and I feel it thumping in your hearts."

The crowd remained silent. It was as if someone had doused them with a bucket of frigid water, fetched from the peaks of the coldest mountains.

"Man of the great faith of *Dini*, what news do you bring to the people of the land of the rebellion?" nature asked as the fist rotated to face the Seer, the only person who remained standing.

"People of the land of the rebellion, I bring grim news to you. I bring news of a malevolent force that has now established itself on a new mountain. The evil rebels have finally found strength to establish a new empire of doom. Soon they will forge the means by which to overthrow the world as we know it. Beware, today marks the beginning of a very powerful dark existence," the Seer announced.

The crowd murmured in frightened and hushed tones.

"But fear not, people of the land of the rebellion. For here before you stands nature in its most glorious manifestation. Repent your sins and nature will forgive you. Remain adamant and you shall perish like your brothers and sisters. Hear me now, oh, people of the land of the rebellion!" the Seer finished and sat down.

"Well spoken, man of the great faith," nature thundered as the fist rotated to face the people. "I hate to destroy the beneficiaries of my bounty. But if man brings his contempt, ridicule, and spite upon my realm, he stands no chance against my power. His best defense is no match against the might of my wrath."

The crowd shuddered even further at the words. Memories of nature's wrath were still raw and fresh in their minds.

"But deep inside, I have mercy. Deep inside, I know man means well. But it comes a time when even the harshest parent will have to put his rod aside and let the rebellious child lead his own life. That is when the rebellious child learns that reality is no benevolent teacher. But I stand before you today in full awareness of your pleas for forgiveness. People of the land of the rebellion, you stand forgiven in my presence!"

The crowd broke into mad applause on hearing nature's words of forgiveness.

"But listen!" nature cautioned. "The era of Sadikia has come to a sad end. The optimal world will be no more. The era of the old ancient is gone forever!"

The crowd quieted in disappointment.

"But this day marks a new beginning for mankind. Today we enter a new phase in world history. I usher in the era of the near ancient. It shall be called, the world of the great penitence of Samaha!"

The crowd bust into raucous applause.

"This new world is yours to protect people. Take care of your new world. You will face insurmountable challenges in your new environment. Nature shall only give you bounty for which you broke a sweat. You will have to learn how to fend for yourselves and your children. You will have to learn how to weather the ravages of nature!"

The crowd murmured in uncertainty.

"But most important, you have to protect your legacy from the evil that now exists in your world. You will protect this world with your life and with my help. I shall bestow special powers upon the five clans along with the responsibility to protect the world from its enemies!"

The crowd jumped in anticipation. No one had an idea what kinds of powers nature was about to bestow upon them. After forgiving the people, nature bestowed upon the five clans distinct powers with which they would use to protect their new world.

To the first clan nature bestowed the power of blacksmithing. Their mastery of the iron mongering skill would be unparalleled in the whole world. Their products would be so superior in quality, great leaders from all over the world would come and beg them to fashion weapons for them. But their products would later be put to the test—against the evil lord's army.

The second clan received the power of light. From then henceforth they would be the keepers of the light. They would use this power to shine out evil in every dark crevice it hid. They would also have the power to deny light to the enemies of nature. But most important, they would also be able to conceal the same light for anyone who needed to move in the stealth of darkness for the right purpose. They too would be tested against the evil lord's might.

To the third clan nature bestowed the unusual power of music. From that day forward, they would have the ability to fashion magical music instruments with extraordinary powers. While to an unsuspecting person the notes from their instruments would sound like regular music, these same melodies had the capacity to work as effective weapons. For one, they could now play music that would send even the strongest and bravest warrior into a deep sleep right in the middle of a raging battle. They would later create drums that when beat, would send tremors that shook the ground violently. In battle, these drums would be an affective way of knocking the enemy off his feet. Their most lethal instruments however would be the flutes that produce deadly notes. As soon as these notes reached the enemy's ears he who would simply expire.

The fourth clan received the gift of the birds. They would forever be able to tame and communicate with all kinds of birds. With this skill they could now train birds to act as effective messengers. But their skill would surpass this. Later, they would also train fighting birds which would become a very useful component of an aerial attack in war. But perhaps the most amazing aspect of their gift is that they would eventually find ways to train birds to speak and understand human languages. A future manifestation of this would be the kite that took Mashaka over Lake Sango the first time he visited the land of the Rainmakers.

The fifth clan received the most powerful gift of all. Upon this clan nature bestowed the power to create rain. From now on they would simply be known as the Rainmakers.

It was after the appeasement ceremony that nature finally left to its own realm, leaving the five clans to their new world. The people watched in sadness as the fist of nature slowly retracted back into the ground. The boulders followed suit, falling into the exact position they were before the manifestation occurred. It was as though nothing happened.

Nature was gone, and it would not manifest for a very long time. In the last spot of its manifestation nature left a full grown tree—the tree of life. This is a tree that nature had preserved since time immemorial. This was also the very first tree to grow on this earth. It is from this tree that the five clans carved out six staves. One stave for each clan and one stave for the Seer. The remainder of the tree was harvested for firewood. This firewood now burned in the form of lightning fire beneath the cauldron in the land of the Rainmakers.

"We are almost done Mashaka," The Rainmaker whispered lightly into his ear

Mashaka did not respond. His eyes were fixed on the horizon. The answers were now coming to him. His thirsty conscious was quenching slowly. Things were now falling in place. Everything now made sense; except for one very important question.

The answer to that was about to come to him. It came in the most bizarre and ironic manner. It came to Mashaka in total darkness.

The darkness that descended upon them would put the one he saw in the land of total darkness to shame. This darkness was so thick Mashaka fondled it with his fingers and it rolled softly in his hands. It felt like a continuous ball of very soft wool. But even in this thick darkness, his eyes could see everything clearly. Nature had just bestowed upon him and The Rainmaker, the eyes of the dark. These eyes looked similar to normal eyes except for one little difference—they did not have whites around the pupils; they were black all around.

Through the dark and from a distance, he could see a group of young girls walking down a well beat path in a single file. They were carrying earthen water pots on their heads, which means they must have fetched the water from the springs. The girls sang merrily as they carried the water home. They balanced their water pots delicately on their heads while their arms hung freely to their sides.

This is just as they do in Amani, Mashaka could not help but think to himself.

He concentrated on the group of girls and as it happened several times before, the ground shifted and zoomed in the scene much closer to him and The Rainmaker. Something was tailing the girls at a distance but none of them seemed to notice. The shadowy thing looked like a thick mist as it floated from tree to tree just behind the girls. Unbeknownst to them, the girls just kept on walking, singing and laughing their way home. The misty thing was now very close to the girls but none of them seemed to notice it even though it had grown in size and was wafting right behind them. As the girls kept on walking, the misty thing finally caught up with them and in a quick spiral it started floating right above them. It must have been invisible to them because it quickly descended and engulfed one girl in the middle of the line. It stayed over her for a few moments before it finally ascended and disappeared into the sky.

The girl collapsed immediately, her pot crashing to pieces on the ground.

Screaming wildly, the other girls ran to her rescue. They called out her name over and again as they tried to get her off the ground. But she just lay still, not moving a limb. Their cries must have reached their village because soon the villagers rushed to the girls' aid.

Still unresponsive, the villagers carried the girl's limb body back to her house. Mashaka and The Rainmaker followed silently.

It was three days later and the girl still lay motionless on her bed. She had lain comatose for three days and three nights. On the morning of the fourth day she finally came to. She rose from the deep abyss of the mysterious sleep in perfect health as if nothing happened to her—at least as far as the villagers could tell.

Weeks later, she would be thrown out of her village in shame, only to be picked up by unsuspecting hunters on the outskirts of a far off village. Their act of benevolence would soon change their lives forever. More so, it would shape the future of her son; a boy born of mysterious conception.

That boy was Mashaka—the son of nature.

CHAPTER 12

The Initiation

He was the son of nature.

He was the product of the unlikely union between a human being and nature.

Mashaka stared into empty space as all the answers finally seeped deep into his thirsty mind. The truth had finally come to him. As he stood entranced by his own thoughts, his mind kept going back to the immediate past. He had suspected that knowing his father would be a total shock to him. He had even anticipated the moment in which the answer would come to him. He played this moment over and again in his mind until it became a mental play he staged day in and day out. He even cast different characters to fit his father's role in the drama he called his life.

Was it the Seer?

Was it someone from the land of the Rainmakers?

Was it a great chief from a far off land?

Even as the council of elders threw him out of the village, the council spokesman's zeal at having him cast out sent a fleeting notion in his mind. Was the man throwing him out because he was the son he never wanted?

The next character he cast in his mind was probably the most unlikely—the evil lord himself. That was a prospect he loathed to entertain but in these strange times he could not afford to put anything beyond reasonable doubt.

Everything seemed to defy—nature.

Not once could he have imagined that the very force that ruled and shaped everything in this world would be the one that gave him life. Now everything fell into place. He was the chosen one for the very reason that nature begot him outside of worldly influences. Nature flowed in his veins. That means that unlike any other human being, he was totally incorruptible.

And the Seer! Mashaka said to himself. He'd been there all the time, just waiting for the right moment to guide him to his answers. But what about the people who laughed at him? The same people who continually threw him scorn, calling him a demented old man with an active imagination. What would they say if they knew what he knew now?

And the Rainmakers! All these years they waited patiently for him to make this journey. He finally made the fantastic journey that took him to the very corners of the world. A journey whose conclusion would make all his adventures pale in comparison. But one thing kept ringing in his mind.

He was the chosen one.

He was the one on whom nature bestowed upon the biggest and most important onus, and that was nature's own legacy. He was now nature's sole protector. It was up to him to uphold the continuity of nature against the insurmountable evil that now lurked in his world. He felt different. He felt braver and more confident. No longer did he feel like the little boy who looked lost as he left him mother's embrace to embark on a journey into the unknown.

"Mashaka, we have to go back." It was The Rainmaker.

He had forgotten all about her.

Yes, they were still in nature's realm. But this was his realm too. This was his legacy, and his new task was to protect it from total annihilation. The whole world now depended on him to defeat the evil that was pulsating inside Mount Elgon. All throughout his journey he walked in the shadow of the evil lord. But now time had come for him to face his nemesis and settle the score once and for all. He never dreamt he would ever be in this situation. But what fifteen-year-old had? No young boy had ever been asked to confront a type of evil so powerful it could easily match nature pound for pound. But again, no boy he knew was born in his circumstances.

Nature had only one son, and that was him, and he was Mashaka.

"Mashaka, I know this is a tough time for you but we have to cross back over," The Rainmaker insisted.

"I am ready to cross back over."

His voice sounded different this time. It was laden with bravery and confidence, the kinds of which one garners only after witnessing and surviving a revelation of apocalyptic proportions as he had just done.

"Okay, now let's join hands and I will summon the others." The Rainmaker then took his hand and started muttering in the ancient language.

Soon the whole place was shaking and trembling as their feet lifted off the ground. Below them, the earth started breaking as huge chunks of the realm's ground started falling into a monstrous black hole. It was as if some powerful force was sucking everything in. Everything within their site was falling into the endless abyss as they floated higher and higher. The clouds whizzed past them as the monstrous void below pulled everything into its bowels. Even the sky in nature's realm started to crumble and give away. Huge chunks of blue came crashing down past their heads, only to disappear into the endless darkness below. Even the air in the realm was sucked down too. It was as if nature was erasing any evidence pointing to the existence of its realm.

Finally the two broke through the water that was the floor of the council's chambers in the land of the Rainmakers. Mashaka could feel his body rising through the water. First he felt his head rise, then his neck, and finally his torso. A sense of calm came over him as he finally lifted out of the water. He was anxious to open his eyes and look at his surroundings but for some strange reason he was unable to move. Something was holding him from opening his eyes or moving his limbs. In panicky desperation, he started lashing out, trying to fight the temporary paralysis that had beset him.

"Its okay, its okay Mashaka," someone called out to him.

He opened his eyes to see who that was. It was the council members trying to restrain him and stop him from toppling off the chair.

"Its okay, you are back with us Mashaka," they consoled him as he shook his head and looked around him. Indeed, he was back on earth, and he was sitting in the chair just as he had been before he crossed over.

"Yes, Mashaka, we are back home," The Rainmaker said. She was standing a few feet away from him, looking very composed. Mashaka quickly looked down at his clothes. They were all dry. He looked up at The Rainmaker as if to ask her how that was possible. She just gave him a knowing smile.

"Mashaka, now that you have all your answers, you know we have a lot of work to do." She went ahead and spelt out instructions for his next mission.

He was supposed to off go to each of the other four clans to spread news of the impending war with the evil lord. But before he could do that, he had to go through the initiation process. If Mashaka thought what he experienced in nature's realm was anything to go by, the poor boy had something else coming his way.

He was about to undergo an initiation process only nature's imagination could conjure.

"Come this way Mashaka. I will take you to the initiation chamber," The Rainmaker said.

"Initiation? What initiation are you taking about?" Mashaka protested as he ran after her.

"You think you are ready just because you crossed over into nature's realm? Ha!" she mocked him as she collected her flowing robes and swept out of the room, head held high and proud. "Nature might have given you the life that runs through your veins but in order to fight its war you have to be ready. It is my duty to make sure you are ready to face the evil lord. Now follow me."

Not sure what was going to happen to him, Mashaka followed The Rainmaker quietly to the initiation chamber. It was not long before Mashaka was standing by the chamber, which was located on the far side of the city.

"This is the initiation chamber?" he asked in disbelief.

"Yes Mashaka, that is the initiation chamber."

"That … that … is a huge hole in the ground," he retorted, pointing at the abyss not too far from his feet.

"Is it? Take a closer look."

Mashaka moved closer to the edge of the hole and almost lost his balance.

"There is a huge fire burning inside. I cannot jump in." He moved back a few steps.

"Then you give up the battle just like that?" The Rainmaker asked, turning away from him. "You will throw away the world's future just because you are afraid of jumping into a hole? Remember, you just said it's a hole, not a chamber."

"Is this the only way to get initiated? I will do anything else you want me to but I can't …" Mashaka protested some more but The Rainmaker cut him off.

"Hush, son of nature. You might carry the forces of nature in your veins but until you undergone the initiation process, those forces are of no use to anyone. Not even you!"

Mashaka peered at the bottomless pit again. The flames were growing bigger inside the huge hole and once in a while they would shoot out like huge red tongues eager to taste food.

"You came here for the answers and you got the answers. You are the chosen one Mashaka. You are nature's legacy to the world. You are the one who will lead the armies of men against the evil lord. You cannot have fear in your heart. Now you have to jump into the initiation chamber!" The Rainmaker, who was growing very impatient, shouted at him.

"But I am just a young boy."

"But a young boy won't do us any good." She was now facing him. "You are nothing but nature's boy right now. But when you jump into the chamber, you will come out as the man nature sent out to the world. You will be the man who will stand up against the worst evil the world has ever seen. You are our only hope Mashaka. But you cannot save us until you go through the initiation process."

Mashaka was shaking visibly. He peered nervously at the burning hole and then glanced back at The Rainmaker. He knew he had no choice—but wait, or did he not?

He could turn back and put all this behind him. He could go back and live in the wilderness. Probably he could make his way back to the land of the one-eyed ogres and stay with them. They would do him no harm. After all, the Seer healed them and they know it is him who sent him their way. They owed the Seer their lives. He could probably make his way back to the village and beg the elders to take him back. But what if they refused? He would never be able to see his mother again—*Mother*! He promised her he would come back to her. He knew he had to do it, if not for the whole of mankind, then at least for his mother.

He turned around slowly, faced The Rainmaker and whispered, "Push me in."

"No!" She was curt. "You have to jump in on your own volition Mashaka. There is no other way."

He turned to face the gaping furnace at his feet. Several images flashed through his mind but one kept hitting him harder and harder. It was the image of his mother the morning he departed Amani. She had been in the firm grip of the village women as they held her back while she flayed her arms from a distance as though to pull him back using invisible ropes. The image rendered his heart into shreds and he did the unthinkable.

"Mother!" he screamed and took the plunge into the fiery chamber.

The Rainmaker, overcome with a variety of emotions, collapsed on her knees and wept like a child.

"Nature, oh nature, please keep him safe. Let him return as a man, ready to fight your war. Let him come back as our long awaited salvation."

Mashaka closed his eyes as he jumped into the red hot pit. He did not dare open them as he fell freely through the hot empty air, towards the bottom of a pit in which he did not know what awaited him. He must have fallen for hours, or so he thought. He opened his eyes eventually only to see the red hot flames all around him. He could feel his skin burning in the heat. The pain was intolerable. But he knew he had to endure it. Just when he thought he could not take it any more, the heat suddenly disappeared and a biting cold took its place.

He looked around nervously, wondering where he was. The air he was flying through was freezing cold. He did not have to worry long about the temperatures because he soon landed on soft ground. He scrambled to his feet and surveyed his new environs. He had never seen this kind of terrain in his life. The freezing wind blew sharply in his face, hitting him with some form of white powder. This same powder seemed to cover everything in sight. It covered the trees and even the peaks of the mountains standing not too far from where he was. He picked up a handful of the powdery substance and studied it curiously. He did not seem to make much sense of it so he decided to walk a little bit farther and survey the place some more. The wind was very powerful and since it was blowing a lot of the white substance in his face, his visibility was limited to just a few feet.

And that is why he failed to see the precipice.

Without warning, he stumbled on the edge and found himself falling down a steep cliff, face first. He threw his arms out and grabbed the rocky edges for leverage. But the wind was blowing too cold, and not having dressed for these types of temperatures, his fingers went numb with the cold and he finally lost his grip. Again he was in a free fall. He felt as if he was falling into the bowels of the earth.

But it was not long before he saw exactly where his fall was taking him. He was quickly descending towards a rocky bottom filled with protruding spikes, ready to impale him in a thousand places. In a futile attempt to save himself he grabbed at the empty air. This only seemed to add to the speed with which he was falling. He looked down as the spikes drew closer. The more he fell, the larger the spikes grew. He was coming down with the weight of a ten ton boulder falling straight from the sky. He was now very close to the bottom; he knew his end was near.

He closed his eyes and thought about his mother. He knew he would see her again—in the after life.

Then something happened.

Suddenly he stopped falling. He felt as if something was holding him up in the air. *Had it been that quick? Death was supposed to be painful.* But he did not feel the slightest of pain. He looked around and to his amazement he found he was hovering in the air, just a few inches above the murderous spikes. He turned his head around and took a look. Not too far from where he was hovering over the menacing spikes, a large mysterious man stood pointing a shiny machete at him.

"Mashaka, welcome to the initiation chamber," the man said in a deep strong voice.

The boy, who was too dumbfounded to say a word, just stared at the man.

"Do you not have the ability to speak?" the strange man asked.

Mashaka remained silent. He was shocked beyond words.

"In that case I will have to teach you how to shed your rudeness!" the man shouted and flung his machete at the boy. Mashaka watched helplessly as the sharp weapon cut through the air, coming straight for his chest.

But it did not hit him.

In fact, it stopped inches away from his chest, but just for a split second. Still bewildered by the events, Mashaka watched helplessly as the machete, without touching him, pushed him to the far wall. He crashed into the wall with a thud. Huge pieces of rock went flying from the huge hole his impact created. The machete remained hanging in the air, still pointed inches away from his heart.

"That will teach you to answer your elders when spoken to!" the man shouted from the other side of the chamber.

Mashaka quivered in fear as he looked at the machete, still hovering menacingly all by itself, inches removed from his heart. He looked at the man on the other side of the chamber. The man showed no emotion as his bloodshot eyes pierced him in a devilishly stern manner. The strange man then held out his hand and in reverse motion the machete went flying through the chamber and back into his hand.

"Mashaka!" the man called out to him. "Walk towards me."

Scared out of his wits, the boy stood up and obliged. Slowly, he made his way towards the man, only to stop short at the edge of the field of the evil looking spikes.

"Mashaka, don't be afraid. Look into my eyes and walk over the spikes of death!" the man commanded.

Mashaka locked his gaze with the man's eyes and gingerly took one step forward. But he was too scared to step on the spikes, so he left his right foot hanging in the air, just inches above a menacing spike. The man extended his arm and with his palms facing up he beckoned the boy forward. Pulled by a mysteriously involuntary force, the boy put his foot down on the spike. It shattered like brittle glass. He took another step and another spike shattered. In a trance-like motion, Mashaka took one step after another and the granite spikes shattered under the pressure of his foot.

"You have done well Mashaka. You have walked over the spikes of death. From now on your feet will be invincible to destruction. Look behind you and see for yourself."

Mashaka turned around and looked at the path he had just created in the field of spikes. His footsteps had created a long trail of broken spikes which lay sparkling in the semi-darkness of the initiation chamber.

"You have passed the test of the hottest fire. You have passed the test of the freezing cold, and you have survived a fall through the bowels of the earth. But are you ready for the rest of the initiation process?" the man asked and laughed softly.

Mashaka looked at him in confusion. Who was he, and what was the worst he could conjure up for him?

"I can read your thoughts Mashaka. I see that you wonder about my identity. My name is Kiboko. I am the ancient initiation man. I have waited since the fall of the era of Sadikia to prepare the son of nature for his arduous calling."

To say Mashaka was besides himself in a stew of terror, fear, trepidation, anticipation, and sheer awe would be an understatement. The poor boy was totally numb. To make matters worse the initiation man was not making the situation any better for him.

"Behold the whip of fire!" the man shouted and raised his hand in the air.

From the empty air a stream of bright orange fire came flying down in a thin long line. Mashaka looked on in horror as the line of fire landed in the man's hand. His jaw dropped open when he realized what it was. It was the same fire whip he saw the evil lord's supervisors use on the lava monsters in the vision nature showed him. Mashaka turned around and ran for his life, only to stop short at the edge of the spiked field. He teetered on the edge momentarily, staring down at the deadly spikes waiting for his skin. Undecided, he glanced back at the man just in time to see him raise the whip of fire. Without second thought Mashaka jumped straight for the spikes. The spikes broke into pieces as Mashaka ran for his life. But not fast enough as the whip cut the air and landed squarely on his back.

The pain was horrible and the impact so great it sent him flying face first into the spikes.

This time the spikes did not break.

"Fear, Mashaka. Fear is what you have. That is what makes those spikes pierce your skin," the man shouted.

Mashaka looked around. He could not move. The spikes were longed deep into his chest, legs, and neck. With all his might, he pushed himself up as the spikes exited his body with grazing sounds. They had torn right through his sternum, through his throat, and through his thighs. He clutched his chest in severe pain. He was bleeding profusely.

"Look at me Mashaka!"

"Why are you doing this to me?" the boy begged in intolerable pain.

"Because you have to be ready to face the evil lord Mashaka. It's the fear I see in your eyes that keeps you in pain. It's the fear I smell in your breath that causes you all this pain. Look at me Mashaka, look at me and draw strength from my eyes."

Mashaka looked at the man's bloodshot eyes and tried to concentrate on them. The more he looked, the more his pain subsided. Soon it was only a dull tingling that was left of the severe pain and this too disappeared very quickly. He looked down at his chest. There was no more blood there and neither was there any blood coming from his throat. Even the puncture wounds on his legs were no longer bleeding. The liquid oozing from his wounds was not crimson. It was a bright orange liquid and is oozed painlessly. It was hot molten lava; exactly the way the monsters he saw up the mountain bled.

"The fear is leaving your body Mashaka. When you are free from fear, your insides will turn hot and burn like the bowels of Mount Elgon. Yes, Mashaka, you will have fire flowing throughout your veins. That is the power of the fearless man. Now get up son of nature, we need to get you ready for battle!" the man shouted in triumph.

Mashaka rose to his feet and walked towards the man. The spikes now crushed even quicker under his step. In fact they crushed so hard this time that wherever he walked he left a trail of fine granite powder. That was the power of the fearless man he was quickly turning into. The initiation man scooped some of the powder in his hands and studied it closely. He held out some for Mashaka to see.

"Look Mashaka, this is fear. This is your fear crushed into a powder. Come closer and take a look."

Mashaka moved closer and took a look at the powder the man now held close to his eyes.

He shouldn't have done that.

"Is this your fear, Mashaka?"

"Yes."

"Well let's see," the man said and without warning he blew the powder into Mashaka's eyes.

The powder went straight to his eyeballs, burning them with such heat that he was rendered blind instantly. He fell to his knees, crying out in pain.

"You still have fear Mashaka. Fear in your eyes. I could see that. The spikes killed the fear from your feet, the whip killed the fear from your heart, but you still have fear in your eyes," the man shouted excitedly.

"I … I … can't see," Mashaka cried out in a painful whisper.

"Of course you can't see. How can you fight the evil lord with your human eyes? You need his eyes to fight him. You need to see what he sees Mashaka," the man shouted, his voice coming from all over the chamber. He must have been running around as he shouted.

"Then give me his eyes. Give me his eyes so I can see. Give me his eyes so I can fight him. I am ready to fight him right now!" Mashaka groped around blindly as if in search of the evil lord's eyes.

"That is the sprit Mashaka. That is the spirit! But you will have to get his eyes by yourself."

"Tell me where they are and I will fetch them with my bare hands," Mashaka said sharply, his voice resolute.

"You will get the eyes when you kill the guardian snake. That is the snake that protects the gates to the evil lord's home."

"And where do I find this guardian snake? Tell me now!"

"I will show you. It's the last of the flying snakes and you will have to kill it for its eyes. Here take this."

Mashaka groped around for whatever it was the man was handing him. It was the flying machete he threw at him earlier. No sooner did Mashaka's fingers touch the machete than his vision changed. It was a sight he'd never possessed before. It was as if he was seeing through fire. Everything in his sight was aflame. He could see a mountain range glowing ominously in the red darkness. It was the evil lord's home, just as he'd seen in the vision.

He looked around and he could make out the edges of the trees in the dark. A strong wind blew past him and as it did so, he could see strands of the red air curving in the current. He stared in amazement at the new vista, clutching firmly to the machete in his hand.

"Massshaka!" a sharp voice whispered behind him. It was Kiboko's voice.

He turned around but there was no one.

"You have to go now. We do not have a lot of time. The snake lies in the cave in front of you. Go now and get the eyes," the man whispered in angst.

Without further hesitation, Mashaka marched towards the cave. The entrance to the cave wavered and swayed in the red darkness as he approached. He tiptoed to the cave's mouth and peeped inside. But the cave was empty. Where was the snake? Or was this the wrong cave? Just then he heard movement from nearby and he instinctively ducked inside the cave. He peeped outside and saw one of the evil lord's soldiers approaching the cave. Mashaka slipped into the shadows. The man carried a gigantic bowl that contained a steaming substance which he placed just a few feet inside the cave before he made a hasty retreat.

Mashaka wondered what the substance could be. The smell of traditional porridge floated through the air to his nostrils. *Why would anyone leave porridge in a snake's lair?* The answer came to him instantly. He'd heard about the legend back in Amani. It was said that snake keepers served porridge to their pet snakes to keep them tamed.

Could the evil lord also …

His thoughts were intruded by a sudden rustling noise coming not too far from the cave. He stepped out and peered into the luminous red darkness that was his new vision but he did not see anything. But the sharp screech that cut through the quiet redness was so powerful it sent him crashing to the floor. It was followed by a powerful drought of cold air, and Mashaka, still lying on his back on the rocky floor, saw the source of both the screech and the drought of air. He watched in sheer terror as the gigantic flying snake slowly landed outside the cave's entrance, its huge bat-like wings flapping powerfully by its sides. It folded its wings and even more amazingly it retracted its clawed legs inside its body before it slithered towards the cave. As it entered, it did an amazing thing. Just like a real snake, it entered head first but immediately turned its head defensively towards the cave's mouth as the rest of its body slithered inside. Mashaka shuddered as the shiny scaly folds slid just a few inches from his hiding spot.

He froze in place, waiting for an opportune moment to make his attack. But as he watched the snake consume the steaming porridge, the fear inside him slowly turned into anger. Within no time his whole body was trembling with rage he had to steady his grip on the machete just to hold back from charging at the snake prematurely. The snake finished its meal and fell sound asleep with its head lying across the cave's entrance. Mashaka decided it was time to claim his vision back. He tiptoed towards the sleeping serpent. He was now so close to the snake he could see huge puffs of reddish mist jumping from its nostrils.

But this was no ordinary snake. This was the evil lord's guardian snake. It possessed powers the evil lord personally bestowed upon it. It could sense an enemy miles away. But its weakness lay in the fact that it sensed, not human smell, but human sight. As long as someone had his eyes open it could quickly sense his presence. But Mashaka was humanly blind. The powder of fear the initiation man blew into his eyes took his eyesight away. There was no way the snake would sense his presence—or would it?

It did.

Mashaka was so close he aroused the snake's sinister Extra Sensory Perception. The snake raised its head and went straight for Mashaka. But this was not the Mashaka who left his village so many days ago. He was not the same boy who fled for his life from the *Gizas* in the land of total darkness. Neither was he the same boy who cowered in fear as a prisoner in Gereza. This was Mashaka, who had just undergone the fantastically unspeakable initiation process. This was Mashaka, the son of nature.

Deftly, he jumped aside and the snake missed him and drove its head hard on the cave wall. This angered the serpent even more. It charged straight for Mashaka again but this time he ducked right under its massive head and ran for the cave's mouth. He was now standing just outside the cave's mouth, face to face with the serpent. He looked on as the monstrous snake raised its head, its eyes shining luminously in the hazy darkness of his newly acquired sight. The eyes were just about the size of a human's despite the massive size of the snake itself. But these were not ordinary eyes. These were eyes that could see right through a victim's skin. This means that when attacking a victim, the snake could see right through his skin and straight through to his thumping heart and quivering liver.

But that is not what it saw inside Mashaka. The initiation had transformed him. What the snake saw was a bright fermentation burning just like the molten lava flowing from the bowels of the mountain. However, this did not deter the aggravated slitherer. It made a last charge for Mashaka. But he saw the serpent coming straight for his blazing heart and his reaction was quick. He jumped high and somersaulted in the air, landing on his feet on top of the cave's mouth just in time as the snake made a mad dash for him. For a split second the snake had its head hanging outside the cave, having missed Mashaka by inches.

He did not waste a moment. With the strength of a dozen ogres he brought down the machete. The blade sliced clean through the snake's girth. The snake's head flew towards a nearby boulder. With its mouth open in a silent screech, the head dug its teeth right into the solid rock. The rock ignited instantly, shining in a bright red color before it exploded into a tantalizing shower of molten lava. Its venom had just melted a solid rock. The snake's head then rolled away, finally resting by its body at the cave's mouth. Cool, calm, and collected, Mashaka got down from the cave's roof, picked up the severed head and raised it high in the air.

"You have done it!" the initiator's voice whispered sharply from within the empty red air.

Suddenly the ground under Mashaka's feet started shaking, finally giving away as a giant fissure opened up in the rock surface beneath him. It was not long after that he was falling into the space below. Still holding the snake's head in one hand and the machete in the other, he descended into the depths of the earth. He whizzed past layer after layer of the earth's crust, finally passing its epicenter. He was now moving vertically upwards, back to the earth's surface, back to the land of the Rainmakers.

But this was not similar to the free fall he experienced earlier when he descended into the initiation chamber. He was in fact coming up the abyss he earlier plunged into. He passed all the places he fell through. He whizzed past the freezing environs, the same ones covered by the cold white substance, back into the fiery pit and finally out of the abyss.

He received a raucous welcome when he emerged from the blazing abyss. By this time the flames were burning more fiercely than ever inside the massive hole. Mashaka emerged slowly and majestically through the boiling flames. First to emerge was his head, then his shoulders, and finally his torso. The people went wild as they cheered the person who went into the depths of the earth as a boy and now emerged as the man who would lead then into the battle for the world. The crowd surged forward as Mashaka raised his hand and displayed the snake's head.

He looked at the crowd and everything looked different. He was seeing things just like the snake. He could now see right through peoples' skins. He watched as thousands of hearts pulsated in joy at his return. His vision was now restored. But this was a new vision he possessed. This was the vision he would soon lay upon the evil lord himself.

The time had come for him to bring back what was due to him—nature's supremacy. He was after all, fighting the war not for himself and the world, but for his life giver, nature itself.

Mashaka walked towards the crowd, treading freely on the flames as he finally stepped out of the abyss and fell into The Rainmaker's embrace.

"I knew you would make it, oh, son of nature," she said, tears streaming freely down her cheeks.

CHAPTER 13

Battle Looms

Mashaka stepped out of The Rainmakers embrace only to fall a happy victim to the reaching hands of other jubilant people. Everyone wanted to get a feel of the son of nature. They waited a long time for his arrival and now he stood right before them. He was the man who was going to take them to battle in a war that would determine their future. He was the only man who could stand against the forces of the evil lord. More so, he was the first person to go into nature's initiation chamber and he had returned successfully.

All the great leaders of the Rainmakers had to go through a similar chamber but no one had ever gone through the one Mashaka just emerged from. This particular chamber was as deep as the earth's diameter. The chamber was so deep it practically cut through the earth's interior. On one side of the chamber was the land of the Rainmakers; on the other side was Mount Elgon. Mashaka went to the very end of the chamber and back. Not only that, he also killed the guardian snake and took its eyes. He could now see just as the evil lord himself.

Hope and joy mingled inside the hearts of the celebrating people. For a long time they lived under the shadow of the evil lord. The more his powers grew over time, the more their defenses weakened. The attack on the rainmaking plant by the evil lord's flying sentinels sent a chilling dose of reality to all the city residents—it was just a matter of time before the evil lord made his move. This time everybody knew it would not be a haphazard rebellion like the one he staged so many years ago. They knew he would launch a full scale war against nature and all who stood behind it. But the days of uncertainty were gone. It was now time to prepare for the future and the one thing that would guarantee that—a grand stand against the forces of the evil one.

Mashaka was now standing by the edge of the boiling pit. But this time not an ounce of fear existed in his body. He turned his head skywards and let out roar. A huge flame burst out of his mouth and the crowd went berserk at the sight. The column of fire kept rising into the sky as if to match the monumental height of the rainmaking plant itself.

And it did.

With thundering force, it worked its way through the clouds, burning a black hole clear through them and finally hitting the sky with a loud explosion. The impact was so powerful and the flame so hot both left a charred smoking dent in the deep blue sky.

The people marveled at the sight as they chanted nature's praises over and again.

*   *   *

But the sight was not exclusive to the Rainmakers. Others saw and felt the flame hit the sky and to them the sight carried a whole different meaning. For them it was time to mourn, and mourn they did.

The mood on Mount Elgon was somber. The guardian snake was dead. To make matters worse its head could not be found anywhere. So far everyone on Mount Elgon thought the snake was invincible. They believed it was meant to defy death by all means. Actually that proposition would sound reasonable to anyone who knew of the snake's origins.

The guardian snake was the last of a species of ferocious flying snakes that once imposed its supreme dominance over the skies. The snakes' control over the skies solidified further when they evolved legs. This meant that now they could hunt both in the air and on land. The effect of these killing machines was disastrous. They consumed almost every living this on earth but one thing they failed to overcome was the human species. Using their innate ingenuity, humans devised a new weapon that quickly matched the ferocity of these snakes. This weapon was not a magic bow or arrow. It was not an ancient machete with such tensile strength as to cut through solid rock. Neither was it a spear that could fly through the air at the speed of light.

No, the humans invented *moshi*, the smoke that kills.

This was a type of smoke the humans of that time developed from the sap they harvested from special trees. When mixed in certain proportions, this rubbery substance formed a thick black compound that produced a pungent smell when burned. This is what finally drove the flying snakes to their extinction. The new compound burned to produce a smell so sharp if one inhaled enough of it he would suffer a severe case of nosebleeding. But to the flying snakes the effect was different. The strong smell quickly lulled them into a deep slumber and hundreds of them came crashing down in mid flight as the compound took effect. The humans then rushed to the slumbering serpents and finished them off quickly.

Weakened by the human onslaught, the snakes decided to migrate to new grounds. But their pursuers were relentless. The humans quickly caught up with the flocks of migrating snakes and brought them down, one by one.

All except one.

It had succumbed to the smell and lay dying. For decades no one found it. Finally someone spotted its fossilized remains. It was the only flying snake the humans failed to behead and it was a prized discovery for the finder. He used his mighty powers to bring the serpent back to life but it resurrected bigger and more vicious than any other that ever existed.

It owed its life to only one man; its rescuer, the evil lord.

But now it was dead. The serpent he expended so much of his power to resurrect was gone by the hand of his nemesis. This was a direct call to war. The mountain residents seethed with anger and anticipation as they cremated the headless serpent. It was only after they finished disposing off the snake that they all turned around and saw the bright light and heard the explosion as Mashaka's flame torched the sky. The mountain shook as the evil lord sensed the immense power his nemesis had gained through the initiation process. He knew he dared not venture outside the confines of the mountain but his anger made him do the unthinkable. It was common knowledge that Mashaka and the land of the Rainmakers were out of bounds for him. But at least he could vent his anger and frustration on the one person he thought was immediately responsible for his current plight.

And so he descended into the depths of the earth.

❈   ❈   ❈

The initiation man sat in the initiation chamber, spent and weary from the session he had just concluded. But despite his exhaustion, his heart brimmed with joy. He knew Mashaka had taken the snake's eyes. He knew that because his alter ego had been right there when Mashaka finished off the snake. Thick rivulets of sweat rolled down his back as he leaned his head on the wall.

Then the noise came.

At first it sounded like the wind, but as it grew louder it became a loud angry hiss. He quickly stood up, holding tight to his spare machete.

Right before his eyes the solid rock chamber walls started fluttering like sheets of cloth in a strong wind. He rubbed his eyes in disbelief as if to wake himself from a dream. *This cannot be happening! Not in the initiation chamber of all places.* This was probably the most secretive place in the whole world. Nature specifically prepared this chamber just for Mashaka's initiation.

But that should have been the least of his worries. With breaking sounds, the spikes on the floor broke loose and weightlessly lifted into the air. They started spinning rapidly like bees, buzzing similarly as they gathered midair in an oval formation. The initiation man looked on in disbelief as the spikes rearranged themselves with clacking sounds. His jaw dropped when the spikes formed a new countenance mid-air—his.

It could not be. It was as if he was staring at a mirror image of his face, only bigger and stonier. He did not have to ponder that for very long. The rocky visage opened its dark mouth wide, rushed towards him at lightning speed and swallowed him whole. Expect for the lone machete on the floor, it was as if the man never existed. A stranger scene was how the stony face that had just swallowed him dismantled into hundreds of spikes that returned to their exact position on the ground, one by one.

♦   ♦   ♦

Back in the city, the celebration came to a halt as the initiation man expired and the boiling fire inside the chamber extinguished with a screeching sound. It was as if the pit was painfully swallowing back its fiery tongue. But that was not all. With a rumbling sound, the pit started to implode as it closed down rapidly. People dashed to safety as huge chunks of earth started falling into the pit. It was not long before the chamber was completely covered.

"They found him," Mashaka said solemnly, looking towards the closing pit.

"Yes they have," The Rainmaker replied. "We have to get ready."

"The council has to meet and make the call to war," Mashaka announced.

He turned around and returned to the city. All around him people milled in confusion. The profoundness of the times in which they lived in now hit them with an impact they could never have fathomed in their wildest dreams. The chamber had existed for as long as the city. It was the best kept secret in the world and the residents were sworn to an oath to protect this secret with their lives. No one dared to utter a word about the chamber to a stranger. The repercussions for this travesty were horrendous.

One foolish resident once tried to divulge the location of the chamber to a stranger. For days, he went around the city mute. Not that he was not able talk as such, just that nature instantly glued his lips together. The man never uttered another word about the chamber. But what pushed more fear into everybody's heart was the brazen manner in which the evil lord invaded the chamber. Since he took his band of castaways into the mountain so long ago, the evil lord never left his fiery home. He always sent his sentinels. But again no one had dared touch his guardian snake. The people knew that by killing the snake, Mashaka had set the wheels of war in motion. What no one knew was how the whole scenario would turn out.

The council members gathered in the same room they had been when Mashaka and The Rainmaker crossed over into realm of nature. But this time the air was thick with grief and sorrow. They had just lost an important member of their society. For a long time they knew this moment would come but as the years went by an uneasy feeling of calm settled in. They knew the evil lord was amassing his forces to make the final confrontation with nature, but no one could have guessed when or who would make the first move. But then word reached the city of Mashaka's birth. They knew then it was not long before the evil lord would try to kill the boy. But it had been a great joy seeing him finally make the dangerous journey to their city, to settle a score that had been simmering for ages.

Now the time had come.

"People of the land of the Rainmakers," The Rainmaker called out to the council members. "We have now reached a point of no return. The evil lord had finally emerged from his home and desecrated nature's work once more. This is not a good sign. It is a direct call to war. Now the battle of the ages looms big upon us."

The council members nodded and murmured in agreement.

"But strong as the evil lord's powers might be, here in our midst sits Mashaka, the son of nature. He came to our city a frightened boy but he stands before us today a brave man. He has gone through the initiation chamber and killed the guardian snake. That is a feat no human ever dreamt of doing. But Mashaka, the son of nature, has taken the eyes of the guardian snake for his. He has undergone the initiation process as instructed by his life giver, nature itself. He is now ready to lead us to war. He is ready to confront the evil lord, once and for all!"

The council members broke into applause at her words.

"But Mashaka, we Rainmakers cannot go to war alone. We need a large army to defeat the evil lord. We have many allies on our side but not all of them are ready for war. Some of them do not believe we can defeat the evil lord's army while others think nature has forsaken them for good. It is now up to you to amass an army big enough to face the legion of evil.

Mashaka, you have to travel to the four clans and spread word of the impending war. We do not have much time left so I bid that you leave on this errand soon."

It was now official. Having finished the initiation process, Mashaka was now responsible for leading the people to battle. But as The Rainmaker said, he had to convince the four other clans of the danger that now loomed over the whole world. It was a task he was now prepared to undertake.

He set off early the next day. His departure was marked by dampened fanfare the city residents mustered despite the gravity of the times. But unlike his departure from Amani so many days ago, he would not have to traverse dangerous lands anymore. He would do it much faster too.

This time he had the talking kite for his transportation.

The kite took of swiftly and was soon airborne. Mashaka took in the crisp clean air as they climbed higher and higher.

"Do you want to fly into the clouds?" the kite asked.

"Yes, that sounds good."

The kite changed course and made straight for the clouds. Mashaka held tightly to the reins as they approached the clouds headlong. The clouds whizzed by them as the kite cut through the fluffy forest that was the clouds.

"You want to go higher?" it asked again.

"Yes, why not?" Mashaka called out.

Soon they were flying well above the clouds. Mashaka looked down at the massive expanse of clouds stretching out as far as his eyes could see. This was nature, and being the son of nature, this was his legacy. He knew he had to protect it with all he had.

"We are almost there," the kite called out. "Hold steady, we are about to descend."

Masterfully, the kite shot downwards and they cut through the clouds again, making straight for the land of the blacksmiths.

The blacksmiths dwelt in a series of villages situated on high altitude rocky terrain. Their houses hung precipitously on the edges of the steep hills and from afar one almost expected them to tumble down to the depths below. But being as skillful with iron mongering as they were, they found ways to anchor the houses to the rocks. These made their houses extremely steady even as they hung on the steep hills.

The kite landed at the foot of a hill and Mashaka made his way up the climb. He finally located the clan leader's house and gently knocked on the door. But then the iron door swung open and there stood the man.

"Mashaka, we've been waiting for you. Come in and sit down," the man said. "What news do you bring to the blacksmiths?"

"I bring grim news from the land of the Rainmakers."

"Then keep us waiting no more. Tell us the bad news."

"The time to face the evil one is upon us. We need to make haste and prepare for war."

"So what makes you think that we need to go to war now?"

Mashaka related the latest developments to him.

"That means we have to double our furnaces for the weapons. But we don't have enough wood at this time to make that many weapons as we need," the man said in deep thought.

"Then you do not have to worry about wood any more. I have brought you special wood from the land of the Rainmakers. This wood burns with the heat of lightning. The weapons you will forge with this fire will be indestructible to anything man creates. This wood burns forever and it can light as many furnaces as you wish."

"You brought me the wood from the tree of life?" the man said in astonishment. "That is the first tree to grow on earth!"

"I am the son of nature and I intend to protect it by any means."

Mashaka bade the man goodbye and headed to his next destination, the clan of the bird tamers. They lived in a forest so dense and thick it looked like one green blanket if viewed from above. But the kite knowledgeably swooped down into the thicket, dodging the branches with ease. After all, this is where she spent most of her life before leaving to serve as a transportation bird in the land of the Rainmakers. Soon an eager flock of birds was flying by her side. These were birds familiar to the kite and they were anxious to know about her travels.

They soon reached the dwelling of the bird people. Their houses were most intriguing. They fashioned their houses after the nesting patterns of the birds. The houses stood way off the ground in the tall trees. This was a safety measure to keep enemies out. Scaling the tall trees was out of question. The bird people did not use guard dogs. They used guard birds; ferocious fliers that could tear an intruder to pieces in no time and these birds kept watch over their masters' houses day and night. The only way to get up to the houses was to hitch a ride on a loyal bird. And that is what Mashaka did. He rode his kite to the clan leader's house.

The man was small in stature but for what he lacked in size he compensated for in intensity and authority. The authority exuding from him engulfed all those who stood in his presence like an aura. He was after all, the leader of very skilled people. His people spoke the language of the birds fluently and they had even advanced their art to teach the birds the human language. But that was not all. He was the leader of an army of fierce fighters—the bird warriors. His army's strength did not depend solely on the skill and bravery of his men; it also depended on the birds. His people went to battle on an army of fighter birds so well trained his clan had never lost in war since nature bestowed its gift upon them.

It is to this army of birds that the leader escorted Mashaka. There were birds of all kinds. They had ostriches that were trained to run at amazing speeds. The leader proudly informed Mashaka that these flightless birds were the fastest animals of that time. These, the warriors used to attack the enemy head on. Since ostriches were not birds of flight, their trainers conditioned them to jump very high. This meant that when faced with a charging army of mounted enemies, the birds would simply leap high over the attackers and turn around in rear attack. Before the enemies could turn around and recreate their formations, the bird warriors would have already drawn their weapons in a fierce countercharge.

These people also trained clever weaver birds that were very effective in war. These tiny birds had the potential of turning lethal if deployed in large numbers. They were especially useful in disrupting enemy armies on the move. These tiny birds, otherwise known for their noisiness, were trained to contain their beaks when facing an enemy. They would quietly lie in wait for an approaching enemy and when he drew close they would erupt from the nearby trees and fly straight for the eyes. It would take a very long time for a blinded and shaken army to regroup for battle.

But perhaps most important and most spectacular were the fighting kites. These birds formed the aerial attack unit of the bird people's army. These gigantic birds could fly at unbelievable speeds and at dizzying heights too. As Mashaka very well knew, the kites could easily fly right into and above the clouds. This was a very advantageous attack strategy. They could fly hidden from view above the clouds for vast distances and then swoop down on the unsuspecting enemy. They were the most effective unit of the bird people's army.

Mashaka's next stop was the clan of the musicians. As Mashaka and the kite hovered lightly over their village, he could not help but hear very light notes of music floating in the air. As they drew closer, the music grew louder and something unusual happened. Mashaka's kite started flying haphazardly, almost throwing him off the reins.

"What is wrong, are you tired?" Mashaka called out to the bird.

"Tired … me … no," the bird slurred.

But Mashaka was very worried. "Are you okay?"

"I just feel a little bit sleepy …" the bird slurred some more as they went crashing hard into the tall trees.

A young boy holding a traditional string instrument jumped out of the way just in time as Mashaka and the kite came crashing to the ground. Shocked but basically unhurt, Mashaka and the kite quickly made it to their feet. The boy stood staring at them in disbelief. He was pointing at the bird, mute.

"This is Mashaka, son of nature, and who are you?" the kite asked the boy.

The boy's hand slowly dropped to his side as his knees gave under him. The sight of a large bird and a strange man falling from the sky was shocking enough for him. But the fact that the same bird spoke to him was too much for him to take.

Mashaka rushed to the boy's side. "Hey, are you okay. Get up, we don't mean you any harm."

Just then the boy's mother came rushing to the site. "What did you do my ... and who are you? And what is that large bird doing here?"

"I am not a large bird. I am a fighting kite," the kite said defensively.

"Oh my, that bird talks. Are you from the clan of the birds?"

"No. I am Mashaka, and I travel from the land of the Rain-makers. I wish to speak to your clan leader."

By this time the boy had recovered his senses and he quickly narrated to his mother what he saw.

"I am sorry about that," she apologized. "The music from my son's instrument must have reached your bird's ears and sent it to sleep. You know our music is so powerful it can send a grown man to sleep right when he is walking."

"I know. And that is why I need to speak to your leader."

"Follow me. I will show you the way."

The leader of the clan of the musicians was a tall lanky man whose pipe never seemed to leave his mouth. He spoke in a slow deliberate manner and chose his words very carefully.

"We are the people who nature bestowed upon, the power of music. We do not use spears, machetes, or arrows to protect ourselves. We use the power of music. We play the music that entertains. We play the music that brings sorrow to your heart. We play the music that lifts your spirits in times of tragedy. But we also play the music that kills. Our music is more lethal than any weapon man ever created."

Mashaka nodded his head respectfully.

"But we rarely use our music to inflict pain on anybody. We are peace loving people. The whole world would be a safer and happier place if people took their time to listen to the soothing notes a musical instrument produces. But we are too busy fighting each other to worry about that. We travel long distances to engage an enemy when the answer lies beneath our very own noses."

The man paused to fill his pipe.

"But these are dangerous times, son of nature. We know the evil lord has garnered enough power to challenge nature once more. We know his evil soul will not rest until he vanquishes all that nature stands for. He will stop at nothing until he rips from this world, everything that represents nature. I don't know what my people would do without our music. I know for sure that is the first thing the evil lord will snatch away from us even before he takes away our lives. We are ready to defend what nature bestowed upon us. We will fight to the bitter end to make sure nature's legacy lives on."

The group of elders who were listening intently broke out into hearty applause.

"Come on Mashaka, let me show you the power of our music."

He led Mashaka to a huge storage room filled with all kinds of musical instruments.

"This is the fiddle that plays the notes that lull," he said, showing Mashaka a strange looking fiddle. The fiddle had but only one string. This string was attached to a short hollow cylindrical bout on one end and to a single peg on the other. The neck was actually a long rounded stick. The bow was made of supple wood and a thick band of greased sisal thread.

"Go ahead and play some music," the elder encouraged him. "Come, stand in front of him," the elder added, ushering a man to stand in front of Mashaka.

Mashaka picked up the instrument and played it briefly, not sure what to expect.

"Play the music louder. Do not be afraid."

Mashaka rubbed the bow harder on the string and as the music wafted through the air, the man standing in front of him suddenly closed his eyes and went into a deep slumber. Amazingly, even as he slept on, he was still standing up straight.

The next instrument the leader showed Mashaka was a set of intelligent thundering drums. These drums were so powerful that when beat, they resounded so loud they shook the ground in violent tremors. But astonishingly enough, even in the most violent of tremors the drummer would still have his feet stable on the ground. Meanwhile, his enemies would lose their balance and tumble down all around him. These drums were called intelligent for good reason. Only in times of danger did they display their uncanny ability to tell friend from foe. This meant that only the enemy felt the earth shifting tremors each time the drums were beat. A slight test of the drums had Mashaka staggering around like a habitual drunkard.

The horns of the winds were another type of instrument this clan developed. They looked and sounded just like regular horns but their power lay in the forceful winds they produced even when blown by a small child. The winds they produced when blown by a grown man were capable of bending even the biggest and most deeply rooted tree. The effect of

these winds on a charging army of enemies could be catastrophic.

But the most lethal weapon was probably the flute of death.
The soft notes from this flute were entertaining to the ear of
the flutist but deadly to the heart of the enemy. These notes
were so lethal they could penetrate a thick wall to reach their
victim. All the flutist had to do was direct one end of the flute
towards the enemy and the notes would rapidly cut through
the air and into the man's chest, ripping a hole right through
his heart. The victim would be dead long before his body hit
the ground. With these lethal instruments, the musicians were
capable of forming a killer marching band capable of taking
on any enemy.

Mashaka's last stop was the clan of the keepers of the light.
It was not long before he was examining their weapons. These
were wondrous weapons that solely used the power of light.
The first that Mashaka saw was the pot of light. It looked like a
regular earthen pot except for the fact that in it was stored
light of such intensity it could have easily rivaled the sun. But
this pot was not used as a weapon. It was used as a source of
light whenever battle prolonged into the night. Then, the lid
would be removed and the light would pour out from below,
shining as bright as daytime.

The eggs of light were other weapons the clan fashioned.
They looked just like regular eggs except that the yolk was
actually a ball of super-condensed light. The eggs of light were
small enough to fit in man's palm but they carried large
amounts of lethal light. When thrown at an enemy, and usually in the face, the yolk would explode and produce an
instant burst of blinding light. This caused white blindness.
The light was so strong it would permeate the victim's eyes,

sticking permanently to his eyeballs and causing the pupils to turn white. In his newly acquired state of blindness, the victim would not see darkness but brightness that drowned everything.

It was these weapons and the men who bore them that Mashaka would lead to battle against the evil lord.

Collectively they would be called the armies of nature. These were the five clans that would stage a last stand to restore nature as the supreme force in the whole world.

CHAPTER 14

Battle

The armies of nature gathered in the ancient valley of *Vita*. This valley held a lot of significance to all those involved in this struggle. It was the site of the evil lord's last stand against nature. It was here, in a last ditch attempt to usurp nature that the evil lord gathered his rebellious followers and staged a fierce and desperate fight. Weakened by the ravages nature had already inflicted upon them they were quickly defeated. Barely escaping with their lives, the evil lord and his band of rebels capitulated and headed into the wilderness.

It was a spectacular view the armies of nature presented as they descended upon the valley. From the west came the army of the musicians. The band of drummers beat their drums lightly and in tune, causing the ground to shake in weak tremors. They were saving their energies for bigger tremors when they would finally engage the real enemy. The flutists played their instruments carefully, pointing them up to the empty sky. Meanwhile, the fiddle players and the horn blowers slung their instruments on their backs, waiting for the right moment.

From the north came the blacksmiths, marching to the sound of their famous battle songs. These are songs they composed a long time ago when they established their new settlement after the rebellion. They carried their bows, arrows, machetes, and spears, ready to do battle with the evil lord. But these were not ordinary weapons. These were weapons forged from iron heated by the wood Mashaka brought with him from the land of the Rainmakers. These weapons were literally indestructible.

From the south came the bird tamers. Their army was perhaps the most spectacular. The ostrich riders led the way, trotting on their birds, weapons held high. They were followed by the young boy warriors carrying cages containing hundreds of weaver birds. But it was the third entrants who drew the most awe. These were the bird fighters who rode the fighting kites. At first no one could see them for the simple reason they flew high above the clouds. But once they reached the valley they swooped down en masse. The gigantic birds numbered in the hundreds, practically blocking out the sun as they swiftly approached ground.

The light keepers approached from the east, carrying with them pouches full of the egg-shaped light missiles. Their role was crucial. If combat extended into the night, and chances are that it would, then the pot of light would provide enough light for all to see. Every man in their army was warned to keep the pot safe at all costs.

From the clouds, the army of the Rainmakers descended. They made their grand entrance in the most astonishing manner. It was the dry rain of *kavu* that heralded their arrival. This was a special rain they released only on very special occasions. And no other occasion could rival this one in significance. They were marching to a war that was bound to shape the whole world's future. Their dry rain was so named because it did not cause wetness. This is because it emanated from some type of special clouds the Rainmakers used very rarely. These were the fast moving silver clouds on which the Rainmakers' army rode to battle.

The armies of nature gathered in the valley of *Vita* to present a breathtaking vista. Mashaka, riding on his faithful kite, took in the sight with overflowing pride. He swooped around the milling masses of fighters, making the call to war.

"My people, the time has now come. We are gathered in the ancient valley of *Vita* on the eve of a very important battle. Not even words can describe the gravity of the battle we are about to engage."

In response, the drummers beat their drums lightly and slight tremors shook the ground. The blacksmiths raised their weapons and the sun's reflection on these shiny new weapons was almost blinding. The ostrich riders commanded their birds to stamp the ground as the whole crowd roared in applause.

"It was a long time ago and in this very spot that our enemy revealed himself for the last time. This ancient valley has witnessed the most atrocious act that could result from the fallibility of the human spirit. The grass on which you stand was once trampled by men so evil, the light of day would not shine on their backs."

The crowd was very silent as it listened very intently to Mashaka.

"But that is not the evil we face today. The evil that was banished into the wilderness from this valley has grown to become powerful. It has become so powerful it has now returned to take what it thinks it lost on this very spot so many years ago."

The crowd murmured in agreement.

"But people of the five clans, not even the most imaginative of you can fathom the magnitude of the power this evil has amassed. This evil has grown beyond proportions. Its power is now beyond the control of mere mortals. But wait, we are not mere mortals." He paused and looked at the armies keenly. "We stand under the sun provided by the most powerful force that there ever was. We stand in the valley cleansed by the greatest force that there ever was. We breathe the air provided by the greatest force that there ever was!"

Mashaka paused again as he approached the blacksmiths.

"People of the clan of the blacksmiths, what do you bring to battle today?"

Their leader stepped forward.

"We bring weapons we forged from the wood that burns with lighting fire. We bring spears we forged from the heat of the tree of life. No man in this whole wide world can destroy these weapons. No man!"

"People of the clan of the musicians, what do you bring to battle?" Mashaka asked, now flying the kite in front the musicians.

"We bring the music that came straight from nature," their leader announced. "We bring the intelligent thundering drums that shake the earth like nature's earthquake. We bring the fiddle that lulls the enemy to sleep. We also bring the horns that blow to produce a gust of wind so strong, no enemy shall remain standing in our face. But most important, we bring the flute that plays the music that kills. We are ready, son of nature. We are ready to do battle!"

"Well spoken leader of the musicians, well spoken." Mashaka went ahead and faced the bird tamers. "People of the clan of the birds, nature gave you a gift to tame the birds. What birds do you bring to battle?"

"We bring ostriches that have long been ready for war," their leader shouted proudly. "These birds have the strength of a bull and speed unsurpassed by any living animal known to man. But we also bring the clever weaver birds. As long as our weaver birds have a whiff of breath in them no enemy shall have the eyes to see our attacking armies. But son of nature, behold our bird fighters. Our men ride the fastest flying birds known to man. Our hearts are anxious to ride to battle!"

With that, the bird tamers broke out into a tumultuous burst of applause.

"People of the clan of the light, what is your role in this war?"

"Son of nature, we bring back the gift your life giver bestowed upon us. It is time to show our gratitude to nature. It is time to prove we are forever indebted. We bring the power of light to this battle. We bring the eggs of light that will blind the enemy's eyes with their brightness. But we also bring the pot of light. This is what will give all of us the light we need to destroy the enemy. Let everyone rest assured that even in the darkest of the night, we, the keepers of the light will nourish your eyes with a light so bright you will think you are battling in broad daylight!"

With that, the pot bearers opened the pot just enough to let a little light through. The whole valley suddenly brightened up so much the light from the pot momentarily overpowered the sun.

"People from the land of the Rainmakers," Mashaka called out to the leader of their army. "Nature bestowed upon you its most powerful gift. But the evil one has gained powers so mighty he almost rivals nature itself. Tell me, how do you plan to use your powers against him?"

"We know the evil lord is mighty powerful such that he mimics the powers of nature," their leader called out. "But he has one weakness. His army cannot stand nature's rain. But such is his sinister shrewdness we know he can divert the rain from falling on Mount Elgon. But son of nature, our intention is to bring the killer rain right into his abode with our very own hands. With us we carry the deadly arrows of rain. Step forth rain archers!"

The rain archers stepped forward and revealed their weapons. Everyone in the valley awed at their ingenious invention. Since the evil lord's lava monsters and kites could not stand water, the evil lord devised ways by which to prevent rain from falling on Mount Elgon. But in counter ingenuity, the Rainmakers devised the rain arrows. These were ice crystal arrows filled with super-compressed rainwater. When shot at a lava monster, the ice was hard enough to penetrate the skin and explode inside, therefore sending jets of lethal water inside the monster. The arrow heads glinted gently from the quivers hanging on the archers' backs.

"People of the five clans," Mashaka shouted as his kite glided across the valley. "I stand before you as the chosen one. I am honored to be the offspring of nature; the one it chose to retrieve its honor and restore it to where it rightfully belongs. But my heart overflows with humility when I lay my eyes on the people who stand before me. I see people who are ready to give up their lives for what is good. I was nothing but a simple village boy when my troubles begun." His voice was now softer with emotion. "It was not long before I was banished from my village. There is no pain in this world as the pain of a boy ripped from his home. I have felt that pain my people. You have felt your pain too. For too long you have lived and cowered under the shadow of the evil one."

The crowd burst into more applause.

"But now is the time for us to redeem ourselves. This is our last chance to restore the supremacy of nature in this world!"

The crowd stamped their feet and shouted their approval.

"I can feel your energy running through my veins. Let me feed on that positive energy because we know we are going to fight hard against a very powerful enemy. We stand as one people. No one can break the bond nature created for us years and years ago. Therein lies our strength. It is the strength to bring back joyful times. Joyful times when mothers will sing to their children freely. Free times when people will work the fields with peace of mind. Peaceful minded people who will look at Mount Elgon and say; there used to be a great evil but now it exists no more!"

The crowd burst into more thunderous applause.

"But words do not beget action. It is going to be a mighty struggle but every man will fight to the bitter end. We have brave men in this great valley today but your bravery will be tested against an evil no good mind can fathom. Our hearts beat fast, but they beat, not in fear, but in anticipation. I know you cannot wait to engage the enemy and bring him down!"

The armies went crazy at Mashaka's words. The air was electrified with emotion as the urge for battle built up and spread across the valley like a volatile forest fire.

"Go to battle with one vision in your mind, people of the five clans. Think about the olden days. Think about the days when nature ruled this world supreme. Think about when man and nature were one and the same. That is what we go to war to restore. Today we will bring back the bygone era of nature's supremacy!"

By this time the atmosphere in the valley was so charged even the birds jumped high in anticipation.

"People of the five clans, are you ready for war?"

The response was so tumultuously loud the valley resonated with the outburst of a unified war cry. The people were ready to fight and restore nature to its supremacy. Their leader had finally sparked and lit the fire of battle in each and every one of them.

With a unified roar, the armies of nature dashed to war.

The massive forces that gathered to battle the evil lord now marched steadily to war. The forces spread out over a large expanse and from afar, one would think it was a large forest in motion. Meanwhile, the army of flying kites was not visible to anyone on the ground. They were now flying high above the clouds, heading to the mother of all wars. The rain archers were not that obvious either. They were riding their super fast silvers cloud right in the midst of the regular clouds in the sky. On the ground, the armies marched over hills and valleys, crossed rivers and streams, and occasionally had to traverse a thick forest or two. But soon they reached Mount Elgon, ready to engage the evil lord.

But this was no ordinary adversary they were about to face. This was an enemy who over time, developed his own powers to rival those of nature. After his defeat in the valley of *Vita* so many years ago, he retreated into the mountain and waited for his opportunity to show up. It took ages but he eventually amassed enough manpower to confront nature and its army. The evil lord was not one to underestimate. Not that any of the five clans did that. It's just that no one really knew of the inner workings of Mount Elgon all this time.

Meanwhile, Mashaka rode his kite bravely at the head of the marching army, giving orders and shouting encouragement. Pumped full of wartime adrenaline, the armies of nature steadily approached the evil lord's home. They were not very far from the mountain when they saw the enemy formations. The mere sight of the evil lord's army took the breath away from everyone's mouth. The dark lava monsters looked gigantic even at a distance. The sheer multitude of the men in red sent cold shivers down the spines of the men on nature's side. Meanwhile, the evil lord's army stamped their feet on the ground and chanted their war cry in unison. It was a dreadful sight to behold.

The evil lord matched nature's army fighter for fighter or even better. This was one foresight they wished they knew. Suddenly, confidence faltered within nature's ranks.

"Son of nature, the evil lord's army outnumbers us," complained one leader.

"His forces might be larger in numbers but there is one thing he lacks. His forces don't have life. That is not life that makes his soldiers move. That is not air his soldiers breathe. That is an illusion. Nature is the sole life giver and that is one thing the evil lord cannot, and will never be able to re-create.

Why do you think he wants to usurp nature? He wants what he can never have as long as nature exists. Those are empty foes you face people. We cannot give up right now. We have to do what we came here to do. Fight this evil and fight it with all your might!"

With that, the armies of nature roared fiercely and rushed to meet the evil lord's men.

Both sides fought furiously. At first it seemed that the evil lord's army had the upper hand. It came as a shock to everyone on Mashaka's side when from behind the charging men from the evil lord's army, a huge army of flying lava kites emerged. They rose high then swooped down, straight for their foes on the other side.

But the evil lord's birds looked different. They did not carry feathers. They carried charred flakes that hung loosely from their crusted skins and whenever they opened their mouths they sent hot flames flying about. But they flew as fast as any kite and fought just as hard. Their sinister riders looked much similar to them in composition. They were just but smaller versions of the larger lava monsters on the ground. The aerial battle was furious. The evil birds attacked with vengeance, cutting though the ranks of the fighter kites with evil skill. Flocks of the fighting kites fell to their death with their injured riders still strapped to their backs. It was only after the silver-cloud-riding rain archers joined the aerial battle that the lava kites fell back to regroup.

Things were not going very well on the ground either. The evil lord's men, accompanied by the gigantic lava monsters, crashed through the ranks of the ostrich riders. The men in red carried spears and machetes almost as hardy as those forged by the blacksmiths. The lava monsters on the other hand swung their crude but deadly smoldering stone clubs at their foes. One by one they brought the ostriches and their riders down. But the men whose birds lay mortally wounded on the ground did not give up. They got on their feet and fought on, cutting down as many monsters as they could.

It was the musicians who almost saved the day. The drummers quickly rushed to the frontline and beat their thundering drums very hard. The earth shifting tremors that resulted from the drumbeats took the evil lord's army by surprise. The soldiers in red lost their footing while the lava monsters tumbled down, crashing to pieces on the rocky ground. But it seemed that their master had anticipated this. More and more of the monsters came spewing out of the mountain. It was if he had endless reinforcements of these loathsome beasts. The fiddle players played their fiddles feverishly but the sleeping tunes only lulled a few of the men in red. The tunes seemed not to have a big effect on the dangerous lava monsters either. Once in a while a monster would come crashing down but for the most part they fought on.

Mashaka rode his kite swiftly, cutting through throngs of the evil lava kites, shouting encouragement to his men. But the evil lord's birds kept regrouping and swarming in attack. He looked down and saw that the evil lord's army had cut deep into his own ranks.

"Fly lower!" he commanded his kite. The bird swooped down as Mashaka flew to the rescue of one drummer who a couple monsters had pinned to the ground. Just about when they were about to bring their smoldering stone clubs on him, Mashaka's machete flashed through the air and he chopped both the monsters' heads off with one powerful swing. The freed man fumbled to his feet and regained possession of his drum. He proceeded to hammer it so hard the resulting shock waves sent dozens of monsters crashing to the ground. All around him lay huge chunks of wasted smoldering lava.

Mashaka then ordered his kite to fly over the horn blowers.

"Blow your horns at their heads," he called out.

The horn blowers directed their horns at the monsters' heads. The wind that gushed from the horns was so powerful it ignited the hot lava inside the monsters' heads, setting them on fire instantly. With their heads ablaze, the doomed mountain creatures ran around confused, straight into the waiting machetes of nearby warriors.

But just when the musicians thought they were overcome by the relentless monsters, the rain archers would speed in, slashing down through the air on their silver clouds. From their bows came a volley of ice crystal arrows headed straight for the lava monsters. The arrows quickly penetrated the monsters, sending them reeling in pain as their insides came into contact with the cold ice—they hated the cold. But they should have been more worried about what the arrows contained. On impact, the heat inside the monsters quickly melted the ice sheathing of the arrows, causing them to explode with splashing sounds. The monsters reeled and contorted some more as the super-compressed rain water extinguished their insides. Soon they were falling to the ground in large numbers and breaking into small brittle pieces.

Encouraged by the counter onslaught, the flutists rushed forth with their death music. The notes were so strong that they cut through both man and monster. The enemies fell in droves. It was the perfect opportunity for the blacksmiths to attack. As fast as their legs could carry them, they charged into the enemy's ranks, cutting and spearing. Monster after monster came crashing down on the rocky mountain floor, exploding into a tantalizing spray of red hot lava. But the heat did not seem to bother the blacksmiths. They promised Mashaka their loyalty and it was evident they were ready to die for nature. They fought on with unwavering zeal.

From the rear, the warriors heard a familiar warning.

"Everybody turn away, here comes the eggs of light!" someone from the clan of the light keepers shouted. Everybody turned away and covered their faces.

The evil lord's men, not sure what it was, stood perplexed as the egg-shaped missiles approached them in long trajectories. In fact one of their commanders laughed in a coarse evil tone.

"Now they are fighting us with eggs?" He was holding one in his hand. "I will show you a real weapon," he said and crushed the egg in his hand.

The shell broke, thus exposing the super-condensed light inside. The resulting light explosion was so powerful it blinded a large radius of the men standing around him. The whole battle field was lit with flashes of the deadly brightness as the tiny missiles exploded. The men in red ran around blind and confused. The blacksmiths moved in swiftly to bring down the disarrayed fighters.

But from the depths of the mountain, more and more enemies emerged. Man, monster, and evil bird seemed to pour out as if from a monstrous overflowing pot. Then the strangest of things happened. The whole place grew dark. Everybody stopped fighting as their eyes turned skyward. The men on nature's side looked on in horror as a dark planet moved in slowly to cover the sun. The evil lord had gained so much power he was about to cause a total eclipse. Mashaka knew for a fact there was no way his men could fight the evil lord's army in darkness. He was the only person on his side who possessed the snake's eyes and the ability to see in any condition. However, each and every member of his enemy's army was equipped with this unique sight.

"People of the light, deploy your pot now!" he commanded.

Just at that moment the gigantic dark planet moved in and covered the sun completely. The whole battlefield was covered in total darkness. It was an eerie sight. Enemy eyes gleamed menacingly in the dark as the evil lord's army charged at the confused victims. Mashaka's men ran blindly into each other, unable to see what was going on. With a clear vision in the dark, Mashaka could see that the scales were now titled severely in favor of the evil lord's side. The evil one's army did not waste a moment of it. The men in red cut down their victims en masse. The lava monsters clubbed Mashaka's men to a quick bloody pulp.

But Mashaka did not see like any ordinary human. He had the eyes of the snake. He could see just as well as any of his enemies could. He knew he had to find the pot of light as quickly as possible. His vision cut through the throngs of fighting men. His men were scattered all over the battlefield as the advantage quickly turned in favor of his enemies. Then he spotted the pot. It was in the possession of a lava kite that was making a desperate dash for the mountain peak with the pot hanging securely in its dark claws. Mashaka made an equally mad dash for the bird.

He used his skill and superior vision to steer his kite towards the fleeing bird. Within no time he was right behind it. He desperately tried to pry the pot from the bird's claws but it held firmly to the newfound bounty. His kite was now flying haphazardly in the dark and Mashaka knew it was very important that he retrieve the pot before the bird delivered it to its evil master. Below him, the monsters were overrunning his men rapidly. In a last ditch effort to grab the pot, Mashaka leaned in too far and lost control of his bird. He frantically tired to correct its flight with the reins but to no avail. In desperation, he lifted his machete high and slashed at the lava kite. He watched slowly as the bird decelerated towards the rocky ground.

Let the pot break, he prayed to himself.

The pot landed soundly on the rocky ground but did not break.

"Oh no, it can't be!" Mashaka cursed loudly.

A soldier in red picked up the pot and looked at it confusion. But as he stared at it and wondered what a pot would be doing in the middle of a fierce battle, the dead bird came crashing down on him. The impact sent both man and pot crashing to the rocky ground.

At last, the pot broke.

The light was blinding as it quickly consumed the darkness, turning the whole battlefield as bright as day. But the light did not emanate from above. It shined brightly from below, turning the rocky mountain surface into a vast fluorescent battle floor. But it was too late for Mashaka and his kite. Having momentarily lost his bearing while watching the pot drop, he failed to see the fiery hole gaping on the side of the mountain. His kite crashed right into the hole and landed into the fiery inside of the mountain. The flames quickly consumed the bird while Mashaka watched helplessly.

He turned around sharply when a strange voice called out to him. "At last, you come to my presence."

He had fallen right into the evil lord's fiery chambers.

❦   ❦   ❦

Mashaka rose to his feet and looked around. He felt as if he was inside a blacksmith's furnace. The heat was so intense it almost melted the clothes on him. The fire inside the chamber burned with such intensity the walls seemed to melt right before his eyes. The walls were made of red hot molten lava and this lava poured and disappeared into the rocky floor on all sides of the chamber in the form of a fiery four-sided waterfall. But still, Mashaka could not see the source of the voice. The shifting voice seemed to emerge from all over the place. First it came from the left, then from the right, and finally it called out to him from above.

He looked up towards the chamber's ceiling. The ceiling consisted of a spectacular display of fire. The huge flames seemed to hang in the air, neither rising higher nor falling to the ground below. They just churned into intricate patterns that for a moment Mashaka was stupefied. Not too far from where he stood was a long table running to the foot of a huge empty throne burning under an intense fire. On each side of the table were three chairs. Just like the throne, these too were blazing. But unlike the empty throne, these blazing chairs were occupied. In them sat six ghostly figures that in unison turned around to face Mashaka.

Then it hit him.

These were not just ghostly creatures. These were the six men of the *Dini* faith, the same men nature revealed to him once. They were the same people who accompanied the Seer on that fateful journey to the land of the rebellion; the same men the evil lord slaughtered in the wilderness and used their blood and ashes to create the mountain. The very mountain inside which their souls now remained trapped and tortured in an eternal and evil prison of fire.

But they did not utter a word. They just stared at him in ghostly silence. *So where is the voice coming from?* The voice called out again. It was coming from right behind his ear. It was so close, Mashaka turned around very slowly expecting to bump into whoever was speaking. But there was nobody. Then the voice called sharply from behind him again. This time it sounded like a young child. He turned around but again there was nobody.

"You will taunt me no more!" Mashaka shouted in anger. "Show yourself if you are worth your salt!"

"So now you are angry?" It was an old woman's voice this time. "You come crashing into my home and you spit anger in my face? Are those the manners your mother taught you Mashaka?"

"Refrain from uttering my name with your evil mouth!" Mashaka spat in disgust.

"My, my, what an attitude we bring with us to battle, Mashaka." Now it was a young girl's voice.

"Show yourself evil one. Show yourself right now!"

"Patience my boy. It takes patience to see the great one." The voice now sounded like an old man's.

"You know no greatness. You cannot speak of greatness!"

He must have struck a nerve with those words because from the empty throne the hazy figure of a young boy lunged at it, hitting him so hard he went crashing to the ground. But the boy disappeared as soon as he appeared.

"I will teach you about greatness!" an old woman's voice hissed.

"You cannot teach me any lesson until you show your evil being. Are you afraid?"

"I am not afraid of any man," a young boy shouted, and with that, the evil lord showed himself to Mashaka.

He first appeared as a wizened old woman doubled up on her crooked walking stick. But this was no ordinary elderly woman. With a shriek, she leapt at Mashaka, sailing through the hot air like a bird and whacked him at the shins with her stick. The stick looked thin and the blow deceptively weak. However, the impact sent Mashaka flying through the air. He somersaulted in the air and finally landed soundly on his back. He writhed and grabbed his back as the pain shot through his body.

He looked up to see a young boy staring at him. The boy's face glimmered wickedly, his eyes nothing but two holes through which the fire burning inside his brain showed.

"If you are the chosen one then let me see you get up from the ground," the boy challenged.

He then opened his mouth wide and a powerful stream of hot air shot through, pinning Mashaka to the floor. Mashaka struggled against the hot wind current the boy was blowing his way but it was too strong for him. As he looked on help-lessly, his tormenter quickly shifted shapes. The boy, who was now sweating profusely, melted into a fiery pool of red liquid right in front of Mashaka's eyes. The thick liquid that was once the boy started boiling violently while it rapidly expanded in volume. As it did so, it kept churning upwards until it formed a thick pillar that reached all the way into the burning ceiling. From it, a voice emerged.

"Mashaka, I will give you a choice. Join my forces and let's rule this world together or you don't leave this mountain alive."

The voice sounded familiar. It was the voice of the eccentric man who led the rebellion against nature so long ago.

"I will never join forces with your kind!" Mashaka shouted back, resolute.

"What has nature done for you? It has had you thrown out of your village. Where is your mother Mashaka? If nature was supposed to be so good to you how come you were left alone to wander in the wilderness? Nature left you to die Mashaka, it left you do die! Now what do you have to say about that?"

"I was never alone in the wilderness. I was protected all the way to the land of the Rainmakers. And that is exactly why your evil forces could not get to me. You don't know me like nature does."

"Mashaka, what plans do you have after the battle is over? Your men are falling as we speak and soon we will slaughter each and every one of them. Now where does that leave you, eh? Where will you be when I finally bring nature to its knees?"

"No amount of suffering will make me join your forces evil one. I am a man who stands by his word, and my word is with nature!"

"I am offering you the last chance to live forever. Join my forces and both you and I will rule this world for the rest of its existence. Decline my offer and forever be damned into the prison of fire!"

"To you I am not Mashaka. I am your worst nightmare come true. I am the son of nature!" Mashaka shouted and sprung to his feet.

He lunged straight at the burning pillar and cut it into two pieces with a quick chop of his bare hands. The pieces fell with a loud metallic clang but the liquid fire quickly recollected and turned into a fiery whirlwind that came straight for Mashaka. But this was not a regular human being the evil lord was battling. This was the son of nature. Suddenly, nature's powers erupted inside Mashaka and he spun around and transformed into a fiery blue spiral of sky material. The spiral went straight for the fiery whirlwind that was the evil lord. The two met with a resounding crash. The molten walls shook violently as the impact sent the evil lord spluttering onto the burning table. The table crashed and disintegrated into little flames that burned weakly on the floor. Mashaka transformed back to his human form.

But the evil one was not done. The disintegrated pieces of the fiery whirlwind collected to form a monstrous fire demon that thundered towards Mashaka. The demon opened its mouth wide and shot deadly fireballs at Mashaka but he dodged them deftly. It then lunged forth but Mashaka grabbed it and sent it flying across the fiery chamber. The fire demon remained on the ground momentarily, dazed and beat.

"Now do you still want me to join your forces or are you ready to die?" Mashaka's voice boomed across the fiery chamber.

"No!" shouted the demon as it raised its right hand in the air and from it a long thin fire whip shot out and lassoed Mashaka at the feet. Before he could do anything, the demon jerked the whip with such mighty force that it sent Mashaka flying across the chamber. The force with which the whip tossed him was so monumental he went crashing through the molten walls and right into a lake of boiling brimstone.

He lay dazed at the top of the boiling lake momentarily, just before the seething red liquid sucked him under.

"That shall be your final resting place. Welcome to the prison of fire!" the demon proclaimed as it transformed back to the wizened old woman. She peered at the boiling lake for a reaction but none came. At last, Mashaka had been cast into the eternal prison of fire.

Did this mean the struggle was over?

🍁   🍁   🍁

Outside, the battle was turning sour for the armies of nature. By this time the evil lord's army was practically having its way, cutting easily through its opponent's ranks. The evil lord's men killed, burned, and clubbed both man and bird. Feeling totally overwhelmed, the leaders were now calling for a retreat.

"Everybody, stop fighting and retreat!" the leader of the blacksmiths called out as he looked at the carnage that was once a group of dexterous warriors.

"But we cannot retreat now. We promised Mashaka we would fight to the bitter end," a tenacious warrior protested.

"Mashaka is gone. Can't you see the evil lord has killed him already?" the leader shouted back.

The battlefield was disadvantageously littered with victims from nature's side. The dying and the dead lay side by side as the lava monsters and the men in red pursued the surviving warriors. The wounded mourned and cried out in mortal pain for help that was unlikely to come any time soon.

❉   ❉   ❉

Back in the land of the Rainmakers, the council members sat in their chambers in nerve racking anticipation. They were anxiously waiting for word from the battlefront. The Rainmaker sat silently at her usual spot at the head of the council table, and for a long time no one said a word.

Once in a while the water that made the floor of the council chamber would ripple slightly. But as time went by, the ripples grew larger and larger until they formed small waves that tossed the ice crystal chairs the council members sat on from side to side.

"Let's join hands and collect our power. Mashaka will need all the power we can garner for him," The Rainmaker called out.

"Do you think it is too late Rainmaker?" asked one old councilman.

"He is the chosen one and we have to have faith in him. Doubt stands to help him in no way councilman."

But the water floor got rougher with time. The waves were now tossing the chairs inches into the air but the determined council members held their hands together firmly. Whatever powers they were trying to collect seemed not to work because the waves increased in intensity, eventually throwing them into the water. The elderly council members were now struggling to keep their heads above water but all this time their hands remained joined.

"Do not give up council members," The Rainmaker shouted as they desperately tried to join hands and simultaneously stay afloat.

Then the warning came.

A messenger rushed in to report that the evil lord's kites were headed for the city. The Rainmaker knew exactly what they were after—three things: To destroy the rainmaking plant, to capture the chief rainsmith, and to carry away the ancient cauldron. *This is not happening,* she agonized silently, looked skyward and let out a frustrated scream.

"Why have you forsaken us in time of peril?"

Outside, a dark cloud of lava kites was slowly approaching the city. Their putrid smell already preceded their arrival and was harassing the noses of the city residents. The birds flew in such numerous flocks they partially blocked out the sun, turning the sunny afternoon into a dreadful dusk.

❦   ❦   ❦

Inside the lake of fire, Mashaka sank deeper and deeper.

But the sight he snatched from the snake enabled him to see his surroundings very clearly. All around him he could see long reaching arms and faces with wide open distended mouths. The faces that formed in the liquid fire were trying to tell him something. He leaned closer and tried to hear what it was they were saying.

"We knew you would come, son of nature," they whispered through the boiling flames.

Mashaka looked closer and realized that these were the faces of the six men of the *Dini* faith. Even in his amazingly indisposed state he could not help but feel the surprise run though his mind.

"You have to go back, son of nature," the faces continued.

But he kept sinking deeper into the burning lake.

"You cannot give up on the world," the faces cried out to him.

The hands were now trying to grab him but try as hard as they could, he was out of reach. Mashaka tried to reach out for the hands but his efforts were futile. The prison of fire was sapping his powers rapidly.

"Try harder, son of nature, try harder," the faces whispered their encouragement.

With a last desperate heave, Mashaka extended one hand and grabbed one of the reaching hands. Soon, six pairs of hands wound around him and starting pushing him back up through the lake of fire.

Back on the surface and high above where Mashaka now lay buried deep in the fiery lake, the old woman stared some more and then turned around to leave. As she turned around, and in mid stance, she transformed into a man. It was the same eccentric man who led the first rebellion against nature. All these years and he had not changed a bit. He looked exactly as he had ages ago.

"At last, nature has been conquered," he stated triumphantly.

But had he turned around to look at the boiling lake of fire he could have seen and uttered something very different. The fiery lake started extinguishing from the center outward. Then slowly, the lake turned into a pool of clear blue water. Mashaka had transformed into water, nature's most powerful element. It was also the most unwelcome element in the evil lord's domain.

"Evil one, behold the power of nature!" a voice boomed behind the retreating man.

It was Mashaka, now speaking in the voice of nature. It was the same voice he once heard nature address him with but now it came from his throat, powerful as ever. It was a single voice made up of several people's voices; a young man's, a young woman's, an old man's, an old woman's, and a young child's voice, all united to form a perfect tone that only one entity could master. Even after amassing all his powers, this was one feat the evil lord failed to accomplish. Yes, he could speak in the voice of different people as he already demonstrated to Mashaka, but he could not blend them to form a unified voice representing all of mankind's diversity.

The man turned around and stared at the site in shock. But he quickly regained his composure and spun around, turned into the fiery demon and made a quick exit on one side of the wall.

But the escape attempt would not come to fruition

The water raised in a huge fist—the fist of nature—that went flying after the escaping demon. It landed on it with such an impact it shook the whole mountain. The water engulfed the evil lord, finally extinguishing him forever.

※   ※   ※

Instantly, the scene on the battlefield changed. First of all the lava monsters froze in their step. The men in red tried to rally them into more battle but the monsters remained transfixed on one spot. No amount of encouragement or whipping could make the things move. What started as a slight tremor soon grew into a violent earthquake as the ground twisted and shifted simultaneously. With powerful tearing sounds, the earth started splitting into numerous fissures. From these crevices, long fiery arms emerged and started grabbing the men in red, pulling them deep into the bottomless cracks.

The men struggled fiercely against the fiery appendages but they were no match for the power that was bound to pull them into the depths of the earth. Screaming and clawing like little children, the men in red were pulled into the deep, one by one.

A much similar fate befell the lava monsters. They all lost their balance in the earthquake and crashed violently to the ground, breaking into little bits of charred stone. Soon, not a single monster remained standing on the whole battlefield.

As soon as the last man was pulled underneath, the earthquake stopped.

The surviving warriors rose to their feet and looked around in shock. It was as if their enemy had just vanished into the thin air. There was not a single man or monster from the evil lord's army left standing.

"Mashaka, it's Mashaka, he has defeated the evil lord!" someone shouted.

The sentence rang repeatedly from mouth to mouth as all eyes turned eagerly towards the mountain peak. As if to answer their thoughts, Mashaka was indeed standing at the mountain peak. But he was not standing in his complete human form. His right hand was raised in the air in the form of the very powerful fist of nature. This time it was not made of granite. It was made up of nothing but the water that had just extinguished both the evil lord and the prison of fire. The men stared at the spectacle speechlessly. They also saw something orbiting the raised fist but none of the men on the ground could tell what it was. But how could they? None of them knew the ancient men of the *Dini* faith. These were their spirits, finally free from bondage.

"People of the five clans, we have defeated the evil lord!" Mashaka shouted loud and clear for all to hear.

The crowd of surviving warriors burst into applause that sent the rocky ground shaking.

Mashaka pumped his fist in the air and from his clenched fingers powerful jets of water shot up like a gigantic fountain. The jets of water rose all the way up to the sky then came crashing down in the form of torrential rain. This was the rain of *safisha*; the rain that cleanses. It was meant to clean and wash away any remnants of evil on the mountain.

The men raised their hands in the air as the *safisha* rain drenched their bloody clothes while simultaneously rinsing their skin only as a healing balm would.

❧   ❧   ❧

The people in the land of the Rainmakers looked up with despair as the birds approached them. The closer the birds drew to the city, the darker the skies grew. The birds were so dark it was as if they were sucking the sunlight right out of the sky. As they crossed over into the city skies, the people went running helter-skelter, looking for cover.

The birds swooped down on them with vengeance begot from an anger pent up inside for a thousand years.

Or did they?

They were practically dropping from the sky in hordes. The running people quickly stopped in their tracks to examine the birds. They were not swooping down in attack. The truth was the birds had expired mid flight and it was the charred pieces of their remains raining from the sky. Just like it happened to the lava monsters and the men in red, every single member of the evil lord's army was gone.

The water floor in the council room suddenly stabilized and the council members quickly helped each other to their feet. They were now standing on the water just like before.

"The evil lord has been defeated, the evil lord has been defeated," The Rainmaker shouted excitedly. "Long live the son of nature!"

Outside, the people of the city watched in happy amazement as the dead birds rained to the ground.

Very soon they would be celebrating a new era of peace.

❦   ❦   ❦

The evil lord's demise ushered a new phase in world history. It was the dawn of the era of the new ancient. It would now be called the world of the great …

Epilogue

… the old man was cut short by the mother, calling out to her children.

"Mother! Mother!" the children shouted and bolted from the room, falling into the warm embrace of their mother.

"I'm sorry I was gone so long," the mother apologized.

"We are so happy you are home mother," the eldest girl quipped.

"Did you behave yourselves children?"

"Yes we did," they chorused.

"Did anyone come by?"

"Just this old man who said he was tired after a long journey," the girl explained innocently.

"You did not let him in did you?"

"Well … he…. he looked very tired and he begged for us to let him in."

"How many times have I told you not to let strangers into the house?"

"But he looked harmless mother," the boy jumped to his sister's defense.

"It does not matter!" the mother scolded some more. "You can never judge a stranger by the way he looks. He could be dangerous. Is he still there?"

"Yes, he is still inside," the girl replied.

The mother rushed into the house to take a look at the strange old traveler.

"I don't see anybody. Are you sure he was in here?"

"Yes, he was sitting right there," the girl said.

"Maybe he went out back," the boy added.

They rushed around the house but the old man was nowhere to be seen.

"Did he tell you his name?" the mother asked.

"No, he just said he was a traveler from a far off land."

"Can you please describe him to me? And please do it very slowly," the mother said in a hushed tone.

The girl went ahead and described the old traveler.

"It can't be …" the mother gasped and dashed back into the house.

"Mother! Mother!" the children shouted and ran after her.

But the girl did not follow them. Something told her to go back into the house and double check whether the old man had really vanished into the thin air. But the man was not there. It was just her and her family in the dark house. But lying on the floor was the old man's walking stick. She picked it up and studied it closely.

"It's the one!" she gasped as she stared at the stave. Not sure what to do, she took a step backwards and winced in pain as a sharp object dug into her heel. She quickly bent down to examine what it was. She could not believe what it was she was holding in her hands.

"The bracelet!" she gasped once more as her hand shot up to cover her mouth.

She peered around to see if anybody was around. She was alone.

The oath!

She knew she had to keep the old man's story secret by all means. But where was she going to hide the stave and the bracelet? Her lips curved into a knowing smile as her mind registered the perfect place to hide the items. She made a mad dash for the thick banana grove that stood a few yards behind the house. She quickly pushed the stave into the thick stems of the banana stalks, out of sight of any prying eyes. She was just about to hide the bracelet when something occurred to her. Mashaka held the bracelet whenever he wished to speak to the Seer. Against her better judgment, she went on her knees, put the bracelet in her palms and gently rubbed it with her fingers.

But nothing happened.

I need to concentrate some more.

She closed her eyes and imagined she was Mashaka, traveling out in the wilderness. But again nothing happened. Disappointed, she just stared at the shiny bracelet in her palms. She was just about to put it away when she felt what she thought was a slight tingling in her palms. She stared down in horror as the bracelet glowed in the dark and the tingling quickly developed into a tantalizing sensation that soon engulfed both her hands and ran up her arms.

"Seer, can you hear me?" The whisper barely left her quivering lips.

"Ssselaaa!" The whisper cut through the night air like a sharp knife.

With a gasp, she dropped the bracelet and the sensation disappeared immediately. She turned around but it was just her in the dark banana grove.

"Sela, where are you?" It was her mother calling out for her.

The girl quickly pushed the bracelet into the banana grove and ran inside the house.

"I am here mother."

Unbeknownst to her, the girl had already made contact. Her life was about to change forever.

#
END

Glossary of Swahili Words

❀

Amani:	Peace/Calm:	/A-Ma-Nee/
Askari:	Guard/Policeman:	/Us-Carry/
Chawi	Night Runner	/Char-We/
Damu:	Blood:	/Duh-Moo/
Dini:	Religion/Sect:	/Dee—Nee/
Gereza:	Jail/Prison:	/Geh-Razor/
Gizas:	Darkness:	/Ghee-Czar/
Hatari:	Danger/Peril:	/Her-Tarry/
Jasho-kuu:	Severe Sweat:	/Jar-Show-Coo/
Karamu	Feast	/Car-Rah-Mou/
Kavu:	Dry:	/Car-Vou/
Kiboko:	Whip:	/Key-Bow-Core/
Kifo	Death	/Key-For/
Korofi	Rogue/Mischie-vous	/Core-Row-Fee/
Maga:	Proper Noun:	/Mugger/
Malaika:	Angel:	/Mah-Lie-Car/

Miti (Plural)	Trees	/Me-Tea/
Moran:	Warrior:	/More-Run/
Moshi:	Smoke:	/Mo'-She/
Raruka:	Tear:	/Rah-Rue-Car/
Sadikia:	Trust:	/Sir-Dee-Key-Ah/
Safisha:	Clean/Cleanse:	/Sir-Fee-Shah/
Samaha:	Forgiveness:	/Sir-Mah-Her/
Sanamu:	Statue:	/Sir-Nah-Mou/
Shimo La Mauti:	Hole of the Dead:	/She-Mo'/—/Lah/—/Mah-Ou-Tee/
Sura:	Face:	/Sue-Rah/
Ukoma:	Leprosy:	/Ou-Core-Mah/
Vita:	War/battle/fight:	/Vee-Tar/
Vua:	Rain:	/Voo-Ah/